Book One of
The Siblings O'Rifcan Series

By Katharine E. Hamilton

ISBN- 10: 0-692-13382-8
ISBN- 13: 978-0-692-13382-8

Claron

www.katharinehamilton.com

Cover Design by Kerry Prater.

This is a work of fiction. Names, characters, places,
and incidents are either the product of the
author's imagination or are used factiously, and
any resemblance to actual persons, living or dead,
business establishments, events or locales is
entirely coincidental.

Dedicated to Charles and Susie O'Neal.

Their 39 years of dairy farming provided insight, research, a legacy of hard work, and even some funny stories that helped shape Claron and the O'Rifcan family into the amazing characters they've turned out to be.

I love you, Papaw and Ninny!

Acknowledgments

It's always hard to think of everyone who's helped shape a manuscript into an actual book. I hope I remember all of you.

My husband, Brad, for supporting me.

My family. It's always amazing how easily you guys support me. I love you all and appreciate you more than you know.

Thanks to my alpha and beta readers. You guys rock! My three Megan's and a Macy. And of course, Erin, Kerry, and Danielle.

Thank you to L.K. Moerbe for allowing me to pick his brain on all things farming and farm life.

Special thanks to my grandparents, Ninny and Papaw for letting me tour the old dairy farm and giving me stories to use as inspiration for Claron.

Thanks to Holstein, the dairy cat, for being one of my fondest memories of spending time in the milk room under Ninny's feet.

Thanks to my editor, Lauren Hanson, for always being willing to help me out no matter the project and no matter where my mind takes me.

And thanks to my readers. I love meeting you. I love hearing from you. And I love writing for you. You guys are awesome.

« CHAPTER ONE »

Tenderly she touched the tinge of yellow under her chin, the discoloration slowly fading back to her normal creamy complexion. Though traces of green and blue still laced the bruises along her collarbone, the sensitivity was fading. It was funny how the exterior of the body could reflect the interior without even so much as a conversation between the two. Though she knew her brain communicated with every inch of her being, she sometimes wondered if her brain and heart did indeed converse. If there ever was a doubt, the battered condition of her heart proved her wrong.

Two weeks. Two weeks had passed since the horrible incident. The man, whom she used to refer to as the love of her life, had chosen someone else, and her stable, predictable, yet enjoyable, life had been altered. The unfairness of it all, the utter disregard for the last two years of her life spent with love in her heart infuriated her. And though she struggled to overcome the anger, it was the hurt and the embarrassment that she was most unable to bear. The looks, the whispers, the sympathetic gestures, all raced through her mind as she replayed the scene for the thousandth time. There was nothing she could do to change the outcome. Oliver's mind was set. He'd made his choice. And it wasn't her. She'd been a fool— A fool in love as the saying goes— and she hated it. Her father had never liked Oliver: red flag number one. Oliver never made time for her family: red flag number two. And the illustrious third strike, red flag, canon shot fired was the fact he'd cheated on her before in the past, and yet she had forgiven him. The night of their anniversary dinner was to be a celebration of their love. The jitters and high expectations of a potential proposal, the long-awaited "what's next in their relationship" conversation, the special table in the far corner where he first told her he loved her, those had been the hopes for that particular night.

She'd been late. Not too late, just ten minutes shy off the mark, which was her custom. She'd worn the plum cocktail dress she'd spent half the day shopping for. The new heels that showcased her long legs, the necklace that graced her delicate neck, all of it meant to make her feel beautiful and confident for what she had hoped would be one of the most romantic and memorable nights of her life. Only it wasn't.

The bitterness that welled up inside her at that particular moment had her snapping the foundation compact closed and tossing it into her make up bag.

"Rhea, sweetie?" Her mother's voice called up the stairwell. "Your father is here with the car. Are you about ready?"

"Be right there," she called, though she felt anything but ready. She zipped up her toiletries and carried the striped bag to her suitcase. Gently, she tucked it in amongst the faded pair of jeans, pajama pants, and all her newfound insecurities. Those were the luxury items to be taken with her. After all, a recently broken heart was bound to have some extra baggage. She pulled the top of her suitcase over and zipped the sides. She heard her mother's footsteps up the stairwell as she neared the door. Forcing a smile, she hefted the suitcase off the bed.

"Ready, honey?"

Though she nodded, Rhea waited patiently as her mother's eyes and fingers skimmed over the last remaining traces of that frightful night. The gesture of maternal concern and fretfulness was meant to help cure the hurts that continued to haunt her baby girl, but instead, it only served to irritate her. "I'm fine, Mom."

"Oh, I know, sweetie. I just hate seeing you like this. Aren't you worried you're moving too fast? I mean, the accident was just a couple of weeks ago. And you and Oliver—"

Rhea held up her hand. "Oliver and I are done, Mom. And as far as the car accident goes, I'm feeling much better. My bruises have faded, my ribs are barely sore... trust me, I'm fine."

Jeanie Conners didn't believe her daughter for a moment, but she let Rhea's pride stand, withholding further scrutiny. "Alright." Jeanie grabbed two of Rhea's smaller bags. "I still cannot believe you are heading to Ireland to live with your grandfather. To say he is overjoyed would be an understatement."

"It's only temporary," Rhea reminded her. "Until I can figure out my next move."

"I know, sweetie. But you know how he is. He's already made a list of things for you two to do together."

"We'll see," Rhea acquiesced. "I just need to get away for a bit."

Jeanie cupped her cheek in understanding. "I know, honey, I know. Maybe the Ireland air is just what you need. I loved visiting there when your father and I were just married. If you happen to visit Galway, be sure to stop in on—"

"Aunt Grace, I know," Rhea added, thinking of her mother's college roommate that had always been Rhea's role model. Though she wasn't of the same blood, she was family. The woman who traveled the world. No man. No responsibilities. A self-made woman, an entrepreneur. Rhea lacked the same courage Grace possessed, but her stubbornness was often attributed to her. And Rhea knew, that even if she were not close to Galway, she'd make the trip to see her aunt regardless of distance.

"There's my girl." Rhea's father entered with a bolstering wave of forced enthusiasm so as to take the sadness off her departure.

Though Rhea had only been staying with them the last couple of weeks, her father longed for days past and having his little girl under his own roof again. He also, despite being warned by her mother, wished to hold Rhea close until he knew her heart had mended over the loss of Oliver. The fact that the man had sat at the dinner table with another woman the night he was to meet his baby girl infuriated him. And not only that, but the scene his daughter had been forced to endure. The embarrassment. The very thought churned his butter and had his temper flaring.

Then, in her haste to escape the pain and heartbreak, Rhea had climbed behind the wheel and rushed to drive home. Her mind was elsewhere, her focus not on the road. And just like that, his daughter— had it not been for the quick response of the medical team— would have been lost. Paul Conners thanked the heavens every day for his little girl, and since her accident he now found himself bending knee both morning and night. He hated to see her leave, but her heart needed mending. Her spirit needed it too, and he knew her grandfather's love and attention, the destination of being as far from home as possible, and the adventure of it all would do Rhea good. So, he acquiesced by lifting her heavy suitcases into the trunk of the car and keeping his mouth shut about his continued rage towards Oliver. "That'll do it." He pushed down the trunk door with a heavy thud.

"That's a good man." Jeanie lovingly tapped her husband's cheek in thanks. She turned to find Rhea staring at the house, taking in that one last view before leaving. Her heart squeezed a bit at the sight and she inwardly prayed the longing for home would stay in her daughter's heart just enough so she would return to them. "Ready, sweetie?"

Rhea inhaled a deep breath and climbed into the back seat of the small sedan and shut the door. "Ready."

∞

The rain pelted the sidewalks, and the sounds of planes landing on the tarmac and tires treading through puddles followed her as she hurriedly made her way through the rental lot of Shannon Airport to find the small car that would carry her onward towards her grandpa. The weight of her bags caused her shoulders to sag, and she mustered what little strength she had left to forcibly roll the suitcase that had lost a wheel somewhere between baggage claim and the rental counter. Thinking dry thoughts, she clicked the key fob and watched as the lights of a small, white car lit up two rows over. She unlocked the doors and struggled lifting her two heaviest suitcases into the back seat. She then opened the trunk and placed her two shoulder bags and her carry-on inside. The door barely closed, but she managed. Wiping her hands on the front of her jeans she then hurried to the driver's side and slid inside. She paused and then laughed at herself as she opened the door once more and walked to the other side of the vehicle. She slid into the proper side of the vehicle behind the wheel and shook her head as she turned the key. She would need to remember that not only would she be sitting on a different side of the vehicle, but she would also need to drive on the opposite side of the road than she was used to.

She programmed the address to an area close to Sidna's Bed and Breakfast, the place her grandpa had sent to her for arrival, into the car's GPS. "You can do this, Rhea," she told herself as she inhaled a deep breath. A bit nervous, she slipped the car into reverse. She navigated her way through the parking area in what she considered a successful trip, only catching herself on the wrong side of the driveways twice.

She exited, praying that the forty-minute drive towards O'Brien's Bridge would not take her the rest of the day. At the speed she was moving, however, her time frame looked doubtful. Not only was she navigating a new country, but she could not pronounce half the signs along the way. She eyed her GPS. "Just follow the blinking dot, Rhea. You're doing fine." She cringed as two vehicles sped by her, her grip tightening on the steering wheel. She briefly took her eyes off the road to survey the landscape around her. Ireland was beautiful. She knew it would be. Despite the rain, the hills were vibrant green set against cloudy skies. The swipe of the windshield wipers brought her eyes back towards the road and she gasped as she hurriedly flicked her blinker to turn onto R463. She wasn't far now. She skirted the boundary line between County Clare and County Limerick. Her GPS would only take her so far before she had to rely on the printed email sitting in the seat next to her: directions from her grandpa to Sidna's B&B in a small village in County

Clare just a little ways northeast of O'Brien's Bridge. She prayed she could find it. And she prayed she made it there in one piece.

She took the turn onto R466 and held fast to the wheel as a van doused her small rental in what she could only assume was the River Shannon. "Just a puddle," she murmured as her mood soured and she waited as another car passed by her and splashed her again. "Just trying to drive here," she called out, her nerves on edge as she eased her car up the road and across O'Brien's Bridge. Turning the knob to hasten her windshield wipers, she braced herself for the downpour that assaulted the glass.

A downpour was just what she needed to reflect her current mood. She scoffed. "*Current* mood?" she asked herself. Full of disdain, she slowed to read an upcoming sign. "More like mood of the year." Sensing that maybe her bad mood had influenced the weather, she attempted to think of happier thoughts. The fact that she would see her grandpa soon should make her happy. And she was eager to see him. She just wasn't ready for his sympathetic hugs and encouragement. Though her mother promised he wouldn't, Roland Conners could not help himself. Rhea was the apple of his eye, always had been. That thought made her smile as she thought of peppermint candies and the faint scent of cigar smoke that he carried with him everywhere he went. And he did give the best hugs, she reminded herself. Her mood slightly lifted and then she heard it. A loud pop and then the flapping of rubber against asphalt. Growling and tampering down the urge to curse Mother Nature, she pulled to the side of the road and turned on her hazard lights. "Just, perfect." She banged her hand against the steering wheel and then yelped at her own stupidity as pain racketed up her arm.

"You're supposed to be good to me, Ireland! Can't you see I need a break?" she yelled upwards to the hood of her car. Huffing, she grabbed the stack of papers from her passenger seat to cover her head, flicked the door handle and stepped out onto the grass— which was more like a bog— as her shoes sank into wet, mushy earth, and slushed her way towards the back of the vehicle. Her right rear tire was blown. Realizing the papers were not helping her stay dry, she lowered them and then gasped as she saw ink sliding down the pages and her directions to her grandpa were lost in the drainage that puddled at her feet.

Defeated, Rhea slid back behind the wheel and began racking her brain to try and remember the remaining directions. How far was she? Could she make it on foot? She remembered her oversized suitcase and its wheel-less base. If she had to, she would make the trek, but she had to know where she was going first. Perhaps there was a store up ahead she could stop in and ask for directions. She looked out the windows and only saw farmland to her left and the River Shannon to her right. And rain. "Okay, Rhea, think. Think, think, think, think, think." Jitters began to take over and she absentmindedly drummed her fingers on the steering wheel. A knock sounded on the window and she jumped in her seat with a small squeal as a man peered into the car. The hood to his raincoat covered most of his face, but a pair of teeth flashed in a warm smile. "You alright there, lass?"

Rhea stared a moment before she realized the man was standing in pouring rain waiting for her response. She reached for the window and rolled it down. "My tire is flat."

His brow furrowed as he looked at the tires on the passenger side of the vehicle. He then held up a finger as he rounded her car and looked at the other two. Nodding, he made his way back to the passenger window. "Definitely have a puncture back there," he motioned towards the direction of the tire. "Whereabouts are you headed?"

Rhea shrugged and pointed to the sloppy stack of papers next to her. "Those were my directions."

He motioned for her to get out of the car. "Best give you a lift then, come along." He did not wait for an answer but expected her to climb out in the middle of a storm and drive away with a stranger. Rhea continued to sit in her car. He appeared on her side of the vehicle and opened her door and she jumped in her seat. "I see you have some bags, I'll grab those if you want to just head towards my lorry." He motioned to the vehicle parked on the other side of the road. She didn't move.

"Not here to hurt you, lass. Just trying to help." He offered his hand and then turned away to yell as a vehicle sped by and splashed him in its wake. Turning back towards Rhea he waved her out. "Come along, I haven't all day."

She caught a glimpse of the devastatingly handsome face beneath the hood and felt herself sliding out of the car. "I have bags in the trunk as well."

"Aye, I'll fetch them. Hurry now, before you get soaked."

Rhea darted across the road and hopped into the passenger seat, only it was not the passenger side. Rolling her eyes, she quickly darted back into the rain to slide into the opposite seat.

A deep laugh filtered through the door as the man opened it. "Yanks always take time to adjust to the vehicles." He handed over her purse. "I'll go get the rest of your bags."

She watched as he patiently walked back across the road unaffected by the downpour and grabbed her two giant suitcases out of the back seat of her rental. She heard them plop into the bed of his truck. He then fetched her remaining bags out of her trunk and tossed them into his truck bed as well. She then saw him unroll a blue tarp to cover them. He slid into the truck and heaved a contented sigh. "That ought to do it."

"Thank you," Rhea said.

He turned as he slipped off his hood and his bright blue eyes sparkled as his raven hair dripped with what little rain bombarded him beneath his hood. "Riley O'Rifcan, at your service." He held out a hand and she shook it.

"Rhea," she introduced.

"Nice to meet you, Rhea. Based on the vehicle and the luggage, I am assuming you just arrived in Ireland?"

"You would be correct." She reached into her purse and pulled out her cell phone. The screen lit up. Pursing her lips, she slipped it back into her bag.

"No service here, lass. You will have better luck closer to town."

"Where exactly am I?" She grimaced at the stupid question, but the stranger responded in kind.

"You're at the county crossing, love."

"The county crossing? As in Clare to Limerick?"

"That would be the one." Eying her, he turned to face her. "I take it that is not where you planned to go?"

"Well, yes and no. I know I'm supposed to be near here, but in County Clare."

"Do you have a village name for me?"

"No, unfortunately I don't. All I know is that I was to cross the O'Brien's Bridge and head northeast. I'm to stop at a bed and breakfast there."

"Would it be Sidna's Bed and Breakfast you're after?"

Relief washed over her face. "Yes! Yes, that's it!" She gripped his hand as if he were her lifeline. Realizing her action, she dropped it immediately. He grinned before turning to face the front. "It just so happens I just left the B&B. We aren't too far off the mark."

She placed a hand over her heart. "Thank you. Thank you for stopping to help me and for knowing where I am."

He laughed. "I'd best know where you are. I grew up here."

"You did?"

He nodded as he drove, the sound of the windshield wipers and peddling rain filled the silences.

"Do you still live around here?"

"Aye, but closer to Limerick. My family is all about though. In fact, I imagine you will meet plenty of them in a few minutes."

Confused, she glanced over at him and he smiled. Rhea couldn't think of ever seeing a man so handsome, even when he was dripping wet.

"Sidna is my mam." He chuckled at her surprise. "She'll be pleased I stumbled upon her guest."

"So you know her," Rhea began.

His brows rose at the absurdity of her reply.

"I mean, I know you know her, you just said she was your mother. What I meant was, well, I was told to go to her B&B and I don't know her. But she apparently knows my grandpa, and—"

"Your grandda?"

"Yes," Rhea started to continue, and Riley held up his hand.

"Who is your grandda, lass?"

"Roland Conners. Do you know him?"

A genuine smile lifted Riley's face as he nodded. "Oh, I know him alright. He's practically family. Though I may disown him for not telling me he had a beautiful lass coming to visit." He winked at her as he turned down a street that began leading them through a small village.

Rhea relaxed as she watched the buildings pass by and several people walked the sidewalks. "I can't believe people would be out and about in this weather."

"It's Ireland, love. If you let a little rain damper your day, you'd never leave the house."

His response made her grin as she continued to watch the scenery roll by. "It's beautiful here," she commented and sat up straighter when he pulled to a stop. "We can worry with the bags in a bit. Let's get inside until the heavy passes."

She reached to open the door, but it would not budge. "Ah, yes, you will have to crawl this way." He motioned towards his direction. "I've got a bit of a stick on that side. It can only be opened on the outside."

"Okay." She attempted to crawl over the console with as much grace as possible, her shoe snagging between the gear shift and the floorboard. She pulled and stumbled forward, Riley catching her as she fell out of his doorway. She swiped her hair out of her eyes and looked up to thank him as he grinned. "No worse for wear." He winked. "Come along." He led her towards a bright red door on a two-story cottage style building. Flowers of all shapes, sizes, and colors graced the stone path towards the front door, and Rhea knew the time for admiring them would come later. She ached for dry feet, and after drenching herself in the rain, she could only imagine the state of her hair and makeup.

« CHAPTER TWO »

Riley opened the door and led her into a warm sitting room with comfortable furniture and not nearly enough wall space for all the framed photographs that sat upon every open shelf or table and filled every inch of the walls. Though it seemed cluttered, the room was welcoming, and Rhea felt her shoulders relax. "Hello to the house," Riley called out. He slipped out of his raincoat and hung it on a stand by the door and Rhea noticed just how tall and fit the man was. He was lean and muscled and striking when he turned to face her. His black hair was long, brushing the edges of his shoulders and collar, and his face was full of sharp lines and angles. She flushed, hoping he hadn't caught her staring when he turned. "Come, they must be in the kitchen."

He led her to a door on the left and swung it open. Rhea entered a large open space, where a round table for four sat to her left as a large island counter stretched along the right side of the room and several heads popped up at their entrance. "Ah, here is everyone." Riley pulled Rhea forward and briefly placed his hand at the small of her back.

Rhea stood, tucking her arm in his, as she waited for introductions. Eyes played over her every feature from head to toe, and her usual confidence fled as she realized what a sore sight she must seem standing next to Riley.

An older woman, plump around the middle and stout in stature turned from the oven. Her smile faded as she eyed Rhea. "Riley O'Rifcan!" she scolded as she stepped forward, tossing her hand towel over her shoulder. "You decide to bring a lass for dinner and you drag her through the pouring rain?" She shook her head in dismay as her eyes turned tender when she faced Rhea. "Hello, dear." She smiled as she reached for Rhea's hand. Gasping, she darted a fierce gaze up at Riley. "Your hands are like ice, love. We'd best warm you up with some tea. Layla, fetch a glass," she called over her shoulder. A tall brunette hurried about the kitchen at her bidding. "Sure, you are a beauty," she complimented as she looked Rhea up and down. Proudly, she tapped Riley's arm. "I always knew my Riley would bring a beautiful woman home one day."

Riley stepped forward, embarrassment flashing across his face as he tried to set the record straight. "I'm just so excited!" The woman snatched Rhea up in a bone-crushing hug. Rhea looked up at Riley in shock as she patted a hand on the woman's back.

"Mam, stop, let her breathe." Riley placed a distancing hand between his mother and Rhea. "This is not my lass, and for the thousandth time, I do not have one."

Disappointment fell over the woman's face and had Rhea stifling a giggle. Riley caught sight of her grin and winked. "Unfortunately, I do not have the same luck as others," he continued. "This lass is here to see Roland."

The woman's gaze widened at the same time as her smile. "Of course! You're his lovely granddaughter, are you not?"

"Yes ma'am. I'm—"

"Rhea," she finished and quickly enveloped her in another firm hug. Rhea held back the grunt as the air fled from her lungs and Riley smirked.

The woman pulled back and smiled. "We are so pleased to have you here. Roland will be so happy to see you. He and my husband are out and about at the moment, God only knows what the two are up to. Shenanigans seem to be their theme for the day. Oh yes, I'm Sidna. Sidna O'Rifcan." She babbled on as Rhea felt Riley move towards the door. She gripped his arm harder, not realizing she still held onto it. "Just fetching your bags, lass. Don't worry, I won't leave you with the crazy woman just yet."

"Crazy woman, am I?" His mother swatted him with her towel and beamed up at her son. "Get on with ye now and fetch Rhea's bags, only then will I offer you a bite to eat."

Riley nodded and walked out, leaving Rhea to look upon the other faces in the room.

"Yes, well," Sidna continued. "These are some of my other children." She pointed to the tall brunette who walked up carrying a mug of hot tea for Rhea. "This is Layla."

"Nice to meet you." Layla smiled in welcome as she handed Rhea the cup. Her eyes were the same striking blue as Riley's, while her thick brown hair in long waves cascading down past her shoulders painted a beautiful picture.

"That gingernut there is our Chloe." Sidna pointed to a spritely redhead who waved from behind the counter as she continued pounding her fists into a mound of dough.

"My oldest, Lorena, there." Sidna pointed to another attractive woman expertly dicing an onion. "And my grand, Emily. She belongs to Lorena." Sidna glanced around. "All my boys seem to be awaiting their meal elsewhere, mostly trying to avoid capture and being put to work I imagine." She patted Rhea on the back just as she began to take a sip of the hot tea. Rhea tried to hide her sputter as the burning liquid ravished her throat.

A rustling noise had Sidna glancing towards the sitting room. "That'd be Riley with your bags. How about we show you your room and you can freshen up a bit before the meal?"

"That would be wonderful." Rhea followed the woman back into the room just as Riley hefted the large suitcases up a narrow, carpeted stairwell. She followed as his mother ranted warnings up ahead for him to avoid knocking frames off the walls as he maneuvered the tiny space. "Room two, Riley," Sidna stated as they cleared the top landing. "Here you are, dear." Sidna opened the door and Riley trudged inside setting the suitcases on the floor. A bit breathless, he turned. "I'll go fetch the rest." Sidna nodded as if that were her expectation and he hurried out of the room. "There's a wash room there, extra blankets in the cupboard. We eat in an hour or so, but feel free to come down when you wish. There is always a gab before dinner any way." She grinned, her hands resting on her plump hips. "We are so pleased to have you here, love. Your grandda has been quite elated as of late, expecting you and all." Watching Rhea, Sidna noticed the faint tinges of bruises hidden beneath touches of makeup. She imagined the girl had successfully blended the marks away at the beginning of the day, but the Irish weather betrayed her mask, and several began to peek through. "We will let you get settled, dear." Riley emerged in the doorway with her remaining bags and set them on the four-poster bed. "That's the lot." He took a deep breath and flashed a smile towards Rhea.

"Thank you, Riley, for... everything." Rhea shyly glanced his direction, unsure of how to thank him properly for all he had done for her.

He waved away her thanks. "You can pay me back later. We'll let your vehicle rest the night where it's at and I'll fetch it in the morning."

Rhea started to protest, but Sidna held up her hand. "No debate," she said. "It will be out front for you bright and early should you need it."

"Thank you," Rhea said again. "I will be down shortly. I would hate to miss my grandpa should he come back soon."

"Take your time, love," Sidna said as she nudged Riley out the door. "Those two old goons will be out right until the meal time. They're over at Clary's, probably being more of a bother than a help." Lovingly, she brushed a hand over Rhea's arm. "See you in a bit, dear." And with that, she shut the door, the sound of her shooing Riley down the stairwell offering a temporary grin to Rhea's tired face.

∞

The room was warm, not just in temperature, but in nature. The hand sewn quilt draped over the fluffy four-poster bed added a touch of home as Rhea thought of her mother's guestroom she'd slept in the last two weeks. The cherry wooden vanity in the far corner was old but polished to a gleam and decorated with lace doilies, and the small television nuzzled inside a looming armoire filled the main wall, a small stone fireplace next to it. Fresh flowers sat upon the mantle and nightstand in crystal vases. Rhea breathed in deep and enjoyed the scent of the place. The scent of a well-loved home. She walked towards the bathroom and sighed in pleasure as she gazed upon an oversized claw-foot tub. On a small table next to it, bath salts of lavender and juniper sat in delicate glass jars. She turned on the water and scooped generous spoonfuls of the lavender into the tub and watched as steam began to fill the room. A hot bath sounded too good to pass up, so she slipped out of her damp clothes and plunged in. A heavy sigh of contentment slipped from her lips as she relished the feel of her cold feet slowly thawing.

Eyes closed, Rhea breathed in the comforting smell of lavender, unsure if it were just the salts she smelled or also the beautiful bouquet gracing the windowsill next to her. She couldn't wait to see her grandpa, especially now that she felt her gloomy mood melting away with each soothing minute in the luxurious bath. She slid under the water and held her breath a full minute before emerging. Her hair clung to her neck and she gently scrubbed her hands over her face before climbing to her feet. She would revisit the bath later, she promised herself, but she wanted to await her grandpa downstairs and possibly talk more with the O'Rifcan family.

All of them are beautiful, she thought. *Even Riley.* The thought of him being a fairy prince in disguise had her laughing. "Don't lose your head, Rhea." Though she had to admit he was unnaturally gorgeous and so were his sisters. Having dried off, Rhea reached for her carry-on and removed her toiletries bag and found her lotion. Lathering up, she then found a fresh pair of jeans and a light cashmere sweater. She sat at the small vanity and brushed through her wet hair and made quick work of drying it. She lightly touched the bruise on her jaw. Almost gone now, she covered the remaining traces with a light coating of foundation. Keeping it simple, she brushed a light dust of blush to her cheeks and ran mascara through her thick lashes. Satisfied that she looked more like herself, Rhea stood and slipped her feet into a comfortable pair of flats. *Dry* flats. She doubted she'd ever take dry shoes for granted again.

Taking one last glance in the floor length mirror in the corner of the room, she smiled, realizing she finally looked more like herself than she had in weeks. She opened the door and slowly made her way down the stairs, taking time to study many of the framed photos along the stairwell. From the looks of the pictures, the O'Rifcans had a large family, not just the three beautiful women and Riley, but six more boys. *Ten children*. She shook her head and smiled as she gazed upon an old photograph full of gap-toothed grins and lanky figures.

She reached the bottom step as the front door to the B&B opened.

"Hello, family." A man stepped inside, shedding his rain coat and hood by the front door before turning and seeing no one in the room. At the creak under her foot, his gaze then fell upon Rhea at the edge of the stairs.

"Hello, there," he greeted, watching her as she nervously wrung her hands together.

"Hello."

"American?" he asked in surprise.

Nodding, she replied, "Maryland, to be exact."

He walked towards her and extended his hand. "Claron."

Rhea surveyed the man before her and appreciated his friendly smile as she accepted his handshake. Warmth spread up her arm at the contact and she found herself temporarily lost in a mossy green gaze partially hidden behind rain spattered glasses. Another O'Rifcan son, she assumed, based on the fact that he looked similar to Riley only with golden hair as opposed to Riley's black mane. And he had dreamy green eyes instead of blue. But the hair settled in a similar fashion along his collar, with an added rogue curl that fell across his brow and he continually swept to the side. He stood around the same height as Riley and was of similar build. Like the other O'Rifcans she had met, he painted a nice picture.

"I'm Rhea," she replied, removing her hand and offering a shy smile.

"What brings you to this crazy house, Rhea?"

"Riley."

His eyebrows rose in surprise. "Is that so? Well, my brother has always had great taste. You heading to dinner?"

Sidna walked into the room and smiled. "Oh Rhea, good to see you freshened up, sweetie. Clary are you going to stand there like a loon or are you going to come and help prepare the table?"

"Yes, Mam, sorry, I was meeting Riley's new lass."

"Oh, I'm not Riley's—" Rhea stepped forward to set the record straight and Sidna chortled.

"She's not Riley's lass, love. Rhea is our guest. Riley rescued her from a tire puncture while she was making her way here to see Roland."

"Ah, I see." Claron smiled as he draped an arm over his mother's shoulders.

"Clary is my youngest lad in the bunch. Come dear, you ready to join us for the meal?"

"Yes, that would be nice."

"Wonderful!" Sidna turned and headed back towards the kitchen.

Claron motioned for Rhea to follow his mother and he brought up the rear. Rhea gasped as she saw her grandpa entering from the back door across the room. Without hesitation and waiting for him to hang his coat, she rushed forward. "Grandpa!" Roland turned just in time to accept the large embrace, his lips splitting into a beaming smile. He pulled back and cupped her face. "Now that is a welcome. Hello, Rhea dear.

"Hi, Grandpa." She caught sight of the puddling of tears in his eyes behind his glasses as hers did the same. He gripped her hands. "I'm so pleased you found your way alright."

She rolled her eyes. "I wouldn't say I made it completely. Riley—" she turned to Riley who sat at the small round table and smiled. "Riley rescued me. My car blew a tire and I was a bit stranded for a while."

Roland nodded his thanks towards Riley. "Well, I'm glad you're here. I see you've met everyone."

"Not everyone." Riley pointed to the loud noises coming from the sitting room as more O'Rifcans began filing into the house.

Overwhelmed by all the new faces, Rhea watched as man after man squeezed into the kitchen, all talking over one another as they greeted fellow family members with hugs or handshakes. Rhea turned towards her grandpa, but he was gone, and she realized she stood by herself. Confusion washed over her face at his absence and Claron stepped towards her. "He went to wash up right quick."

Relieved, Rhea nodded. "Thanks. So, you're Clary?"

He flushed at the nickname. "Well, that is what everyone seems to call me, but yes, that would be me."

"So, you live around here?"

"Aye, not too far, actually."

"Your mother had mentioned my grandpa was over at your place helping today. I assumed you were... well... not her son."

"An old buggar?" He grinned, and she chuckled.

"Yes, actually."

He waved her assumption away. "It doesn't help much that my Da and I have the same name. He is Claron Senior. Most call me Clary just to distinguish between the two."

"I see." She stepped closer to him as a small boy rushed by them into the crowd only to be lifted into the air by one of the other brothers.

"Aye Clary, you going to introduce us to your lass?" One of the other O'Rifcan brothers called out causing everyone to turn their heads. Rhea and Claron both blushed at the mistake.

"Actually, Jaron, this is Roland's granddaughter, Rhea. She's visiting."

"Ah." The man walked forward and shook Rhea's hand, his stormy gaze washing over her. "A beauty. I knew she couldn't possibly be with you." He nudged Claron's shoulder and laughed heartily as he moved out of the way for the remaining brothers to introduce themselves. Rhea's head swam with names and faces she knew she would never keep straight.

Claron Senior stepped into the room, his presence as looming as his voice as he barked out. "Are we eating or just putting it on the long finger?" He walked towards Rhea. "Ah, a beautiful lass distracting the lot of ye, I see. No complaints there." He winked as he kissed the back of Rhea's hand. "Welcome, Rhea. We are pleased to have you with us."

"Thank you, Mr. O'Rifcan."

"Ah, call me Claron." His gaze traveled to the younger Claron standing next to her. "Or Senior. Most people call me that anyhow." He slapped a hand on Claron's shoulder as he nodded towards the dining room. "Let's eat, Sidna love," he called over his shoulder as he walked toward the dining room followed by the others. Claron lightly tapped the small of Rhea's back as he led her towards the table and pulled out a chair for her. Everyone settled around the long table, her grandpa at one end, Claron Senior at the other. A dry red wine was passed around and Claron expertly filled her glass and his own before passing it along. Roasted lamb, potatoes, carrots, and warm bread rotated around the table as everyone filled their plates. Senior raised his glass. "To our newest guest, Rhea."

Flushing a bit at the extra attention, she toasted with the others as they all repeated her name in welcome. She forked a bite of the tender meat and closed her eyes to relish in the delicious flavors melding on her tongue.

"Good?" Claron's voice tickled her ear as she turned to see him watching her.

She nodded. "I think it's the best I've ever had."

He chuckled. "Don't tell my mam that, she might become a gloater."

Rhea tore a piece of the bread and dipped it in the thick brown gravy. Rolling her eyes back in pleasure, he laughed as he took a sip of his wine. "I could eat this every day," she whispered.

"You're in luck to be staying here then. I am only fortunate enough to receive supper here each evening, but you will have the luxury of every meal." Claron took a hearty bite of potatoes as conversations whirled around the table.

"So, Rhea," Layla leaned across the table, "if you are up for it tomorrow, Chloe and I can show you around the village if you like?"

"That'd be great, thanks." Rhea smiled and appreciated the invitation.

"And then we can introduce you to the local." Riley winked.

"Local?" Rhea asked. "Local what?"

Several of the siblings snickered.

"Ah, the pub," Riley corrected. "If you're going to live in Ireland, you'd best know where to find the best plain."

"Plain what?" Rhea's brow wrinkled as she tried to decipher what Riley was saying. A couple of the siblings laughed at her expense, but not in harshness.

"A Guinness, lass," Riley explained with a wink.

"I see. Well, that sounds fun, Riley, thanks." She turned towards Claron.

"Do you go to the local pub, Claron?"

Her question surprised not only him, but several O'Rifcans as they waited with grins for their younger brother to respond. "Aye, I do."

Nodding, she turned back towards Riley. "Count me in." Not realizing her reply seemed in acceptance of Claron's company rather than Riley's, the look of amusement that passed between the siblings escaped her notice as she continued eating her supper.

"So, do you have grand plans whilst here, Rhea?" She wasn't sure which brother asked the question. She tossed around a few names in her mind and then settled upon Declan.

"Not really. I just came to see my grandpa for a while."

Roland beamed. "It is my job to convince her to stay." He winked at her as he took a sip of his wine and she grinned.

"We'll see about that, Grandpa."

"An old man can only wish." Chloe, the youngest out of the entire O'Rifcan family squeezed his hand and smiled at him. The sweet gesture had Rhea smiling at the sister.

"It is beautiful here, despite the rain," Rhea admitted. "I tried to look around while I made my way here."

"Just wait until you see it on a good day," Roland explained. "Simply breathtaking. Especially at Clary's place." He motioned towards Claron beside her. "He's got the best spot in County Clare, if you ask me."

"Aye, indeed," Senior replied.

Rhea looked to Claron, but he continued eating without comment.

"We'll take you by there tomorrow," Layla chimed in. "The gap is best seen during the day."

Not sure what she meant by "the gap," and not wanting to give the family further reason to laugh at her expense, Rhea simply nodded in response before taking her last bite of roast.

"Dessert is waiting in the sitting room. Chloe, top off the glasses on their way," Sidna ordered, as she waited for everyone to rise to their feet and make their way out of the room with their glasses. Chloe stood at the door leading to the sitting area and refilled each glass as one after the other passed into the other room. Sidna began gathering dishes and Rhea began to help.

"Oh no, dear, you go on into the other room with the others."

"I don't mind helping, Mrs. O'Rifcan."

"It's Sidna, and don't you worry. I have plenty of help." She motioned to three children sitting at the small table in the kitchen finishing off their own dessert before hopping to their feet.

She felt a tug on her free hand as Claron pulled her towards the doorway to exit. "Best not to argue, Rhea. My mam has a nasty temper." He winked at his mother as she swatted him with her towel on their way out of the room. Rhea accepted more wine and the slice of lemon cake as she allowed Claron to lead her to a seat on one of the sofas. Sitting between Claron and Riley, Rhea looked to her grandpa. He grinned and wriggled his eyebrows as a loud conversation between Layla and Riley boomed across the room.

"Well, let's leave it up to a mutual party then, shall we?" Layla waved towards Rhea. "Rhea," she continued and waited until she had Rhea's attention. "Do you think it unfair for a young woman to date a friend of one of her brother's?"

Put on the spot, Rhea glanced to all the brothers' faces, not one revealing their thoughts. "Well... I guess it would depend."

"On what?" Layla asked, crossing her arms.

"On age, for one. Is the woman close in age to the friend?"

"Yes. Only a couple years off."

"Alright." Rhea tapped her fingers together. "And I guess it would just depend on the relationship between the friend and the brother. If they are best friends—"

"Which they *are*," Riley stressed in annoyance as he stared at his sister.

"Then the woman would need to be careful," Rhea continued. "So that should it not work out, that the relationship between her brother and his friend isn't compromised."

"Which it's bound to be," Riley added. "Because we all know it's not going to work out."

"Don't be so blue, brother," Layla tossed back. "Gage has had a glad eye for me for years. I just had to make him suffer a bit before I acquiesced." Layla winked towards her sister, Chloe, though Chloe only frowned. Layla grunted at the firm slap on the back of her head from one of her other brothers.

"Ouch!" She whirled and parried two consecutive punches into the man's shoulder before turning eyes back to Riley. "Trust me, Riley, I do not intend for things to go wrong."

"Isn't that what you said about my mate, Patrick?" Another brother— *Jace*, Rhea thought— replied. "He barely speaks to me anymore."

Layla waved his comment away. "He was too sensitive."

"And what about my mate, Owen?" Declan chimed in.

Layla flushed and then a guilty smirk crossed her face. "Yes, well there was him, wasn't there."

"Layla!" Chloe swatted her sister. "You didn't tell me about him."

"I'll tell you later, sister." She winked before all the brothers groaned.

"Layla," Sidna warned. "Mind yourself. Can't you look outside your brothers' friends for a lad? Is it that difficult not to stir feathers?"

"Mam, it is not my fault there are not many men in this town."

"You could always try Limerick," Riley suggested with a bite to his tone.

"Or Shannon," Rhea offered, receiving a friendly pat on the knee from Riley in appreciation.

"Shannon, bleh." Layla, disgusted at the thought, stuck out her tongue. "Besides, whose side are you on, Rhea?"

Rhea's eyes widened not knowing how to answer the question.

"I'm only slagging you, love." Layla grinned wickedly as she took a sip of her wine.

"I tell you I don't like it, Layla. Clary doesn't either."

Rhea heard Claron choke on his wine at being brought into the conversation at hand. "I don't recall commenting, brother."

"Gage is your mate too, you should feel the same as I do."

Claron sighed and bit back a grin as Rhea made a funny face at him while the others waited for his response. "I think," he began, "that Gage and Layla are two grown individuals that can—"

"Ah, forget you, brother." Riley waved away the rest of Claron's peaceful response. Claron received a wink from his sister and a small nod of approval from Rhea at his answer.

"This conversation is now closed," Riley said as he stood to his feet. "I'm leaving now. Have to work in Galway tomorrow."

"Whatever for?" Sidna asked as he bent to kiss her cheek.

"A new project, Mam. I'll be back late so don't expect me for sup tomorrow."

Rhea stood as he started to walk towards the door and followed, everyone watching as she waited for him to don his raincoat. When he caught sight of her standing close to him, he startled a moment and had her flushing.

"You alright now, Rhea?" he asked quietly. "Feeling comfortable?"

"Yes," she nodded in affirmation so that he knew he left her feeling content. "I just wanted to say thank you again for helping me today and getting me here."

"Ah," Riley chucked her chin with his knuckles. "I was glad to do it." He reached towards the small entry table and grabbed a pen and pad. "If you need anything tomorrow, don't hesitate to call me, yeah?" He handed her his phone number.

"Oh, I'm sure I will be fine, but thanks. I appreciate this." She held up the small note. "Good night."

"Night, lass. Later, family," he called as he tossed a wave over his shoulder and darted out into the rain.

Rhea stood by the door a moment and looked down at his number. Odd how a simple gesture of kindness could make her want to cry. *She'd spent too many nights crying the last few weeks*, she decided. So, she accepted the simple gesture with a glad heart. She took a deep breath as she made her way back to the sofa and sat next to Claron only a moment before he stood. "Well, it's my turn. I need to head back to the cottage."

"So soon, Clary?" his mother asked, disappointed.

"Aye, Mam." He leaned down and kissed her cheek. "Early mornin' for me." He nudged his glasses up his nose a bit and shook Roland's hand as he passed by him towards the door. "Rhea, it was a pleasure meeting you, lass. I'm sure our paths will cross tomorrow." He nodded towards his sisters. He waved and walked out the door shouldering on his rain coat.

Rhea wasn't sure what she felt, but the empty seats beside her made her wish to retire to her room for the night. She caught her grandpa's loving gaze and smiled. Walking towards him, she gripped his hand. "Breakfast tomorrow, Grandpa?"

"Unfortunately, I won't be able to, Rhea dear. But I could meet you for lunch." He beamed up at her, though she could see he was disappointed. "You can meet me on the patio there." He pointed to the opposite side of the house. "Just off the kitchen."

"It's a date." She kissed his cheek and turned to face the room. "It was nice meeting you all, but I feel jet lag is catching up with me."

"Oh, of course, dear." Sidna stood to her feet and hugged her tightly, Rhea almost getting used to the woman's hard embraces. "You rest up. If you need anything, anything a'tall, you just ring for me, yeah?" She pointed to a bell on the entry counter.

"I'm sure I will be fine, but thank you. I will if I need anything."

"We'll come by and steal you away after breakfast," Layla called to her.

"Sounds great. Thanks." Rhea waved farewell and headed up the stairs. She had high hopes for another warm bath, but when she spotted the comfortable bed, exhaustion slammed into her and she immediately decided a bath could wait. She needed rest. Tomorrow would be her first full day in Ireland, and she wanted to absorb as much of the country's beauty as possible. As her mind began to wander over the day's events, she felt herself smile before drifting into a deep sleep.

« CHAPTER THREE »

Tossing his glasses onto the bench, he grabbed the water hose and immediately started hosing off his shirt and pants. The stench of manure was overpowering. Not that he wasn't used to it, but the fact that he had slipped and fallen in the lot was undeniable evidence of his distracted mindset that morning. But it was hard not to think of the beautiful stranger that happened to walk into their lives the day before. *And Rhea was beautiful,* he thought. The dark, soft waves of hair around her shoulders, the smooth caramel color of her eyes. The elegant face with full lips and high cheekbones had haunted him all morning, as did the sadness that seemed to loom over her. He suspected she didn't realize it, but Claron could tell Rhea was in the midst of overcoming something. *It was none of his business*, he reminded himself, as he ran the hose through his hair and combed his fingers through the mixture of manure and cold water.

"Do you not have a shower for that?" Chloe's teasing had him glancing up to find not only his sister, but Layla and Rhea staring at him as well. All had curious expressions on their faces. He reached over to the faucet and turned off the water.

"I had an accident." He grabbed a small towel and began running it through his hair. "Blasted cows had me slipping and falling flat on my face in the lot."

"Yuck." The word slipped out before Rhea could stop it and it had the sisters bursting into laughter at the embarrassed look on their brother's face. "I'm sorry, I didn't mean for that to come out."

Claron shook his head as he grinned, "Well, I agree with you, lass. It's disgusting." He reached for his glasses and then began polishing the frames with the towel before slipping them back on his face. "So how is the grand tour of town going?"

"Good." Layla plopped onto a work stool and crossed her legs. "Pretty sure every man in town has fallen in love with Rhea."

Blushing, Rhea shook her head and eased onto the grass next to Chloe.

"I imagine so." Claron laughed. "Did you take her by O'Malley's?"

"Of course we did," Chloe said. "Besotted, he was."

Rhea laughed at that and shook her head. "He was very sweet."

"The old flirt is a pure picture of our Riley when he grows grey and old," Layla pointed out.

"Riley looks nothing like him," Rhea replied, confused, looking to Layla for explanation.

"Ah, not looks." Layla waved her finger. "Those two are the biggest gossips and biggest flirts in the village. Mark my words, Riley O'Rifcan will be a Thomas O'Malley one of these days. Nothing better to do than earwig on conversations and turn a glad eye to any pretty female that walks by."

"I don't know how Mrs. O'Malley stands it." Chloe added. "The woman is a saint. Her patience bar none."

"Do not speak poorly of the man," Claron defended. "He's a good man at heart and only means well."

"Says a man," Layla joked. "You don't have to wander into the market and expect to be haggled."

"All in good fun," Claron pointed out.

Layla shrugged.

"And take it as a supreme compliment," Claron continued. "It means he thinks you're a beauty."

Layla smiled at her brother and swatted his hand. "And just like that you make a lass feel gorgeous."

"It's a gift," Claron teased as he slipped his hands into his wet pockets. "So, what else do you three plan on accomplishing today?"

"Besides annoying you, brother, we plan to hit the local tonight." Layla looked to Rhea and she grinned.

"The local being the pub," Rhea recited, Layla and Chloe nodding in approval.

Claron laughed. "I see they are teachin' you the way of things, Rhea."

"Trying to." Their gazes lingered upon one another a moment and had the two sisters sharing a quick knowing glance with one another.

"So, will you be up for joining us, Clary?" Chloe asked.

"Maybe. I've just finished first milking. I need to visit the fields today, not sure how long that will take."

"So, you're a farmer?" Rhea asked.

Layla waved her hand over the barn behind her. "What gave it away, Rhea?"

Embarrassed, Rhea's cheeks warmed. "I mean, I didn't realize that was his job until we arrived, and I didn't realize he did cattle *and* fields. You know what, never mind." She finished her rambling and had all the O'Rifcans grinning at her.

"Don't be discomfited, Rhea." Claron walked over and extended a hand for her to grab and helped her to her feet. "Come, I'll show you about. You two, go and fetch us a drink." He motioned to the inside of the barn for his sisters and began leading Rhea towards a grassy field.

The grass swayed in the breeze, and Rhea reached down to her knee to run her hand over the top of the blades. The vibrant green was just as lush as she had imagined. Claron reached for her elbow and stopped her pursuit. She gasped as she looked out over the steep cliff that was at her feet.

"Welcome to the gap." He grinned.

"Wow." Breathtaking beauty of plunging cliffs and hills of green descended to a beautiful valley of vibrant flowers and choppy banks of the River Shannon as it weaved its way through the countryside. "How do you— What— Wow." Rhea's fumbling had him laughing.

"It has that effect on people," Claron said.

"And you live near here?" Rhea asked.

He nodded and pointed over her shoulder. She hadn't noticed the cottage on top of the hill when they arrived, but now she saw that it sat amongst the beautiful scenery, as if an artist had completed the picturesque scene with a personal touch. "Wow." She laughed at the absurdity of her own repetition. "I mean, it's so breathtakingly beautiful. I could not imagine waking up to this each day."

"It isn't difficult, that is for certain." Claron felt Rhea studying him and turned towards her. "Welcome to Ireland, Rhea."

A slow, wide smile spread over her face as she turned to survey her surroundings once more. "It's going to be good for me here." Her words were quiet, as if she meant them for herself and not for someone else to hear. She absentmindedly rubbed a hand over her collarbone as if tracing over an old wound.

"Do you plan to stay a while?" Claron asked, noting she immediately dropped her hand to hide whatever she felt she had given away.

"I'm not sure yet. To be honest, I just needed a change."

"Change is good. Sometimes," he added.

Nodding in agreement, she faced him, the wind tossing her hair into her eyes. She tucked it behind her ears. "This place suits you, Claron."

"I find it does as well. I'm too much of a hermit to live in town, but I'm too much of a family man to move too far away. I dreamt of owning this place when I was but a wee lad, and now I do."

Impressed and moved by the obvious love he held for the place, she stepped closer to him as they stood next to the drop off. "Can I make a suggestion?"

"Aye, go on."

"Perhaps a railing of some sort would be good right here."

He laughed. "You think so?"

She smirked as her gaze wandered the length of the cliff and surveyed the churning water down below. "If you hadn't guided me, I would have walked right off the cliff without even blinking. And how do the cows not fall off?"

"Usually the grass isn't so tall, and you can see the edge, but I've been a bit lazy with trimming the blades as of late. Besides, I don't normally have beautiful strangers coming to my cliffs."

She took the compliment in kind and held a hand over her eyes to block the sun as she peered over the edge once more. "The flowers are stunning. It looks like a garden down there."

"The fairies stay busy, that's for certain."

Amused, she cast him a curious glance. "Fairies?"

"Don't tell me you've come to Ireland and don't believe in fairies." Claron flashed a quick grin. "Legend has it that these very cliffs are where fairies are born."

Rhea tried to bite back her smile, but she couldn't help her grin. "I see. And have you ever seen one?"

"Aye, all the time." He winked at her as his sisters walked towards them and handed them each a glass of lemonade. "So, whereabouts are you ladies headed next?"

"Lunch with Roland," Chloe replied. "Luckiest gent in Ireland today, that man."

"Care if your lowly brother tags along?"

As the sisters said yes, Rhea said no she would not mind, and Claron smiled. "Bang on then, I'm going to grab a quick change and will be ready soon." He made his way towards his cottage and Rhea watched as he stooped to pet a furry bump sleeping on the stoop of his front steps.

"Isn't that something, sister?" Layla began looking directly at Rhea. "Our older brother weaseled an invitation out of our new friend. Should we warn her of his ways?"

Rhea turned to them. "What ways?"

Chloe laughed and waved away Layla's comment. "Clary has no ways. He's as genuine as they come. Layla just annoys easily when our brothers interfere with our friends."

Rhea smirked and placed a hand on her hip. "Oh really? And can you now see how Riley might feel that way about you?"

Layla's eyes widened in surprise at Rhea's gumption and Chloe burst into laughter. "Aye, she's got you there, sister." Hooting with laughter, Chloe accepted the slap on her shoulder in good humor as Layla's mortified face flushed crimson.

"You should be grateful, Layla, that our brother has taken a glad eye for Rhea. It shows his heart is mendin'."

Layla acknowledged that with a nod of agreement. "Aye, I guess so."

"I'm confused," Rhea admitted and had both sister's smiling.

"Our brother suffered a heart break about a year ago," Chloe explained. "He hasn't quite moved on from it."

"He has too," Layla defended. "It's that poisonous doxie, Amelia, who has not moved on her way." Disgusted, Layla jabbed her hands in her pockets as they walked towards her car. "Houndin' Clary like she's not the one at fault. It was her caught in another man's arms. Now she begs for Clary's affections? I don't think so."

Understanding, Rhea slid into the back seat of the car to wait for Claron.

"He is handling it," Chloe offered. "He does not seem interested in her tactics."

"And why should he be?" Layla continued. "No woman can cheat on an O'Rifcan and then expect us to welcome her back into the clan. I never liked her any way, but now when I look at her, I just want to pound her face."

Chloe patted her sister's arm to calm her down as Claron made his way back towards the car, freshly showered, hands in his pockets.

"Enough for now, sister," Chloe warned quietly as the back door opened and Claron slid in beside Rhea. She smiled in greeting.

"You smell better."

Grinning, he buckled his seat belt. "Aye, I did not think I wanted you to suffer the smell of cow manure in such close quarters."

"We are all thankful, Clary." Layla shifted into drive and made her way down the road towards town.

∞

The simple act of riding in a car with friends had Rhea feeling thankful and free, she realized, as she laughed at more jovial banter between the O'Rifcan siblings. She felt at peace as Layla wound their way through the narrow streets of Castlebrook towards the B&B. Friendly faces and waves provided opportunities for stories of the local residents. The businesses lining the street bustled with every day buzz and activity. "Wait," Rhea called out, and Layla slammed on the brakes, tires screeching, and turned in her seat.

"What the devil, Rhea?! You gave me a fright."

"Sorry, look, there's a bookstore." She pointed to the small building on the corner and had the sister's exchanging a nervous glance. "You guys didn't tell me there was a bookstore."

Layla turned back in her seat and waved an apology to the truck behind her as she eased into a parking space along the sidewalk. "You guys mind if I go take a look around really quick?" Rhea was already unbuckling her seat belt.

"You can go, but I will be staying here." Layla crossed her arms in defiance.

Rhea paused. "Is something wrong, Layla?"

Chloe turned in her seat and looked to Claron. "We do not shop at the bookstore."

"Oh." Rhea eased back into her seat. "Is there something wrong with it?"

"You could say that." Layla peered ahead as if even offering a glance to the cursed building would turn her into stone.

"Come, Rhea. I'll take you." Claron unbuckled his seat belt to the sounds of his sisters demanding him to stay in the car. He held up a hand. "Enough. We are going. Come along, Rhea."

"Are you sure?" Puzzled, she eyed him warily.

Offering a relaxed smile, Claron nodded. "Aye, come." He slipped out of the car and Rhea followed. He placed a guiding hand to the small of her back as he led her to the entrance. A sign out front bragged about excellent coffee and pastries, and the bell greeted them with a friendly ring.

"I love to read," Rhea commented. "I was thinking last night while I was snuggled up in bed that all I needed was a good book to read, though that was before jet lag set in and I passed out."

Claron smiled and quietly followed her inside.

"Oh wow!" Rhea looked around as if she stepped into a wonderland. Heavy velvet drapes of deep maroon hung in front of curved glass windows. Deep cushioned couches scattered about the store, tucked into nooks and settled in sitting areas with oversized chairs and coffee tables creating a warm and inviting place to snuggle up for a long read. The smells of coffee grounds and leather beckoned her forward. "I feel like I'm in a hobbit hole."

Chuckling, Claron led her towards the first row of books. "Aye, it does have that feel to it, doesn't it?"

"Very much so. It's so cozy. I could read here every day."

"I imagine that is the goal," he pointed out.

"True. Worked on me." Rhea ran her hand over the spines of books in front of her as she wandered up and down the shelf. "I'm not sure what I want to read. Any suggestions?"

He slipped his hands into his pockets as he followed alongside her. "That's tough to narrow down."

"Ooooh," she turned to him in excitement her hands softly clapping together. "You can help me." Grinning, she linked her arm with his. "I'm in Ireland, so I might as well read up on legends, folklore, and... fairies." She wiggled her brows at him and had him laughing.

"Perhaps you should." He walked them towards a separate cove of shelves. "Here's where you will find those."

"My goodness." Her eyes darted from book to book. "There's so many. Where do I even start?"

He pulled a book from a shelf and handed it to her. "This should get you through a few nights."

"Have you read this one, or did you just pick the first one you saw?" She eyed him suspiciously and he laughed.

"Hey now, love, I believe you have confused me with Riley. I give things more consideration than that. That be a classic regarding Irish lore."

"Oh." She smiled appreciatively. "Thanks."

He bowed slightly as she began flipping through the pages. "It even has pictures. Bonus!" She grinned up at him before flipping through a few more pages. "I'm sold."

"An easy sell." He took the book from her and tucked it under his other arm so she could continue to graze the shelves. Rhea kept her arm in his as they walked around the store. "The selection really is impressive, especially for a small village."

"Clary?"

Rhea felt Claron stiffen beside her at the sound of his name. They slowly turned and a petite brunette with bright blue eyes stared back at them. Her gaze slightly hardened at the sight of Rhea linked with Claron.

"Amelia," Claron greeted.

Rhea felt her heart race. This was Amelia, the woman who'd broken his heart.

"Who's your friend?" the woman asked.

"Ah, sorry, I'm being rude." Claron turned a genuine smile on Rhea. "This is Rhea Conners, Roland's granddaughter. She is visiting from America."

"I see." The woman's smile was polite, but stiff, as she extended a hand towards Rhea. "Amelia Biden."

"Nice to meet you, Amelia." Rhea said in kindness, though she now realized why the sisters did not want to venture into the shop. Perhaps Amelia liked to read there.

"Amelia runs this shop," Claron explained.

Rhea's eyes lit up. "Oh!" She smiled, though she now realized the full extent of Layla's disposition. "I was just telling Claron how wonderful it is. You have a great place here."

Amelia, though aggravated to find another woman with Claron, could not help but appreciate Rhea's kindness. "Thank you."

"He's helping me pick out some great Irish folklore to read the next few days."

"Is that how long you will be staying?" Amelia's question, though odd, did not deter Rhea.

"Oh no, my trip is open-ended at the moment. I just wanted something to keep me busy." She shrugged as her gaze wandered to a display over Amelia's shoulder. "Oh, look at that." She slipped her arm from Claron's and walked towards the books in front of her. She turned before reaching them, "I'm sorry, I—"

"You're fine, lass," Claron grinned. "Look around a bit. There's no rush."

Grateful, and also torn as to whether or not she should stay near him due to Amelia's presence, Rhea faltered. He waved her onward and Rhea kept an ear to the floor as she looked through the books.

"How've you been, Clary?" Amelia asked.

"Good, Amelia, thanks."

"You haven't returned any of my calls."

"I've been busy."

"Well, I can see that." Amelia's voice held a sting as Rhea felt the woman's eyes bore into her back. "If you aren't busy tonight, maybe we could—"

"Claron!" Rhea rushed towards them with a wicked grin on her face and handed him a book. "This one is for you." She handed him a novel. Fairies, dragons, and a touch of magic were promised in the bold script along the cover. "I got me one too." Rhea squealed as she handed him her copy as well. Claron shook his head. "I should never have brought you in here, lass."

"I'm in heaven." She lightly placed a hand on Amelia's arm as she said it. "I think this is my favorite place so far."

Amelia smiled in thanks but diverted her gaze to Rhea's arm now linked with Claron's once again. "I should stop while I'm ahead." Rhea patted his arm. "Ready?"

"When you are, lass."

She pointed towards the counter, and Amelia followed, slipping behind the cash wrap. Rhea fished in her purse for her wallet. She grabbed Claron's book and set it on her stack. "My treat. Agh—" She lifted her purse higher to dig around inside it. "It's in here somewhere. Give me a second."

Claron handed money to Amelia and she began wrapping up the transaction. When she had finished placing the books in a bag, Rhea fished out her wallet. "Okay, here we go." She slipped out her credit card and held it out, but Amelia shook her head.

"My treat," Claron said, as he grabbed the bag from the counter and held it out to her.

Rhea fisted a hand on her hip. "Claron."

"Don't Claron me, lass."

Her lips tilted as she fit her card back into her wallet. "You did not have to do that."

"I know. I wanted to. We'd best go now, Layla will be impatient, if she hasn't already left us behind. Thank you, Amelia."

"Yes, thank you." Rhea smiled sweetly as she slipped her new purchases into her free hand so as to slip her hand around Claron's arm as he escorted her out of the store. "And thank you, Claron, for not only buying these, but for accompanying me inside."

"It was a pleasure, lass."

When they rounded the corner, Layla's car was gone. "Aye, I figured as much." Claron shook his head. "Looks like we'll have to leg it from here."

"It's a pretty day, I don't mind. I'm just sorry you lost your ride."

"I'm not," Claron said. "I've better company now any way." He waved a greeting to an older man passing them on the sidewalk. "It's not too far a walk anyhow."

"So, will you be at the pub tonight?" Rhea asked.

"I've a mind to, but I need to see how the remainder of the work goes for today."

"No more falling in manure," Rhea added.

"Very funny." He nudged her as she grinned.

"I hope you can come. I won't lie, I'm a bit nervous about going."

"Why's that, lass?"

"Because I still don't know anyone. And everyone stares at the new person. I've been stared at all day and it's a bit discomforting."

"Ah, they only stare because you're beautiful." He complimented.

Rhea shook her head and rolled her eyes. "You Irishmen and your compliments."

Claron chuckled. "Aye, but we only speak the truth."

"Is that so?" Rhea looked up at him as they stepped onto the large patio of the B&B. Rhea, distracted by the large crowd and bustling activity froze a moment. "It's a restaurant."

"It is," Claron answered.

"Your mother owns a restaurant?"

"Aye. She operates for breakfast, lunch, and afternoon tea. Ah, there's Roland."

She allowed him to weave her through tables and chairs. "See," she whispered. "Staring."

Laughing, Claron pulled out a chair for her. She flashed Roland a welcoming smile. "Hey, Grandpa."

Layla and Chloe sat around the table as well, and Claron sat next to Rhea.

"How's your day been, Sweetie?"

"So great." She set her purse onto the ground beside her, followed by her book bag. "I owe it all to these three."

"Do not give me credit for that last stop." Layla sulked, taking a sip of her water.

"Layla," Claron warned under his breath.

"Oh, well, yes." Rhea offered an apologetic look to Layla. "But thanks to Claron I am set with a few books for the next week or so."

"That is good to hear." Roland waved a hand and Lorena sped towards them placing a fresh bowl of bread and butter in the center of the table. "Thank you. Lorena, right?" Rhea looked up at the sister and she smiled approvingly as she hoisted a tray onto her shoulder. "That it is, Rhea. Good memory. I'll be along shortly with your chips."

"Have you learned everyone's names yet, dear?" Roland asked.

Rhea shook her head. "Not exactly. I mean, I think I remember all the names, I'm just not sure I can place them with the right person."

"Well, you have us three figured out," Chloe offered. "And Lorena and Riley. Five out of ten is not too bad, Rhea. Most people in the village still get us O'Rifcans confused."

"Let's hear it then," Layla waved a hand for Rhea to tell what she knew.

"Okay, well, Lorena is the oldest and her daughter is Emily, not sure if she's married or not."

"She is. Her husband is Paul," Chloe provided. "He travels for work most of the time."

"Ah, okay, another name to add to the memory bank." Rhea tapped her temple. "Lorena and Paul. Then Declan?" Uncertain, she looked to the siblings for approval. Claron nodded.

"Okay, Lorena, Declan, Jaron, Jace..." She paused a moment. "Oh... tall, sandy hair, Claron's eyes and a cleft in his chin... think, Rhea, think."

The siblings grinned. "Agh, I cannot remember the other brother's name."

"Murphy." Chloe answered.

Rhea snapped her fingers. "Yes, Murphy. Then the redheaded brother…" She looked to Claron as if he would give her a hint. "Tommy!"

Roland chuckled at her enthusiasm. "Then Riley, Claron, Layla, and then Chloe. Phew! That's a lot to remember."

Layla clapped. "Well done, Rhea."

"If anyone else is married, I do not recall meeting any other women yet, so I should not be held responsible for leaving them out."

"Only Declan is married, the rest of us are all still single birds." Chloe explained. "Dec's wife is a nurse. Her name is Aine."

"Do they have children?"

"A boy, Rilan," Claron provided.

"Ah, the little boy from the other day. There was one more child though. Another girl," Rhea pointed out.

"Lorena has two children. Emily and Rose."

"Rose," Rhea said as if to bank it in her memory. "That's pretty."

"As is she," Claron stated.

Chloe rolled her eyes. "She's Clary's favorite."

"Not so," he defended. "I do not have favorites. That would be wrong."

His sisters looked doubtful and Rhea smiled.

"Rosie just has a way with me," he admitted, "that makes me want to give her the world."

"Mm hm," Chloe replied. "Wrapped around her finger, he is."

Rhea chuckled as he shrugged.

"And what of you, Roland?" Layla sidled up next to Rhea's grandfather. "Do you have a favorite O'Rifcan?" She batted her eyelashes and Roland tapped her nose.

"It's a grand tie between the lot of you. I couldn't choose just one."

"Ah, posh," Layla teased. "We all know it's me." She winked as Lorena swept by and placed meals in front of each of them. "Fish and chips." She rushed away in a blink.

"Chips?" Rhea looked confused as she stared down at her plate. "These aren't chips." She held up a potato fry.

"Such a Yank." Chloe teased. "It is a chip. What you Yanks call chips, we call crisps."

Rhea shrugged and popped a fry into her mouth. "Still delicious, whatever you like to call it."

"So, you still on for the pub, Rhea?" Layla asked.

"I think so." She looked warily at Claron and he draped an arm over the back of her chair.

"You will be," he said, tilting his head to her and waiting for her to feel confident about her decision.

Sighing, Rhea rolled her eyes. "Yes, I will be."

"Good." Layla clapped her hands. "Best rest up until then. Wear something sexy. We have the rounds to make, want to make sure we bring around the best talent. Or at least I need to, since Gage will be in attendance."

Rhea just shook her head. "I have no idea what you are talking about, but okay, I will do my best." She noticed Chloe's lack of enthusiasm at Layla's statement about Gage, but the younger sister grinned and patted Roland on the back. "We will only introduce her to the best, Roland."

"I'm counting on it." He tweaked her nose. "Clary, you will keep an eye on them for me?"

Though he had yet to confirm his presence for the evening, he nodded. "Riley will be there and is sure to be watchful."

"Ah, good." Roland stood. "I think I am going to take a walk by the river. Rhea, would you like to join me?"

She placed her napkin on the table. "I'd love to, Grandpa." She reached for her purse and bag.

"Go," Layla said. "We'll take this to your room for you."

"Thanks." Rhea nudged her chair under the table. "Thanks for today."

The sisters smiled.

"And thanks, Claron, for taking me into the bookstore."

"My pleasure, Rhea."

"See you guys in a few." She waved and darted after Roland.

« CHAPTER FOUR »

He watched as Rhea linked her arm with Roland's and laughed at something he said. She gently rested her head on his shoulder as they walked, Roland's cane keeping time with their steps and a contented smile on his face. Claron popped his last chip into his mouth and wiped his hands.

"So, how was the bookstore?" Layla asked. "Did you see Amelia?"

"We did."

"And?"

"And what?" Claron leaned back in his chair and took a sip of his drink.

"And did she speak to you? What did she think of you with Rhea?"

"I don't think she thought anything of it," Claron said. "Why would she? And besides, what do I care?"

"Atta lad." Chloe gripped his hand in pride.

"Amelia and I are over. She made her choice. She can pester me all she likes, but my mind will not sway."

"Riley told us she's been calling on you," Layla tested.

"Aye, but that does not mean I've changed my mind."

"I hope you don't." Her opinion hung in the air as Rhea's laugh floated on the breeze. Claron watched as she sat by Roland on a wooden swing hanging under a tree on the bank of River Shannon.

"Do you fancy her, Clary?" Chloe asked.

He turned to find that Layla had left the table to go speak with friends and his youngest sister studied him closely. "I do not know her."

"Aye, but do you fancy her? You can fancy someone without really knowing them," she pointed out.

Claron stood, tossing his napkin onto the table. "True. And how are you dealing with Layla pursuing Gage?"

Chloe shook her head on a sigh. "Doesn't seem to matter how I feel. She's got her mind made up on him. Besides, we both know Gage has never seen me as more than your younger sister."

"Perhaps he might if you shared your feelings with him."

Chloe shook her head. "It's not the right time for that. His eyes are on Layla, not me." Disappointed, but not deflated, Chloe shrugged with a smile. "I'm starting to believe there is someone else out there for me."

Claron laid a hand on her shoulder. "Aye, and he will be grand, Chloe."

She patted his hand. "Thanks, Clary."

"I think I will go join Roland and Rhea for a bit. If I'm able to come to the pub tonight, I'll see you there, sister."

Chloe nodded, worried that her brother, despite what he said, still troubled himself over Amelia. She could sense a bit of interest between he and Rhea and she hoped he did not let his wounded heart hold him back and that he would recognize the possibility right in front of him.

∞

"And so here I am," Rhea explained. "Sitting with you in this beautiful countryside. I can't say I'm too disappointed. It's a nice change for me, Grandpa. And for once in a long time, I feel at ease."

"I'm glad to hear it, sweetie." Roland squeezed her knee. "And have you heard from Oliver yet?"

"He's emailed me a couple of times... and called," she admitted. "I haven't responded to either."

"Good for you." Roland draped his arm over the back of the swing and Rhea snuggled into his side. He handed her a peppermint, and she smiled at the predictable offer. Unwrapping the candy, she popped it into her mouth as she lay her head on his shoulder.

"You know what's funny?"

"What's that, dear?" Roland asked.

"I don't even miss him. I thought I would. I thought I would be thrilled to hear from him. Thrilled that he would want to make amends. But I'm not."

Claron stood silent as he eavesdropped on the conversation. He knew it was wrong, but his feet did not echo the thought to walk away. So, there he stood, planted, and listening to Rhea share what he assumed was the reason for her visit to Ireland.

"I'm not even sad anymore. When I walked into the restaurant and saw him with her..." She paused, shaking her head in disgust. "I was devastated. When I was in the hospital recovering, all I could think about was that moment and the loss of what we had. But now, it just makes me mad. He makes me mad. The fact that I wallowed over him makes me mad. I'm just mad, Grandpa." Her hands fisted as she turned to see her grandfather's reaction. "Is that normal? Should I not feel something other than anger? I did love him... but was I not as in love with him as I thought? Should I not be more devastated about losing him to another woman?"

Surprised, Claron leaned against the edge of the rear porch railing, his hands in his pockets. So, Rhea had been cheated on as well. From the sounds of it, her situation was similar to his and Amelia's. He understood the anger that seemed to taint every memory, even the good ones. He also understood the feeling of rejection. The embarrassment of being in the dark. And the anger at being fooled.

"Rhea honey," Roland began, "I'm going to tell you something, and listen closely to what I have to say."

"I'm listening." Rhea reached for his hand and held it.

"You are free to feel however you want to feel, sweetie. There's no wrong or right way to handle the situation. You just have to handle it. If you do not wish to have anything to do with Oliver, then don't. But do not let his calls or emails anger you. Just let him go. If you wish to reconcile, that is up to you as well. But you feel and handle this the way that's best for you."

Rhea leaned back on a sigh and stared at the river. "I know for a fact I do not want to be with him again. Fool me once, shame on you. Fool me twice, shame on me. He's cheated on me twice, Grandpa. There's no reason for me to settle for a man that does that."

"I agree." He chuckled at her surprise to his response. "But I will support you no matter what, dear."

She gave him a tight hug. "Thanks, Grandpa. Thanks for letting me come visit you here. I will admit it's growing on me. And this is only my second day. I can't imagine how I will feel after a few weeks."

He patted her hand again. "I'd like to think you would consider staying."

Her eyes widened. "Really?"

"Why not?"

"I don't know, I just... I never thought about it. I've been operating on the assumption that I'd be heading home soon."

"Your ticket is open-ended, is it not?"

"It is."

"Then take your time to enjoy it here. If you choose to stay, I will help you any way I can. If you choose to leave, then I want it to be the best time of your life that you've spent here."

She kissed his cheek. "You're pretty great, did you know that?"

He winked at her and nudged his glasses up on his nose. "I've been told that once or twice."

Claron began walking towards them, his steps louder than normal so they would hear him coming. Rhea's head popped up and she smiled.

Roland turned. "Why, hello there, Clary."

"Roland." Claron offered a quick nod. "I was about to head back to the farm. Just wanted to tell Rhea goodbye."

"Ah, well don't let me stop you." Roland began to stand.

Rhea and Claron both shook their heads. "You don't have to leave," they said in unison.

"Grandpa, you can stay." Rhea accepted the quick squeeze to her hand as Roland grabbed his cane. "Nonsense. You two chat a bit. I've got to go bother Sidna for a munchy sweet anyhow." He patted Claron on the shoulder as he passed. "Still coming by tomorrow?"

"Wouldn't miss it," Claron answered, the two men exchanging a glance. Claron knew he was discovered, that Roland knew of his presence during Rhea's private conversation. He accepted the pat and eased into the spot Roland had vacated.

"Sorry to run him off."

"Don't worry about it." Rhea leaned back in her seat. "So, you're headed home?"

"Aye, here soon."

"Still not sure if you're coming to the pub tonight?"

"Depends on the state of my fields unfortunately."

"Need help?"

Amused, he turned to her. "You offering to tend to my fields?"

"If you need help."

"Do you know what to do?"

"No, but I'm a great listener and a fast learner."

He grinned. "I wouldn't want to ruin your first full day in Ireland, love. Perhaps another time. Besides, if you are to attend the pub this evening with Layla and Chloe, you'll need your rest."

Regret flashed across her face. "Oh no, is it going to be that bad?"

He laughed. "Not a'tall. I just imagine they will want to introduce you to everyone, and I do mean *everyone*."

Groaning, Rhea leaned back against the bench and bumped the arm Claron had placed there. She didn't move, however, and he found he didn't mind. "Only teasing, Rhea."

She turned to face him, their faces close. Her caramel gaze poured into his as she searched for truth. "No. You're not," she said, and then on a sigh ran her hands through her hair. "I'm a bit overwhelmed with meeting people at the moment. It's all I've done today."

"Aye, it's but a season."

"True."

"It's not every day we have a new person in Castlebrook. Pretty soon the polish will wear off and you'll be just another tarnished coin like the rest of us."

"Tarnished? I don't think so." Rhea crossed her arms. "I will keep my shine."

He playfully tugged on her hair and laughed. "Aye, I imagine you will, especially with that attitude."

"To be honest, I haven't fully allowed my body to rest from the flight. I'm feeling a bit sluggish."

"Then rest it is. See, working with me would only make it worse." He winked at her.

"Somehow I doubt that, but I will forfeit the idea for today. I'm actually eager to start reading my new books. Thank you again for those."

He waved away her thanks.

"Oh! Your copy is in my bag upstairs." She placed a palm to her forehead and went to stand.

"You can get it to me another time, lass."

"No, hold on. Just give me a second." She started to rush off and turned back to him. "Don't leave. I'll be right back."

He waved her onward and watched as she rushed through the back door of the B&B. He felt comfortable, too comfortable, sitting on the swing with his arm draped lazily over the back listening to the sounds of the river and the soft chatter coming from the B&B. Too comfortable and at ease with Rhea for only knowing her a short time. Not trusting this feeling, he slid his arm off the bench and slowly stood.

She came jogging out the back, his book in her hand. Breathless she held it out for him. "We should read it together."

His brows rose.

"I mean, we could." Her cheeks flushed. "You're busy," she fumbled. "I didn't even ask. That was foolish. I meant, if you have time, we should. But don't feel like you have to. It seems a bit silly now that I say it out loud."

Claron watched as she rambled, embarrassed with herself.

He gently took her hand and brushed his thumb over her knuckles, the gesture causing her to stop talking. He kissed the back of her hand. "I'll do my best, lass. I'd better head on now."

"Oh, right. Sure." Feeling self-conscious, she clasped her hands together and began walking with him towards the café patio. "I hope I will see you later tonight."

Again, a tightness in his chest told him to take a step back. She was too intriguing, too tempting, as vulnerability emanated from her in giant waves. "Me too, lass."

An awkward silence fell between them as they stood on the cusp of the patio and just stared at one another. He offered a small wave. "Until then, Rhea. Have a good day." With reluctant steps, he weaved through the tables and out towards the street. He felt her watching him but did not turn around for fear of lingering longer. He'd already spent too much time away from work. If he had any hopes of attending the pub for the night, he needed to busy himself the rest of the afternoon. Unfortunately, he felt the work may be tedious due to his mind focusing upon the woman who seemed to knock him out of sorts.

∞

Rhea stepped out of the shower shouldering on her robe and winding her wet hair into a towel-styled turban atop her head. When she stepped into her bedroom, she jolted. Chloe and Layla both sat on her bed. Chloe reading the back of Rhea's latest read, and Layla surveying her nails that she had just painted with Rhea's polish she had found on the vanity.

"You two scared me to death." Rhea's heart had yet to slow down.

Chloe set the book aside. "Sorry about that, Rhea. We thought we would come and dress together. That's what Layla and I normally do."

"Oh."

"Is that alright?" Layla looked up from her coral tipped nails.

"Sure." Rhea smiled, relaxing her shoulders a bit as she walked to her vanity and sat down. She didn't have siblings. Her parents had married later in life and Rhea came as a surprise several years after that. Her father, on more than one occasion, teased that she was all they could handle. So, having two sisters rush about her room as if it were their own was new. And as Chloe emerged from her closet draping the hanger of a sequined, copper-toned top over her head, Rhea smiled. "That would look great on you with your hair color, Chloe."

"Oh, I couldn't." She started to remove it from over her head until she caught sight of herself in the floor-length mirror. "Or..." She tilted her head. "Perhaps I could." She grinned.

"I have my outfit all picked out." Layla stood and walked towards a dress bag hanging along the top of the bed post. She unzipped the bag and withdrew a slinky— *and very short*, Rhea thought— navy dress.

"Layla!" Chloe gasped. "That won't cover your knickers!"

Rhea laughed in the mirror as she rubbed cream over her face. Layla, smug, draped the dress on the bed. "Aye, isn't the point of these legs to show them off?"

"Not always," Chloe admonished. "At least, not in such a dramatic way."

"I happen to like dramatic." Layla grinned wickedly as she winked at Rhea in her reflection. "What about you, Rhea? What do you have planned for tonight?"

Rhea spun around on her chair. "I'm not sure yet. I have a few dresses to choose from." She pointed to her closet, and Chloe walked back inside. The sound of hangers scooting along the rack told Rhea her wardrobe was receiving a thorough comb through.

"Ah." Chloe emerged carrying a simple black dress.

"That's boring." Layla waved her hand as she settled on top of the bed to paint her toenails.

"'Tis not." Chloe wriggled the dress at Rhea. "It's elegant. It's short," Chloe narrowed her eyes at her sister, "but not too short so as to look desperate."

Layla's blue eyes sparked as she growled at the insult.

"And it's, what is this fabric, Rhea? It feels like a dream."

"It's Peau de Soie." Rhea turned back toward the mirror and began smoothing foundation over her face.

"This is what you should wear," Chloe added, laying the dress gently across the bed. "You sure I can borrow this top?" She pointed to the sequins still hanging from her neck.

"Yes." Rhea nodded.

"I have some black skinnys I can partner it with." Chloe reached into a small duffle on the floor.

"You guys came prepared." Rhea appreciated the easy way in which the sisters welcomed her into the fold and she felt them becoming close friends though she'd only known them a day.

On the nightstand next to the bed, Rhea's cell phone rang.

"Ah, who do we have, Chloe?" Layla leaned forward to be nosy as Chloe peered down at the phone. "It's a Heidi for you, Rhea."

Excitement flooded Rhea's face as she hurried to the stand and snatched up her phone. "You are so late in calling me!" she exclaimed into the phone.

"Well hello to you too." Heidi's voice was loud as Rhea covered the mouth piece. "Sorry, this is my best friend from back home."

The sisters waved to her not to worry.

"I have to drive by your parent's house to learn that my best friend has traveled all the way to Ireland? What's that about?" Heidi asked, warmth in her tone. "I'm proud of you!"

"Don't be." Rhea eased into her vanity chair. "I'm not as brave as it sounds."

"Yes, you are," Heidi stated. "Oliver called me." Her tone grew serious. "He's worried about you. Said he's tried contacting you but hasn't heard back. Said he went by your parent's house but your dad wouldn't tell him where you were."

"Go, Dad." Rhea chuckled into the line.

"Seriously," Heidi agreed. "Any way, he's pathetic. Oliver, not your dad," she amended. "And so am I now. What am I going to do with you out of town? How long you staying over there, anyway?"

"I'm not sure. My ticket is open-ended."

"Wow." Disbelief rang in Heidi's tone. "You really did go all out on your escape, didn't you?"

"Not escaping, just... needed a change. Well, maybe I'm somewhat escaping Oliver."

"I don't blame you. Well, you have to call me from time to time. Life will be weird without our daily lunches."

"I know what you mean. You could always come see me."

"Ha! And miss out on the fabulous lifestyle of an accountant? Please." Heidi laughed into the line. "If you're there longer than a month, I'll consider it."

"Done," Rhea agreed.

"You're seriously thinking of staying that long?"

"Not sure. It's pretty great here, Heidi. It's beautiful. Grandpa is here. The people are fantastic."

The two O'Rifcan sisters perked up at that description and smiled at one another.

"It would be hard not to give it at least a month."

"Well, keep me posted. And send me pictures, dang it! I need to live vicariously through you as I start preparing for tax season and have no life."

"Done." Rhea laughed.

"Alright, well you have fun, Rhea. I have to buy groceries, ugh. I've stalled long enough sitting in my car in the parking lot."

"Just do it and get it over with," Rhea encouraged.

"Yep. Alright, chat with you later."

"Bye." Rhea hung up and smiled down at her phone. She then remembered the sisters. "Sorry about that. My friend, Heidi, didn't realize I was already gone."

"She should come see you," Chloe invited.

"That's what I said. But this is our busiest time of year, so she won't be free for a couple of months."

"*Our*?" Layla asked.

"Oh, accountants. I'm, well, I *was* an accountant before I left."

"And how's that?" Layla asked. "Crunching numbers for a living?"

"About as exciting as it sounds."

Chloe cringed and had Rhea laughing. "Let's just say I am thankful for a break."

"Well, the best way to start a break or break up..." Layla eyed Rhea with a narrowed gaze to relinquish a hold on her tongue.

Sighing, Rhea turned to face them instead of staring into the mirror. "Yes. I've recently come out of a serious relationship."

Chloe, her green eyes full of compassion sank to a seat on the arm of a small love seat in the middle of the sitting area. "Sorry to hear that, Rhea."

"Don't be. It needed to happen."

"What happened?" Layla asked, fanning her fingers beneath her mouth as she blew to dry her nails.

"He chose someone else." Rhea shrugged her shoulders as if the situation could not be helped.

"Rumbly fool," Layla insulted.

"Excuse me?" Rhea asked.

"Your Oliver. He's a fool if he gave you up."

The fierce loyalty in Layla's tone made Rhea's heart dance. The rallying of support elated her. "Thank you. Yes, he was and is. I don't know why I wasted two years with him. He'd cheated on me before too."

"He cheated?!" Layla stood straight to her feet. "Why, that—"

Chloe placed a restraining hand on her sister's arm. "We are sorry to hear that, Rhea."

"I don't understand why I didn't get a clue the first time."

"Because we're softies," Chloe admitted. "We like to believe the best in people. Especially those closest to us." She reached into her bag and grabbed a hair brush and began combing through her thick red hair, the glossy locks falling about her shoulders.

"I guess you're right." Rhea turned back towards the vanity and grabbed her eye shadow. "Despite him being the cheater, he made me feel like the fool. I have never been more embarrassed than standing there in the dining area watching my future unfold before me. I felt helpless to stop what was soon to be a train wreck. Or actually a car wreck, in my case."

"You were in an accident?" Chloe stood and walked over towards her, laying a hand on her shoulder. Rhea tilted her head up and pointed at her jaw line. The faint bruising barely noticeable. "Yep. I ran out of the restaurant and hopped in the car and floored it."

Feeling pity for her, and also tending to a friend, Chloe unwrapped Rhea's hair and began combing out the mass of wet chestnut.

"Men can be pigs," Layla spat.

"Not all men are," Chloe added. "Just some. You should count yourself lucky, Rhea."

"How so?" Layla scoffed at her sister.

"She sorted through him and now can move on to the right one. If the situation had not happened, then you would still be blind to his ways. Perhaps you married the man and his ways came to light later?"

"That would have been even worse," Rhea admitted.

"Exactly." Chloe parted Rhea's hair and continued brushing. "Now you don't have to worry about that. One pig out of the way leaves room for a better man."

"Or another pig," Layla pointed out.

"Layla," Chloe scolded. "Don't listen to her, Rhea. There are plenty of wonderful men out there."

"Chloe's always had a wistful heart," Layla explained.

"As opposed to Layla." Chloe rolled her eyes. "Who acts like sifting through men is a sport."

Rhea grinned at the sibling debate and the unaffected way Layla shrugged. "A sport I'm good at. And speaking of, my eye is on Gage tonight."

"Riley's friend?" Rhea asked and noticed Chloe's hesitant brush stroke at her sister's proclamation.

"Aye." Layla stood and tentatively pressed a finger to one of her nails. Satisfied they'd dried completely she walked towards the bathroom. "I'm going to shower." She shut the door and the muffled sound of water filtered through the room.

"She's determined, isn't she?" Rhea asked.

"It would seem that way." Chloe handed Rhea her brush.

"Thanks."

"No problem." Chloe smiled as she grabbed her own make up bag and set up shop next to Rhea, the two women sharing a seat.

"Do you have a fella in mind tonight?" Rhea asked.

Chloe shook her head. "Believe it or not I actually enjoy the pub just to visit."

Rhea chuckled. "That's how I'm approaching it as well."

Chloe grinned. "Besides, I don't think my brothers can handle two of their sisters latching onto their friends. That might cause a riot."

"Oh, do you have an eye for one of their friends?" Rhea asked quietly, though she felt she already knew.

Chloe darted a quick glance at the bathroom door. "I've always thought Gage a handsome lad. However, he has always had a glad eye for Layla. I'm just the little sister in his mind."

"You can't be that far apart in age, right? Or at least, you don't seem to be," Rhea added.

"I'm twenty-five," Chloe stated. "Layla is twenty-six almost seven."

"And how old is Gage?"

"Twenty-nine, I believe." Chloe's brow furrowed as she tried to remember.

"Have you told Layla?"

"Oh no," Chloe brushed the wand of mascara over her lashes. "Then it would be a competition, and I do not compete for a man's affections. I'd rather wait it out. But you—" She picked up a tube of Rhea's lipstick and quirked a brow. Rhea nodded that she could use it. "I imagine every man in the place will be vying for your attention tonight."

"Let's hope not." Rhea shook her head. "I honestly just want to have a good time."

"You will. Did we tell you our brother Murphy owns the place?"

"No!" Rhea perked up at that news.

"He does. He's always been a social one, our Murphy. It was no surprise when he opened the place. Bringing people together, that's his way."

"Seems to be the O'Rifcan way," Rhea added, and Chloe smiled.

"Aye, I suppose it is."

"Thanks for including me tonight and for showing me around today." Rhea caught Chloe's gaze in the mirror and both women smiled.

"To new friends." Chloe raised her perfume bottle and Rhea reached for hers and they clicked them together.

"To new friends," Rhea repeated and spritzed.

« CHAPTER FIVE »

The rain had dampened the soil, but not too much, Claron appreciated, as he lifted a hand from the tractor's wheel to acknowledge it was now his turn to plant the seed spuds. He'd rallied the help of his father for today to destone the soil so his farmhand, Buddy, could fertilize and then he could follow along behind and plant. Perhaps the efficiency would pay off and he would finish in enough time to shower and head to the pub with Riley and the gang.

He loved the smell. Damp earth freshly churned. He loved the look of a field freshly planted. The rows. The endless rows of possibility, of growth. And thanks to Ireland's climate, his potato crop yielded steadily. And if the fairies had a mind to boost his work along, he didn't mind.

What he did mind was the mist that began to splatter onto his windshield, and with its every drop, robbed him of his chance to dance with Rhea at the pub later. Hissing and restraining his tongue, he turned off the tractor and hopped out, climbing to open the bonnet to find the source of the leak.

"Problem, Clary?" His dad stalked through the freshly tilled soil and propped a foot on the wheel.

"Got myself a leak in the hydraulics, I believe, Da."

Senior leaned over and looked in as well. "I'll give'er a crank and you see where she's spoutin'."

"Aye. Go ahead." Claron watched as his dad climbed into the cab of the tractor and cranked. As it sputtered to life, Claron caught sight of the troubled area. He waved his hand for his da to cut the engine. Fishing around, Claron waved his hand again and Senior started it up.

Groaning, he waved his hand and the engine died. Senior hopped down. "Well?"

"It's going to take a bit, sorry Da. Thanks for your help today, but you'd best make it back to Mam for fishing. Her heart's set on fish for supper for the two of you tonight, and it looks like I may be here a while yet."

"Aye, you'd be right about that. Your Mammy," he clarified. "the woman loves her weekly fish date with me." He winked and slapped Claron on the shoulder. "If you need me, just give me a ring."

Claron nodded and watched as his da climbed into his lorry and headed towards the B&B. Claron could have used his help a bit longer, but he could see the fatigue lying beneath eyes the same green as his own. Da was best resting after a full afternoon of farming, and if the condition of the hose was any indication, Claron would be making a trip to Limerick for a replacement. *No pub tonight*, he thought.

Fishing out his cell phone he propped an elbow on the front of the tractor while wiping sweat from his forehead. "Aye, Aengus, Claron O'Rifcan here. I've a need for a hose." He shared the measurements and fittings and listened as Aengus tallied up the time frame in which to order a replacement. "What about Seamus? Wager he could cut me one today? I'm fresh in the middle of planting."

He listened as Aengus called out to his brother over the line and waited. "Aye, he can do it," Aengus said. "Head on this way, Clary, we'll have it ready."

"Thanks a portion." He hurried over to his lorry and set out towards Limerick. He'd just crossed O'Brien's Bridge when his phone rang. Seeing the caller id as Riley, Claron turned towards the County Limerick line and answered. "Brother, what has you calling?"

"Clary." He heard papers rustling in the background as Riley worked on whatever project had him sidetracked in Galway. "How's planting?"

"A complete disaster. And your building?"

"About the same."

"Seems we are both having a bleeding awful day of it then."

"Aye. Will you be makin' it to the pub then?"

"No. I am currently driving towards Limerick for a new hydraulic hose. Didn't even finish half the first field. It needs to be done by nightfall in order for me to remain on schedule before the next rain passes through."

"You will have disappointed ladies, brother."

"Layla and Chloe will understand."

"I wasn't talking of them." Riley grinned into the phone at the uncomfortable silence Clary carried through the phone. "Teasing, brother. Just teasing. I should be back in time to fill your spot for the evening. I promise to spin Rhea a few times in your honor."

"That'd be grand. I'm sure she would enjoy it."

"Is that all you have to say about it then? Why, I guess I will do more than spin her then. And here I thought you held a spark for our new Rhea."

"Easy now, Riley. I do not know her. And besides, I do not have time for a lass, no matter how pretty."

Riley cringed. "I don't even know how to respond to that, brother. I'm officially out of words and only feel pity for you. You have fun tinkering with your tractor then, and I will have fun tinkering with the ladies."

"Best keep to spinning instead of tinkering," Claron warned and grinned at the deep belly laugh of his brother. "Aye, I'll try to remember that. Have a care, Clary."

Hanging up, Claron continued through Castle Connell and onward towards Limerick, praying the usual half hour trip would roll by quickly on the M20. No matter how long the trip took, he knew he would miss out on a playful evening with his friends and Rhea. Which was a pity, he thought, because he did indeed want to give her a spin or two.

∞

"Don't be such a jibber, Rhea." Layla prodded her forward through the entrance of the pub, the heavy wooden door closing behind her. Music, so loud it pulsed against her chest, had Rhea short of breath as Chloe clasped her hand and began winding her through a thick crowd of people to a small table in the back. Several men threw darts as drinks passed freely between friends.

"Good to see you out, Rhea." Murphy smiled. "Welcome to the pub."

She smiled. "I was just told you own it."

His grin widened. "Aye. What's your drink?"

"Oh, she'll have a plain, Murphy, be on with ya." Layla waved away his hovering as he flipped a hand towel over his shoulder and nodded on his way back to the bar. Layla's eyes ever watchful, she straightened in her chair when a man walked towards their table. "Now is this the Yank your brother was rattling on about?" A man with smoke grey eyes and onyx hair winked at Layla as he approached and extended a hand to Rhea.

"Rhea." She shook his hand.

"Gage O'Donaghue. Pleasure to meet you, lass."

"And you as well."

"Chloe." He nodded a greeting towards the other O'Rifcan sister before turning his attention towards Layla. "I must say, Layla, you're a vision tonight. Shall we take a turn on the dance floor?"

Lashes pruned for sultry glances, Layla nodded. "You have my hand." She allowed him to escort her from the table just as Murphy returned with pints of Guinness for Chloe and Rhea. He watched Layla drape her arms around Gage's shoulders and slowly move with him on the dance floor though the music's tempo called for a faster pace. He shook his head and rolled his eyes. "Riley won't like that one bit."

"It was bound to happen." Chloe took a sip of her beer.

"Do you have a lady, Murphy?" Rhea asked.

His brows lifted slightly at her question and Chloe grinned. "What's it to you, Rhea?" she asked.

Realizing the way her question must have sounded, Rhea placed a hand on her heart in embarrassment as her cheeks flashed scarlet. "Oh, no, I didn't mean to imply I... I meant... Well, I'm still learning names, and if you had a girlfriend I would like to meet her and know her, is what I meant." Rhea trailed off as Murphy winked at her.

"No worries, Rhea. I understood you, lass. And the answer is no. I'm a free bird. A lonesome bachelor in these parts."

"Lonesome." Chloe rolled her eyes heavenward as she took another drink.

"How about you save me a dance, Rhea, darling. I'll swing by in a few to snatch you away."

"Sure." She nodded and watched as he headed back to the bar. "I like Murphy."

Chloe grinned. "He has a friendly way about him. Always has."

"Yes. He does. All of you do, really. In your own ways." Rhea's gaze traveled to the dart boards lining the back wall and watched as one man hit a bullseye, his friends celebrating his triumph with a round of high fives and shots. "I'm surprised Riley and Claron are not here yet."

"They will be." Chloe bumped against Rhea's shoulder as someone slipped up behind her and draped an arm over her shoulders.

"Why if it's not the most beautiful coppertop in all of Ireland sitting here without a dance partner." Chloe and Rhea both looked up to a ruddy face covered in a vibrant red five o clock shadow and sparkly blue eyes. A friendly squeeze about Chloe's shoulders and he slid into the seat across from them. "Is this the Yank then?" He asked, vigorously shaking Rhea's hand in greeting.

"This'd be Conor McCarthy, a great fool of a man who smiles when it rains and spreads his cheers to all those he passes." Chloe toasted towards him and he clinked his pint with hers.

"No kinder words, Chloe." He clinked his glass with Rhea's as well before chugging half his pint. "Your brothers about, Chloe?"

"Murphy at the kegs, of course. Riley be on his way. Not sure about the rest."

"I see Layla has enraptured our Gage."

"Of course. As was her goal."

He laughed in a wheezy gasp as he bobbled his glass on his next sip to make room for another person at the table. "Aye, and there one is." He grabbed the available hand and pumped heartily as he shifted over for Riley.

Relief eased Rhea's shoulders at a familiar face and she accepted the kiss to her cheek as he did the same to Chloe. "Looking beautiful tonight, my darlings. And where's our Layla?"

Rhea pointed towards the dance floor and watched as Riley's jaw tensed at the sight of his friend draped with his sister. "I see."

"Don't let it spoil your night, brother." Chloe patted his hand.

All of them watched as Layla and Gage walked back towards the table, Layla greeting her brother with a wink. "Good of you to show up, brother."

"And where's the other half of your dress, sister? Did you leave it at home?"

Layla looked down and then twirled. "Not a'tall. This is the new style."

"Really? I don't see Chloe or Rhea sporting such a look."

"They're old fashioned." Layla grinned at the girls before sliding onto a chair next to Rhea. Before Riley could respond, Chloe held up her hand. "Alright you two. We are to be showing Rhea a fun night, and we can't very well do that when you two are at each other's throats."

"Agreed." Rhea pounded a fist on the table in agreement and Conor laughed heartily at her judgment ruling. "Would you like to take a turn, lass?" He held his hand towards Rhea as he stood.

"A turn?"

"To dance." He snagged her hand and all but pulled her off her seat and had her spinning as they made their way to the dance floor.

"He'll be a good first dance." Chloe grinned as she watched Rhea try to keep time with Conor's sloppy steps. The radiant smile on her face told them she did not care that her feet were getting clomped on as they went.

"I'll give her a go here in a bit." Riley took a sip of his beer. "Save her from further bruising."

"And have you a word from Clary?" Chloe asked. "I know Rhea was hoping to visit with him."

"Was she now?" Riley's brow rose as he watched their new friend laugh as Conor spun her out and she almost rammed into another couple. He winked at her when she caught his eye and she waved on her way back into Conor's arms. "Well, he had farmer problems so he will not be making it."

"Pity." Chloe beamed as Rhea walked up breathless and tired from Conor's style of dancing and slid into her seat.

Conor took a long sip of his beer. "Best dance I've had in a long while, Rhea. I thank you." He toasted towards her as he finished his pint. "I think I will go bother Murphy for another."

"You're a saint, Rhea." Gage nodded towards her. "Nobody ever dances with Conor."

"And why is that? Other than the obvious fact that he cannot dance." She laughed as they did.

"He'as a good heart, Conor does." Chloe patted Rhea on the back. "And you made him feel special by allowing him the privilege to dance with a beauty."

"Well he asked." Rhea shrugged her shoulders.

"Well, if that's all it takes." Riley set his pint on the table and extended his hand and bowed. "Rhea, my love, would you do me the honor?"

"Now how could I refuse that?" She placed her hand in his and laughed as he mimicked Conor by spinning her uncontrollably towards the dance floor before straightening up and allowing her to catch her bearings before he glided her over the floor in expert fashion.

"You look lovely tonight, Rhea, darling."

"Thanks. You don't look so bad yourself. How was Galway?"

"Middling."

"And that would mean?"

He laughed. "Not bad. Not good. Just... middling."

"I see." She grinned and allowed him to spin her a couple of times. "I plan to visit Galway in a week or so."

"Is that so?"

"Yes. I have an aunt there I would like to see."

"Would that be Grace, then?" he asked.

Surprised, she nodded. "You know her?"

"Roland's ventured to Galway a few times over the years to visit with her."

"Oh, well, great. Yes, that's who I wish to visit."

"Perhaps we can plan a trip then. As I will be working up that way for some time, I could show you around while you are there."

"That would be fun." She smiled as the song ended and clapped with the rest of the patrons as the band announced a small break from playing and recorded music began blaring from the speakers. Her gaze wandered around the bar.

"He's not able to make it tonight, lass," Riley explained.

"I'm sorry?"

"I wager you're looking for Clary?"

She blushed slightly but tried to hide it and Riley found that truth quite telling. And endearing. "He had a mishap on the tractor and was traveling to Limerick for a fix."

"I see. Well, maybe another time. I have you to dance with, and that's a good thing." She nudged him. "Or Conor." She grimaced as she pretended to rub her ankle and had Riley laughing. "That you do. Forever and always, I imagine. Conor is a loyal one after all."

"Lucky me."

Rubbing a hand over the back of her neck and giving a reassuring squeeze, Riley kissed her cheek. "You're a sweetheart for it, Rhea, make no mistake."

And at that, Conor slid into his seat and slid a fresh pint towards Rhea. Riley winked at her as she offered a grateful toast and took a sip. The woman was a gem for accepting Conor and the rest of them as friends, and he watched as she paid particular attention to Chloe as well, as he knew his younger sister nursed a slight disappointment at Layla and Gage interacting. And interacting they were, he realized, as he saw his friend's hand rest on Layla's exposed thigh as if it were meant to be there. And in Riley's mind, it wasn't. Not at all.

∞

Rubbing a tired hand over his eyes, Claron finished washing his hands in the barn sink, splashing cold water on his face, and toweled to dry. The chime of his phone had him reaching for his pocket. "Hello, Mam."

"Clary." His mother's straightforward greeting had him hoping it was a social call and not a request for him to fix something at the B&B. After the day he'd put in, he was done for.

"You will come by the B&B and fetch a meal to take home. I know you must be melted after the day you've had."

"Thanks, Mam. I'll be there shortly." He was suddenly thankful for her call. He could muster enough energy to grab a hot meal before heading home. Though home was closer, the idea of cooking up something to eat did not rank high on his agenda. His bed, on the other hand, was at the top of the list. So, he dragged himself into his lorry and made the short drive to his mother.

As promised, she awaited him in the sitting room with his da and Roland, her knitting underway as she added blanket after blanket to the pile she had knitted for the future grandchildren she claimed to have one day. "Each would have their own." She always said. And she did her best to knit one blanket after the other to fulfill her promise. The fact her pile held over twenty blankets and she only had three grandchildren did not slow her down.

"Ah, Clary, you look completely buggered. Come, have a seat." She pointed to a comfortable chair next to Roland's. Predictably, Roland sat with his crossword as his father sat with his. They'd work the same puzzle and compete, and even place money on who would complete it first. And as always, his mam would have the final judgment on completion and correct answers.

"Did you fix her up, Clary?" his father asked.

"I did. And finished the field. *Just* finished, actually."

"Atta lad."

"A good day's work for you then." His mother set her knitting aside and ventured to the kitchen and came back carrying a bag of containers full of food. The warmth of it seeped into his hands as he set it on his lap. "Thanks, Mam."

She gently rubbed a hand over the top of his hair and then glanced at her hand. "Blimey, Clary. You'd best head on and wash up. And don't be leaving that in your hair. Best take the time, no matter how tired, to clean up before bed. You'll rest better."

At the clucking, the men all rolled their eyes and had Sidna's back straightening. "Don't be mocking me, you great fools. I only speak the truth of it."

"If I could sleep all night and all of tomorrow that would be grand." Claron stood. "But field two awaits me in the morning and then the milking."

"You work too hard, Clary," Roland said. "You need to hire a hand or two."

"I do, when need be."

"Your da does not count, and neither does Buddy some days," Sidna added. "You've the wages to support another hand, do you not?"

"Aye, but I struggle with trusting a man's work. One day I will, but after I've overcome the great disaster of Declan and Murphy from two years ago."

"Ah, now." Sidna chuckled as everyone tried to contain their merriment over the memory. "Your brothers were never meant for the work you do."

"Tis not their fault they were outsmarted by a cow," his father burst into laughter.

"Yes, well their being outsmarted cost me two days extra work rounding up *all* the cows and a new fence." Claron grinned as the front door opened and Rhea entered, her high heels in her hand. She froze as curious faces stared back at her.

"Oh, hello. I wasn't expecting anyone to be up and about." She glanced at her phone for the time. "Ah, I'm still slightly off on my time, I guess."

"No, you are accurate, I assure you. We just like to enjoy our nights as well." Roland beamed up at her as she placed a kiss on his forehead. "You are also back rather early, dear. Everything go okay at the pub?"

Rhea nodded. "It was fun. I'm still just a bit tired from traveling."

"Did no one escort you home, lass?" Claron Senior asked with a tinge of worry.

"Murphy did, though I'm afraid he didn't linger to say hello. He wanted to get back to the pub as quick as he could."

"Good."

"Hi Claron." She soaked in the image of him covered head to toe in dirt, oil, and manure. And though he smelled and looked frazzled, she found his presence a comfort. "I heard you had a long day."

"Aye. Sorry I wasn't able to come to the pub."

"Completely understandable." She waved away his apology. "Nothing too exciting happened. I met new faces. Layla and Gage were putting Riley in a mood, and Chloe found a friend in Conor for the evening, so overall, I'd say it was a full night."

"Oh, Conor McCarthy, bless him," Sidna said as she continued to knit. "Well, you look lovely dear. Just beautiful, doesn't she Clary?"

She eyed her son over the top of her glasses and he took the hint. "Yes, of course. Beautiful." He cleared his throat and held up his bag. "I'd best be going. Early morning and all. It was good to see you, Rhea."

She followed him to the door and opened it for him. "I hope you get some rest tonight, Claron, and that your day runs smoother tomorrow."

"Thanks." He offered a tired smile and ran his eyes over her dress and face, the small act causing her heart to beat one drum faster. "Night, Rhea." He nodded a farewell and she watched him climb into his truck to head back to the gap.

Sighing, she closed the door and went and sat in the seat he'd vacated. "He looked tired, didn't he?"

"Aye," Sidna said. "He's had a rough day so forgive him for not being social, lass."

Rhea waved a nonchalant hand. "I understand." She leaned over the arm rest of her chair towards her grandpa and focused upon his puzzle a moment. "Four across is Milan."

"Ah," Roland beamed.

"Cheating, he is, Sidna love. Best mark it down."

"Not if you use it too." She nudged Senior's book down and saw he had yet to solve that one as well and swatted his hand. "A fair freebie, then."

Rhea grinned as Mr. O'Rifcan sent her a wink. "Do you have grand plans tomorrow, Rhea?" he asked.

She rubbed her ankle that still throbbed from Conor's stomp. "Not yet."

"You will have supper with me at my flat," Roland invited. "On Saturday's I eat at home."

"I have yet to see your house, Grandpa. That will be fun." She smiled and squeezed his hand. "I look forward to it." She stood. "And on that note, I think I will head on up and get my own shower and rest. You all have a good night." She kissed her grandpa's cheek and headed up the stairs.

"A wonderful little bird you have there, Roland." Sidna nodded towards the stairwell.

"Agreed," Senior commented. "She'd do one of our boys just fine."

Roland laughed at the hopeful glance of Sidna. "Rhea is of her own mind." Roland warned. "And she is coming out of a serious relationship. In time, she may be ready for something new, but she needs healing."

"Healing is important," Sidna agreed. "But to be blind to opportunity should not be the way of it either."

"Blind to opportunity?" Senior shook his head in mock dismay. "My wife, the matchmaker. Calling our boys opportunities."

"Aye, and you after just saying she would do nicely. Do you wish for more grands?" Sidna eyed her pile of blankets and had Roland and Claron laughing.

"Plenty of time for that." He squeezed her hand. "Roland says the girl needs healing, that's what she needs then. Just like Clary. It takes time for a heart to mend."

"Aye, that's the truth of it." Sidna set her knitting down. "But a mammy wishes what she can in the meantime."

"Nothing wrong with a wish." Roland closed his crossword and stood, gathering his cane. "Until tomorrow, my friends. I think I shall take my leave as well." He tucked the book inside his jacket pocket as he headed towards the door. "Good night to you."

"Good night to you, Roland," Sidna called after him. The door closing with a quiet thud. "And I'll be doing more than wishing," she mumbled, causing her husband's roll of laughter to bring a smile to her face.

« CHAPTER SIX »

Odd, Rhea thought, as she walked along the edges of River Shannon behind the B&B, that she felt so at home and at peace in a new place. The light breeze teased her hair, and the filtered sunlight added a touch of refreshment to what had recently been gloomy days. The small stone path that ran alongside the river wound through shady oaks and small outcroppings of benches, hammocks, and swings that the O'Rifcans had strategically placed for their guests to enjoy. And by the soft chattering of an elderly couple occupying one of the benches, Rhea knew Sidna had hit the mark. Mrs. O'Rifcan's personal touch to the bed and breakfast lingered everywhere. The warmth, the personality, the intimacy of family all enraptured the guests and made them feel at home and as part of the large family she already possessed. The elderly couple would feast alongside all the O'Rifcan family that night for the evening meal. It was custom for all the O'Rifcans to join together for supper if possible. A tradition, but more importantly, an enjoyable time with family.

Tonight, Rhea remembered, she would join her Grandpa at his apartment, or flat, as he called it. She reminded herself to call him and ask if she needed to bring anything. *Like food*. She wondered about his life here. Wondered how he made such a commitment to a country not his own. Though as she continued her walk and her stay in Ireland, she felt she was beginning to understand. But her Grandpa had lived in Ireland for over thirty years. Rhea never knew her grandmother, and since her passing, it was said her grandpa immediately moved to Ireland and never looked back. Well, except to visit. But she never visited Ireland as a child. Her parents never vacationed to visit him once she came along. It was always Grandpa showing up on their front steps out of the blue to shower his love and attention on a lonely Rhea. She longed to know more of his story, what he'd spent the last thirty years doing in Ireland. *Why Ireland in the first place?* she wondered. She felt a vibration in her pocket and pulled out her cell phone. Not recognizing the number, she answered.

"Rhea?"

She froze. Debating whether to hang up or just toss her phone into the river, she stood silent a moment longer. She was rather fond of her new phone case, so opted for growing a temporary backbone that would force her to converse with the man who'd broken her heart. Oliver.

"Oliver," She finally said, her greeting lacking warmth, but her voice held steady. She slid her free hand into her front pocket of her jeans and continued to lazily make her way down the stone path. "What can I do for you?"

"I've called you a dozen times. I've emailed you, why have you not returned my calls?"

"I've been busy."

"So I hear. I finally talked to Heidi and she told me you were traveling. Where are you?"

"Does it matter?" Rhea bent forward and picked up a small stone and tossed it into the river.

"Of course it does. We need to talk, and our conversation would be better had in person."

"Unfortunately, that is impossible." Rhea felt relief at that statement.

"And why is that?" Oliver's tone turned condescending as he continued. "I'll just wait until you come home then. I can wait. No matter how long."

"And you're sure I'm actually coming home?" Rhea's question lingered a moment as she shook her head at his smugness.

"What do you mean you are not coming home?" Oliver asked. "Did you move?"

"It's still up in the air."

"Where?"

"Like I would tell you, Oliver. Why is this important? And why do you think we need to talk? What is there to say? To me, you made your feelings pretty clear when I saw you kissing another woman."

"That was... a mistake, Rhea. Obviously, I only want to be with you."

"*Obviously*?" Rhea laughed into the phone and found the nearest swing to sit. "How in the world would it be obvious that you want to be with me *when you are kissing another woman*?" she stressed.

"You misread the situation."

"Oh really? So, when I was in the hospital recovering, why did you not come and see me?"

"Your stay was so brief, Rhea, by the time I heard of the accident you had already been released."

"I was there a week!" Her voice rose, and she paused to compose herself. She heard a whistle making its way up the stone path and offered a wave as Riley meandered his way towards her with a friendly wave. "Listen, it's not important now. I have to go."

"Wait, Rhea, wait," Oliver interrupted. "I want us to work this out. We need to—"

Riley walked up and Rhea smiled. "So sorry, have to go." Without saying goodbye, she hung up and patted the seat next to her. "Perfect timing."

"Is that so?" Riley sat down onto the swing and draped an arm over the back completely at ease as he tugged her ponytail.

"Oliver." She gestured towards her phone.

"Ah, the eejit."

"I'm assuming that's insulting, so I'm going to say yes."

Riley grinned and nodded. "And what did Mr. Oliver have to say?"

"Oh, that he wants to talk to me. That he wants to work things out. The usual spiel."

"And you don't want to?"

She turned horrified eyes to him. "Why would I? He cheated on me. He chose someone else."

Riley held his hands up in surrender. "I was only asking, love. Seems to me he's not used to taking no for an answer."

"He's not. Oliver has always gotten his way." Rhea leaned back and rested her head on Riley's shoulder.

"Tell me what I can do to make you feel better." Riley rested his cheek against her hair and squeezed his arm around her shoulders.

"Can you go beat him up for me?"

Laughing, Riley turned her face towards his. "Consider it done. And I'll do you one better than that, Rhea, I'll take all the O'Rifcan lads with me. That's seven against one."

"I like those odds." She grinned as she leaned forward and rested her elbows on her knees and her chin in her hands. "It's hard not to feel insulted when someone doesn't want you, but at the same time you are grateful to know so that you can move on. It's just the act of moving on that seems to be hard, even though you remind yourself of the circumstances. It's a weird thinking pattern. Cyclical if you're not careful."

"Aye, believe it or not lass, I understand your situation."

"You've been cheated on?" She looked doubtful and then rolled her eyes when he shook his head.

"No. But Clary has, and I've witnessed firsthand how that very cycle operates. It's a brutal one, it is. And none too easy to shake off."

"So, how did he?"

"I think he still is."

"Layla said it was Amelia. I felt terrible yesterday making him go to the bookstore. If I had known she was the owner, I would not have pushed to go inside."

Riley waved her worries away. "Don't you worry about that, lass. It's good for Clary to face her down every now and then. Amelia is like your Oliver. She's been houndin' him. Wanting to patch things up. But she made her choice, and Clary did too, and he does not want to play second fiddle."

"And I don't either," Rhea added. She rubbed her hands over her ponytail. "It's so frustrating that you can feel confident in who you are one second, and then one person's opinion of you can completely reshape your opinion of yourself. Why do we let that happen? Why do we question our worth just because one person doesn't find us valuable?"

"Good question. Though I think you need to focus on the first part of your statement there, Rhea." Riley turned to face her. "If you feel confident in who you are, what does it matter what anyone else thinks? Just be you and be happy about it. And those who do not appreciate you for who you are be damned."

A small smile tugged the corner of her mouth. "You're right. I shouldn't care so much. Especially if I no longer want him in my life any way. I just need to *be*."

"Exactly. And I've only known you but three days and I can tell you now that Oliver is a fool." He playfully squeezed her knee.

"Thanks." Reluctantly she stood. "I should head in. I'm to meet Grandpa at his place for supper tonight."

"Ah, good 'ol Roland. Yes, I'm sure you will have a grand time."

"Thanks for listening, Riley. And thanks for being a friend."

"It's what I do best. Well, one of the things I do best." He winked at her and laughed as she rolled her eyes. "I'm an amazing architect, did you know?"

"Oh, is that what you were talking about?" Doubtful, Rhea laughed as he grinned wickedly. "Riley O'Rifcan, something tells me you are a heartbreaker in these parts."

"I don't know what you mean, love." He winked. "Come, I'll walk you to the house and you can see I am a perfect gentleman."

And perfect gentleman he was, though three women had stopped to chat with him and Riley had a pleasant kiss to the hand to offer each of them, along with dashing compliments that had them scurrying away flushed with interest. Waving goodbye to Riley, Rhea hurried passed Sidna and Senior in the sitting room to run upstairs and change for her evening with Roland.

"She is in a tizzy, is she not?" Sidna continued knitting on yet another blanket and waited for her husband's response.

"I'm sure it has nothing to do with our son, now does it Riley?" He eyed his son from across the room.

"Not a'tall, Da. Just walking her home after a spell."

"What sort of spell?" Concerned, Sidna lowered her needles.

Riley shrugged. "Seems her Oliver called while she was enjoying a walk and upset her."

"The poor dear." Sidna placed a hand over her heart. "And you cheered her up, darling?"

"Of course, Mam." Riley winked.

"At's a lad," Senior said.

"She's a wounded little dove," Riley continued. "Much like Clary was at the beginning. Makes me want to strangle the man who made her so."

"There are no strangers in heartbreak," Mr. O'Rifcan stated. "She'll heal in time, as has our Clary. He be a good example to her of healin'."

"She doesn't really even know what happened between Clary and Amelia, Da. And besides, I don't think she knows any of us well enough to be taking advice as of yet."

Senior shrugged. "She's a strong one, that Rhea. I believe she will bounce back to her feet in a short time. Just needs extra care for a bit."

"I agree," Sidna added. "And perhaps more time with Clary would do just that."

"Clary?" Riley asked. "Misery deserves company?"

"Oh no." Sidna waved away his comment in a huff. "Oh no. I've picked him for her."

"Is that the way of it?" Mr. O'Rifcan looked at his wife as if she'd grown an extra head. "You can't just force two people together, Sidna. Clary has his own mind, as does Rhea."

Sighing, Sidna shook her head. "When two people share similar experiences, it can lead to a good foundation."

"Mammy..." Riley leaned against the chair.

"Don't Mammy me," she warned. "I would have chosen her for you if you weren't such a flirt. You're worse than Tom O'Malley at the market."

Unoffended, Riley grinned at his father. "Rhea is quite bewitching, but as you say Mam, she is not for me. Whether or not she is for any of us will have to wait and be seen, but she is family already, and that is for certain."

"Aye, agreed. Whoever belongs to Roland is family indeed." Senior nodded his approval towards his son. "Now on with ya. Your mother and I wish for some peace."

Riley trudged towards the back entrance through the kitchen, snatching an orange from the counter bowl as he went. "Low on oranges," he called over his shoulder, as he stuffed an extra in his pocket and headed home.

∞

A knock sounded on the door and Roland eased to his feet and crossed the carpeted floor to the entry. "No cheating," he called over his shoulder as he opened the door to a smiling Rhea. "Hello, dear. Come on in." He stepped back for her to enter and she paused while shedding her coat. "Claron?"

Claron glanced up from a chess board and smiled in welcome. "Evening to ya, Rhea."

She eyed her grandpa curiously.

"Clary and I have a standing Saturday night supper. Also gives me the chance to beat him a few rounds at chess."

Concentrating on his next move, Claron scoffed as if offended, but he wore a friendly grin as he nudged his bishop forward. "Your move." He then looked up at Rhea as she studied him. "I hope you are better at this than I am."

"I haven't played in a long time."

"Besides, Rhea is my card player." Roland eased back into his chair and motioned towards the glass of wine on his table. "Wine is in the kitchen, Rhea dear, if you wish for a glass. Pizza should be here shortly."

"Pizza, beer," she motioned towards Claron's bottle, "wine," she motioned towards Roland's glass, "and chess." Grinning she sat on the sofa as she watched them. "You two are just regular party animals, aren't you?"

"Is she making fun of us, Roland?" Claron faked offense and had Roland chuckling as he nudged his glasses further up his nose and moved his rook. "I believe so."

"Not poking fun. Just making an observation." She rose as another knock sounded on the door.

"Money is on the table, Rhea." Roland motioned without glancing up and Rhea shook her head on a grin.

Opening the door, she beamed when Conor McCarthy stood on the other side holding a pizza box. "Conor," she greeted warmly.

"Well, if it not be my favorite dance partner. How's the evening, Rhea?"

"Great. And yours?"

"Oh, just keeping busy." He handed her the pizza as she handed him the money.

"Conor's family owns one of the best restaurants in town." Roland stood and thanked the young man for the pizza. "It's a real treat."

"Thank you, Roland. Though we can only hope to hold a candle to the lovely Mrs. Sidna." He nodded a greeting towards the table. "Clary, good to see ya."

Claron walked forward and shook his friend's hand. "Missed you at the pub last night." Conor nodded towards Rhea. "I have me a new dance partner." He winked and had Rhea laughing.

"The best dance of the night," Rhea bragged.

Conor flushed as he pocketed the money. "Oh now, I don't know about that for you, Rhea love, but it was indeed for me. I thank you, and you as well, Roland." He nodded towards the pizza. "You three have a good night."

"You too, Conor." Rhea shut the door and turned with a thoughtful expression. "What do you think about Conor and Chloe?" she asked, and had both men look at her as if she'd beamed down from another planet.

"What on earth gave you that idea?" Claron asked.

Rhea shrugged as she headed towards the sofa and set the pizza on the coffee table. "He's friendly, kind, and fun to be around. He seems to have a solid friendship with the family, and he seemed to appreciate Chloe last night."

"The day Conor McCarthy dates an O'Rifcan woman will be the day I die of unbelief."

"Why?" Rhea asked.

Claron laughed. "Let's just say that Conor isn't the smoothest of men when it comes to... anything."

"So? His heart is in the right place," Rhea pointed out.

"True. There be no better heart in the county," Claron continued. "But I'm not sure if that is enough for our Chloe."

"I'm going to mention it to her." Rhea helped herself to a slice of pizza as Roland handed her a napkin.

"Do not meddle, Rhea, dear," Roland warned.

"I'm not. Besides, Layla attempted to pawn me off on about a dozen different men last night."

Roland noticed the stiffening of Claron's jaw at her statement and bit back a smile.

"Is that so?"

"Yes. It was quite exhausting really and partially the reason I came back early. I just wanted to visit with everyone, but it seems matchmaking is on her brain. Chloe, however, was more pleasant company. I learned she is the town florist. I didn't know that."

"Aye, loves flowers, our Chloe. She has a way with them." Claron took a hearty bite as Rhea extended a napkin towards him. He nodded his thanks. "She also knows all the town gossip due to most new or secret relationships involving the gifting of flowers. I imagine you will have a few bundles come your way after last night."

"Why would anyone send me flowers? All I did was dance with a few people."

"Ah, but we Irishmen love gifting flowers to a pretty lass, even if it's just for dancing."

"Oh boy." Rhea leaned back against the cushions and sighed as Claron grinned and Roland laughed.

"Don't worry, dear. The O'Rifcan boys will look out for you."

"I don't need looked after, Grandpa." Rhea sat up straight.

"I didn't mean you did. I just meant that they will make sure that the gentlemen who decide to show you attention are decent fellows." Roland looked to Clary and he nodded he would if need be.

"Right, well, I don't need that either. I'm a grown woman. I can look out for myself."

"If that isn't Grace coming out of your mouth, I don't know what is." Roland's voice held a sharp edge to it that had Claron briefly turning to him in surprise.

"And what is wrong with that?" Rhea asked, as she walked towards the kitchen and poured herself a glass of wine. "Aunt Grace has a great life, and she's never married. Clearly it is possible for a woman to be happy without a man."

Roland stood to his feet and walked towards the kitchen with his own glass. Rhea topped it off. "Rhea, you listen to me." Roland's voice lowered, but Claron still heard every word. "Grace made her life choices because they were what's best for her, or so she thinks. But you are not Grace."

"Maybe I wasn't before, but maybe I'm more like her than you realize, Grandpa."

"Impossible." Roland made his way back to the table and Rhea leaned against the door jam watching him move a chess piece and Claron politely waiting his turn.

"Why would that be impossible?" she asked. He moved a pawn and then looked back towards her and sighed with a tender smile.

"Because you are a gift, Rhea. A wonderful woman meant for a loving family. Grace chose her path, but I guarantee there are moments she wishes she had chosen a different one. You, dear, are just hurting. Once you see past the hurt, you will be able to look towards the future. Or *a* future with someone else."

Embarrassed that Claron was present for a brief glimpse into her personal problems, she flushed as she sat on the couch and reached for another piece of pizza. "We will see," she murmured around the bite in her mouth.

"Check mate," Claron called and leaned back in his chair with a smug smile as Roland leaned closer towards the game board to observe the circumstances of his loss.

"Thanks for distracting him, lass. You just gave me a win." Claron stood and walked over to the couch and snatched another piece of pizza as he sat beside Rhea. "You can look at it all you want, but I won," Claron taunted towards Roland.

Roland nudged his glasses back up his nose as he continued studying the board. "I'm astounded, but I believe you did." He looked up and grinned. Claron held up his beer in a toast towards Roland.

"Time to celebrate." Claron took a long sip of his beer and laughed as Roland shook his head and made his way to a worn recliner and sat.

"So, is this how you two party animals usually spend your Saturday nights?" Rhea asked, tucking her feet underneath her on the couch and peeling a pepperoni off the top of her pizza and popping it into her mouth.

"Is she saying we are not fun?" Roland asked Claron.

"I believe she is. I'm insulted, lass, for Roland and I are always fun." He winked towards her grandpa as he laughed.

"The truth is, Rhea, dear, that Claron takes pity on an old man and comes to keep me company."

"Ah, now Roland, you know that's far from the truth. I come to beat you at chess."

Roland laughed again, lightly rubbing his thumb under his eye as they watered with joy. Claron leaned towards Rhea and dropped his voice. "I'm not sure if you can tell, love, but this'd be my first time besting Roland." He grinned wickedly as Roland guffawed in his chair.

"He is not a humble winner." Roland laughed.

Rhea's lips tipped into a smirk. "Gloating does not become you, Mr. O'Rifcan."

On hearty laughs the two men grinned and had Rhea's mood lifting significantly. She was thankful for Claron. Though he did seem to genuinely enjoy her grandpa, she also knew his weekly visits were, in a small way, his way of keeping an eye on the older man, and for that, she was grateful. And she also found his willingness to do such a thing endearing.

"Rhea dear, turn the volume up a notch, won't you?" Roland waved a finger towards his television and nodded in approval for when she needed to stop turning the dial on the ancient box set. An announcer's voice flooded the room as the two men settled back with their respective drinks to watch whatever sport graced the screen. Rhea watched the remaining portion of the game and munched on her pizza in silence as she tried to figure out the concepts of the sport in front of her.

She took extra time to study Claron's profile as he sat on the opposite side of the couch. The defined jawline, the nice nose with a slight hump that spoke of an unfortunate incident in the past that had left its permanent mark. She would have to remember to ask him how he broke it. The mindless task of nudging his glasses up that slightly crooked nose had her lips tilt in a small smile. He, like the other O'Rifcan siblings, was nice to look at. As if he felt her staring, he turned and offered an encouraging smile as though he knew she was bored out of her mind watching the sport. She felt her cheeks flush and hoped he didn't realize she had been watching him instead and that she was anything but bored with the task.

∞

"You're a gem, Rhea." Claron placed a hand on her back as he led her down the small staircase in front of them as they departed Roland's flat. "I think Roland enjoys having you here."

"And you're a gem," Rhea added. "For spending your Saturday nights with him. I'm sure there is much more you could be doing, but it's sweet of you to keep him company."

"You act as if it's charity." Claron slid his hands in his pockets as he walked up the sidewalk to escort her to the B&B, though she didn't ask. It was an unspoken gesture that had him feeling content. She slid her hand in the crook of his elbow, another gesture that seemed natural and pleasing to him. "Truth is, Roland is one of my most favorite people to hang around with. There's wisdom in the elders, and usually better company. Roland offers the best of both."

Rhea studied him as he spoke and leaned over and kissed his cheek. Surprise had him turning. "You're sweet, Claron. And I appreciate your caring about him."

"It's a mutual caring, I believe."

"I saw that," Rhea agreed. "There is one thing I need to ask you, though."

"Of course, lass, ask away." Concern had him slowing his pace.

"What in the world is *hurling*?"

Laughing, Claron lightly patted her hand as they rounded the corner onto the street that would then lead them to Rhea's destination. "Were you confused a bit?"

"Very much so. I mean, I tried to figure out the game you guys were watching, and believe I did for the most part, but… it's a bit dizzying to watch." She looked up at him as they walked. "I understand throwing the ball through the goal posts scores you points, much like it would in any other sport, but why bounce the ball on the end of a stick?" She paused a moment in thought. "Did you ever balance an egg on a spoon as a kid?"

"Can't say that I have." He looked down at her as if she'd grown an extra head.

A light giggle slipped past her lips. "There's a game, usually played at kids' parties, a relay of sorts. You place an egg on a spoon and you have to run with it a ways and turn around and come back. You then hand the egg to the next in line and they do the same. The point is to not drop the egg, or it cracks, makes a mess, and you lose."

"And this be like hurling to you?" More confusion as he tried to piece together what she was saying.

"Sort of reminded me of it, yes. Especially when they'd run tapping the ball on the edge of their sticks and it began to run away from them a bit. Like, oops, uh oh, here we go now, ah, ah, annnnnd tap. Score!" She pulled him in zigzags up the sidewalk as she spoke and had him laughing.

"I am sure the GAA would appreciate you thinking their highly competitive and historic game equates to party tricks for children."

"I didn't say it equates," she amended. "Just that it reminded me of it. I see the athleticism in it. I like that the players can still be tackled by one another. Adds a bit of excitement to it when there's a chase happening."

"Aye, we'll make you a camogie player in no time."

"What is camogie?" Rhea tilted her head up and caught the small smirk before he replied.

"It's hurling, but the women's variety."

"Then why can't they just call it hurling?"

Claron's brow narrowed as he peeked over the top of his glasses at her.

"It's a long story?" she asked.

He grinned.

"Okay then," Rhea continued. "In America we love our football, baseball, and basketball."

"And which is your favorite?" he asked curiously.

"Oh…" She thought a moment. "Well, I guess I lean more towards baseball. My dad and I usually keep up with it, watch games together, especially the World Series."

"And did you play?"

She shook her head. "For women, it is called softball. But no, I didn't play." She smiled. "I tried out for the team once, but I was terrible."

"I don't believe it." He nudged her with his shoulder, and she laughed.

"You should. I'm pretty sure my terrible aim and the black eye the coach received will forever live in infamy."

"Away with ye…" His eyes widened in disbelief, and he watched the slight blush stain her cheeks as she stifled a giggle.

"For safety's sake, the coach's and my own, I opted out of playing."

"I should hope so." He turned up the walkway to the B&B and guided her up the front stoop. Stepping into the warm interior, the friendly faces of Senior and Sidna welcomed them. Rhea smiled.

"Why, hello dear." Sidna's smile broadened as Claron stepped in behind Rhea. "Clary," she greeted warmly.

"Mam. Da." He nodded and then slipped his hands into his pockets as Rhea turned to face him.

"Thanks for walking me home."

"Home now, is it?" he asked with a smirk. She flushed, not realizing her mistake. "It was my pleasure, lass. You have a good night. Perhaps I will see you at the meal tomorrow."

"Oh Clary, don't run off in such a hurry now." His mother stood to her feet. "I've a bit of milk cake keepin' warm. You two will have a slice with tea." She bustled away before either had time to respond. Claron just shrugged in apology as he motioned for Rhea to lead the way towards the kitchen. Mrs. O'Rifcan set two plates on the small table nestled in the kitchen as she began pouring two hot cups of tea. "And how was Roland, Clary?"

"Nursing a sore ego at the moment would be my guess." He winked at Rhea.

"Still so humble," she murmured, making him laugh.

Sidna watched as they bantered back and forth and quietly made her exit to give them time to chat further. Her heart warmed at the sight of them together, and she just knew her inklings were correct when it came to the two.

"Don't look so smug, love. You will jinx the fates." Senior flipped a page in his book and peered disappointingly over the rims of his glasses at his wife as she bustled back into the sitting room looking pleased with herself.

"It's a mother's way, Claron, to see to it our children are well matched."

"Should they want to be," he reminded her.

Ignoring him, Sidna grabbed her latest knitting project, another blanket, and sat smugly in her chair, tuning out her husband's advice, and hoping for the best.

« CHAPTER SEVEN »

It was half past midnight when Rhea climbed under the handmade quilt that covered what she considered now to be the most comfortable bed she'd ever slept on. Though she considered it was just her tired body's way of letting her know it needed rest, she relished sinking into the deep mattress and comfortable pillows with a long sigh of pure pleasure.

She and Claron had sat talking in the kitchen for over three hours and two slices of milk cake each. She pulled the covers up over her shoulders and smiled blissfully into the dark, her stomach fluttering at the thought of him. She warned herself not to read too much into their interaction and tried to fight the giddy feelings floating around her gut, but like her softball tryouts, she failed, and her mind raced over every detail from the previous few hours spent in the company of a certain handsome Irishman.

Rhea also tried to muster up some sympathy for Claron as she realized he had to wake up in three hours to start his morning milking for the dairy cows. She grimaced and felt a pang of guilt for keeping him up so long. And the fact he would still have to drive home to the cottage at Angel's Gap, cutting into his sleeping time as well, did not escape her notice. She would just have to take him a hot breakfast tomorrow morning. With coffee. *Lots of coffee,* she thought. She found, in the small time they sat together, that despite his mother's attempt at tea, that Claron much preferred coffee instead. Black, with a touch of cream. Fresh cream, too, from his dairy.

Rhea shook her head in disbelief. He worked the land and milked cows for a living. Much different than her desk job back home in the city. She crunched numbers and helped people with their taxes. She also helped with a bit of bookkeeping here and there, but for the most part, her life was spent behind a desk tapping away on a keyboard and glaring at a computer screen. She couldn't fathom waking so early in the morning and tending to cows. Then spending the entire afternoon working to produce crops on several fields, and then milking cows again. She learned he did the milking twice a day. Every day. The thought baffled her.

Not that she didn't know it needed to be done. After all, milk had to be made. *Made?* she wondered. *Probably not the right terminology*, she realized. But she knew in order for there to be milk in the refrigerator or at the supermarket that farmers had to somehow retrieve it from the cow. *And butter too*, she thought to herself and then had her mind wandering down a separate rabbit hole of questions on how butter was produced and manufactured. She would just ask Claron. That thought cheered her, as she loved hearing him talk about his work. Loved hearing him talk, period. His voice was lyrical. The melody of his Irish accent mixed with odd jargon she had yet to fully understand, but enjoyed, soothed her. The way his green eyes lit up when he spoke about his grandparents and helping them run the dairy when he was younger. It was in his blood: the farming, the cottage, the Gap. All of it encompassed who he was, and she realized she had never met someone so at home *in* who he was and what he did. He was happy with his life. With his family. With his work. And she envied him of that.

She knew he had overcome a heartbreak due to Amelia, but they had yet to rip that band aid off. Perhaps when they did, she'd have to do the same and speak of Oliver. But right now, she enjoyed getting to know the charming man she now considered a friend. And as her eyes grew heavy, she also enjoyed that her last thought of the day was of him.

∞

"I must say, brother, I was surprised at your call." Murphy shuffled around the milk parlor, dipping teat cups into sanitizer and flushing them with water as he and Claron readied for the first round of cows to milk. He watched his younger brother wipe a palm over his tired face, the exhaustion evident as Claron walked towards the door and opened it up without enthusiasm. They stood in the milk parlor, on the lower level known as the pit so the cow's udders hung at eye level and within easy reach. They worked quietly, the small radio in the corner playing music to soothe the cows against Murphy's unfamiliar voice. The small area normally did not bother Claron, but he wasn't used to having someone in his space. And though he appreciated Murphy's help, his head ached, and he really didn't want conversation. However, he also knew that if he didn't want to talk, he'd chosen the wrong brother to help him. It was in Murphy's nature to chat and joke around. It was his way, to be friendly and amiable. One of his best attributes, Claron admitted, but on a morning with only two and a half hours sleep under his belt, the sound of Murphy's merciless chatter only irritated him and made the drum in his head pound even harder.

"You're not yourself this morning, Clary. What's got you so out of sorts?"

Claron stepped down into the room and cringed as his foot landed in a bucket full of sanitizer Murphy had forgotten to move.

"Aye, sorry about that brother," Murphy swooped in and removed the bucket, placing it out of the way. "Got a bit of a posser now, don't you?" He grinned, restraining a laugh at Claron's miserable expression. He slapped Claron on the back. "Come now, Clary, it's just a wet boot, nothing to damper your entire morning."

"Tis fine, Murphy." Claron grumbled as he made his way to the door and opened it. "Morning ladies," he greeted the first few cows with pats on their sides as they filed in one after another lining seven cows on each side of the parlor room. The brothers worked smoothly, Murphy casting curious glances Claron's way as they worked. As if the silence were too unbearable, Murphy plopped his hands on his hips and turned towards Claron with a frown on his face as Claron led the next group of cows into the room. "Tell me your woes, brother, because this mood you're in is dampering my mornin'. I did not offer help just to surround meself with a grouch." Scolding was not in his nature, and Murphy shifted uncomfortably under the weight of it as Claron turned to him with an apologetic shrug.

"Just tired, Murphy, nothing more. No mood here. My own fault for staying out too late."

"You and Roland party to the wee hours?" Murphy's scowl turned into a chummy grin as he began dipping cups to sanitize again before placing them onto the fresh cows.

"Not Roland. Rhea." Claron blocked off the entry with a rope and set to work as well, as the cows shifted their weight and then settled comfortably under his familiar care.

Murphy's brows rose as did his smile. "Oh really? Late night with our new Yank, hm? Is there something brewin' between you and our Rhea?"

"Just long conversation, Murphy, nothing to blabber about." Claron turned a serious face towards his brother and pointed. "No gossiping about it and making it more than it was."

Murphy held up his hands in innocence. "I do not gossip. I'm not Riley. I just... explain things to people... elaborately."

"Exactly." Claron fought back his grin as he turned back to his work.

"Do you know how she takes her tea?" Murphy asked. If his brother memorized that tiny detail about Rhea, then it was more than just a friendly conversation last night and more of his brother wanting to spend time with their new Yank. A lot could be said with just a simple cup of tea.

"Milk and two sugars. What does that matter?" Claron looked confused as he brushed a dirty hand through his hair and slipped his glasses off to wipe away water droplets.

"Nothin' a'tall." Murphy shrugged at his brother. "Call it me own curiosity. So, what did you and Rhea *discuss* for so long? Was it her recent break up? I guess you two would relate on those grounds, come to think of it."

"What? No." Claron pointed a finger at his brother. "Gossiping," he warned. "And besides, Amelia and I have been over for quite some time. So I wouldn't call that recent." Aggravation tinted his tongue as he slipped his glasses back on.

"First, it is not gossiping if it is a fact, little brother. We all know Rhea is visiting because she had a rough time of it after her relationship with a man named Oliver came crashing down. Literally crashing on her end."

"I'm not listening," Claron chimed. Though he was, and blast, curiosity finally got the best of him. "What do you mean by crashing?"

Murphy grinned to himself as he turned to reply. "Her car accident, of course. Have you not noticed the faint bruising on her face?"

"Yes, but…" Claron trailed off. "I just assumed the relationship was a volatile one."

"Oh, no. Our darling Rhea was in a car accident. Word has it that she discovered her fella Oliver cheating and ran out and drove away. Distracted, or blind with fury, would be my guess, she ended up in an accident that very night."

Sympathy settled in Claron's chest for Rhea. The heartbreak of such a discovery. It was a raw pain he knew all too well. And though they covered large ground in getting to know one another the night before, neither of them mentioned their past and most recent hurts. It was none of his business, he reminded himself. But he couldn't help wanting to know more. After the previous night, he found himself wanting to know everything about Rhea. And God help him, he wanted Murphy to tell him what he knew. "What else have you heard?"

Pleased with himself, Murphy stopped whistling his tune and patted a cow on her side as he grinned. "Hmmm… what would you like to know?"

∞

Rhea groaned at the pounding on her door. Her feet, with bricks tied to the bottom, or so it felt, trudged their way over the softly carpeted floor. Opening the door, she squinted at a beaming

Riley. "Mornin' lass," he greeted, charging by her and into the room.

"Riley, please come in." Sarcastically she waved a hand at the empty doorway and then turned to face him.

"Best dress, love, for I am stealing you away for the day."

Rhea didn't bother stifling her yawn as she eased onto the side of her bed. Slowly, she started bringing her legs back up into a curling position and plopped down against her pillows. "Can you come by again later?"

Her eyes were already drifting closed when she felt a sharp sting on her thigh and a loud pop sounded through the air. Riley stood, much too proudly, she surmised, as he held her towel from the night before that had been draped on her chair. She rubbed her leg. "That hurt."

"It was meant to." He winked. "Up and about, Rhea love. I am taking you to Galway for the day."

She turned her face into her pillows. "I can't today, Riley."

"And why is that? Stay out too late with me younger brother, did ya now? Well, I won't be letting Clary steal all your time, lass. It's my turn for today. Dressed and ready to leave by eight. I'll be waiting for you downstairs with a mug for travel."

She heard her door shut and she moaned as her achy body reluctantly slipped into a sitting position. She glanced at the clock. At least he had the decency to give her a solid hour to prep herself for the day. She stretched and sighed as relief flooded to her lower back and tired muscles. She reminded herself to pull back on the late nights, no matter how fun, so her body could receive some much-needed rest. But then she thought of Claron and her plans to take him breakfast. Which then led her to the shower where she replayed their entire evening over again in her mind.

He'd be wrapping up first milking and be headed to the fields soon, she thought, as she stepped out to towel off. She expertly applied her make up and scrounged around her closet for a pair of jeans and a light sweater to wear over her blouse should the early spring weather take a chill or rain during the day. She wondered if Claron felt tired too, or if he was used to such late nights. That thought bothered her more than expected. For why would he have consistently late nights? Why was she even thinking about it? Why did she even care? He was his own man. His own person. Had his own life here in Ireland. Just because she showed up didn't mean he should change his ways. Now he had *ways*. She shook her head in disgust at her train of thought. Not all men had *their ways*, she reminded herself. Not all men were Oliver.

Even more disgusted with herself for thinking of her ex, she slipped into a pair of flats and grabbed her purse before heading out the door and down the stairs. True to his word, Riley finished stirring her travel mug as she walked into the kitchen.

"Good morning, dear!" Sidna greeted. "Trust you were able to get some brief shut eye last night." Her pleased smile had Rhea blushing.

"Yes, thank you."

Riley handed her the mug. "And how pretty you look, lass, even with ten minutes to spare." He winked as he grabbed a small paper bag off the counter. "Breakfast. For the road. Come along."

"You haven't even told me why you're taking me with you. Don't you have to work?" Rhea grumbled after him closing the door behind them and making Mrs. O'Rifcan chuckle as she listened to their trailing conversation.

"I figured it was time for you to get out of Castlebrook."

"I've only been here a week."

"Aye, and you haven't already gotten the itch to explore?"

"I have yet to see all of Castlebrook." She held up her hands in defeat as she waited for him to open the passenger door.

"Plenty of time for that. We have a drive ahead of us, but I think you will enjoy the city for the day."

"And what am I to do in the city?"

"Why, I figured I would drop you off at one of me favorite restaurants, so you can eat a proper breakfast, and then after that it is up to you. Because as you so sweetly pointed out earlier, I have to work."

"If you're working the whole day, why am I going? I don't want to spend my day alone. I had plans for today, Riley. I was going to be taking breakfast to Claron this morning, hopefully get a full tour of his farm, and then I was go—"

"Ah, planned to see my brother, did you now?" He watched as a blush stained her cheeks.

"I take it my mam's comment about shut eye was because you and Clary had a late night at Roland's?"

"No. We sat in the kitchen and talked... until late. It was stupid, really, knowing he needed to wake up early to milk."

"But..." Riley prodded and lightly squeezed her knee as she turned away to look out the window and to hide her embarrassment.

She swatted his hand which made him laugh. "You fancy me younger brother, lass?"

"No." She answered too quickly.

He laughed which made her wish to disappear into thin air. Or perhaps the wispy clouds that dominated the sky at the moment.

"Can't two people of the opposite sex just have great conversation?" she asked.

"I'm hoping so, considering we have over an hour of driving time." He glanced at his watch and smiled.

"And why is it, just because two people can talk a while that everyone assumes they '*fancy*' one another? And why is it always *fancying*?" Annoyance flowed from her in droves, as Riley continued down R466.

"Most of it is teasing, lass." He signaled to pass a slow car that occupied an elderly woman barely able to see over the top of the steering wheel. "It would be the same if you had been talking to Murphy, Tommy, Jaron, or Jace."

"And you?" she asked.

"And me, no doubt." He winked at her. "My family tends to play matchmaker regardless of whether or not two people wish to be matched."

"I have noticed your mother's attempts at sort of... nudging me Claron's direction."

"Nudging, is she?" he asked in surprise.

"Okay, more like pushing," Rhea admitted and laughed when he did the same.

"Mam loves a good love story. She especially loves it when it is one of her own in the write up."

"Has she ever *nudged* you towards a woman?"

"Oh plenty of times, yes. However, I'm a fish that can't be caught."

Rhea sputtered before she laughed. "Is that so?"

"Aye. I'm just a man about town. A mild flirt with no desire for deeper relationship."

"*Mild* flirt?" Rhea narrowed her gaze at him and he grinned wickedly.

"Of course."

"I haven't even known you that long and I know that is a downright lie."

"No fooling you, hm?" He chuckled, completely unashamed. "It's my way. The way I see it love cannot be rushed or pushed upon a person. It just sort of happens. My Mam just tends to think all love stories should be like her own."

"And what is her story?"

"She fell quickly, madly, and deeply in love with me Da and they were married right off. I will save you the details as I am sure she will tell you of it herself come time for it."

"I'm a sucker for a good love story myself, but I'm not interested in my own at the moment."

"Ah, the infamous Oliver," Riley began. "Heard from him again?"

"Every day." She crossed her legs in the seat and rested her hands in her lap.

"Still not giving up, is he?"

"Not a bit." She tried to hold back a smidgen of disdain, but by Riley's frown she could tell she failed.

"Can't fault the man for trying." He waved a hand to ward off an attack as he saw the sparks fly from her eyes. "Not saying he has a right to you, lass, just that I can understand his groveling. I've taken a shine to you and I've only known you a week. I can imagine the heart strings you grip when a man's known you longer."

"In an odd way I think you're complimenting me."

He laughed. "Aye, though obviously not very smoothly."

"I appreciate the sweet words, Riley. But Oliver is just playing his game. That's all I ever was to him. One big game. I'm gladly passing him off to the next girl. Whatever her name is."

"As you should," he agreed. "Though it must be somewhat satisfying to see him beg."

"Not really. I mean, don't get me wrong, I kind of thought it would be. But it's not. It only makes me angrier and more resolute in my decision to come here. I cannot imagine how inescapable he would be if I were back in Maryland."

"Good thing you are here, then. Indefinitely." His sly smirk had her grinning.

"Not sure about indefinitely, though I will say it's growing on me."

"We'll see how you feel in a few weeks. Once you're an O'Rifcan, you're always an O'Rifcan."

"Who said anything about becoming an O'Rifcan?" Baffled, Rhea turned to face him.

"Lass, the moment you walked into the B&B you became an O'Rifcan. Like it or not you are family from here on out. What's Roland's is ours."

The conviction behind his statement had her eyes glistening. "That's sweet." She reached over and squeezed his hand. "And believe it or not, it's exactly what I needed to hear right now."

He returned the hand squeeze and kissed the top of her knuckles before returning his hand to the wheel. "If Oliver continues to bother you lass, you let me know."

"He's harmless, Riley. He'll get the hint soon enough, or he'll move on to another woman, either one. But thank you." She fisted her hand and rested her elbow on the window sill and chin on her fist as they passed rolling green hills. "No matter where I look there's beauty here."

"Aye, you will have to convince me on an off day to take you around, or the girls, or perhaps Clary could. Castles and ruins every turn it seems. Nice to look at."

"I can't imagine living near castles." Rhea's eyes softened as they passed through a small village and locals waved in greeting from the sidewalks.

"You're an American, of course you can't. Your country is a wee baby compared to Ireland."

"That's true," Rhea agreed. "The fact you guys have buildings and structures that date back to the 12th century is hard to imagine when our oldest buildings are just over 200 years old. It's amazing really, that there are castles still standing after all this time."

"Been reading your books, have you?"

Rhea nodded. "Before you know it I will know everything about Ireland. Myth, legend, and history. It's rather fascinating. Although, I have to say I am fonder of Irish folklore than history right now. Mainly because those were the books Claron bought me at the bookstore the other day. So once I'm finished reading those, then I can move onto history."

"You're a studious one, Rhea."

"I'm curious, that's all. If I'm going to live here, I might as well know all about it."

"Live here?" he asked in a leading tone.

"For the next few weeks," she amended on a wistful sigh as they passed an old cratering building that looked to date back hundreds of years. "Or months," she whispered under her breath as Riley eased around a wide curve in the road leading them on towards Galway.

« CHAPTER EIGHT »

His feet were barely keeping up with his steps as he walked towards the cottage. Rugby, his lazy Irish Setter, raised his head as Claron trudged up the front stoop and opened the door to the house. "Been waiting for me, have you?" The dog lazily stretched its front legs and yawned, the action causing Claron to do the same. He shook the tiredness away as he stepped inside to a ringing telephone. He grabbed it on his way to the refrigerator for a cold bottle of water. "This is Claron," he answered. The bottle froze half way to his lips. "Excuse me?" he asked. "Who is this?"

He listened as the female voice carried over the line and had Rugby's ears perking at the sound. Claron motioned to the dog to sit and Rugby complied, accepting the pleased pats to the head as a result. "I am sorry, lass, but my cottage is not for rent. Not for a weekend or a day. I live here. I don't know where you got the idea to rent me home, but—" he listened. "A website? I'm not on a website... what's the site address?" He grabbed a notepad and jotted down the information with a scowl. "I'll be looking into this." He hung up the phone and shook his head. "Odd."

Rugby tilted his head. Flopping his ears with a hearty pet, Claron led the way towards his living room, kicking off his shoes along the way. Normally he wasn't so untidy, and he valued things in their prospective places, but he was so exhausted all he could think about was a hot shower and his bed. At least for a few hours until the next milking. Field work would have to wait until tomorrow. He just didn't have it in him for today.

Though he hated feeling sluggish, Claron did not regret the time spent getting to know Rhea the night before. Though their conversation centered mostly around his youth and growing up in Castlebrook, the few insights into her life were interesting as well. He couldn't imagine being an only child. Having such a large family, though at times a nuisance in regard to having privacy, the chaos and comradery was a staple in his life. He loved that no matter what life threw his way, he had family beside him. His siblings were his best friends, and though Rhea spoke of her good friend Heidi, he couldn't imagine not having siblings.

The water pounded against his back and he concentrated the spray at the base of his neck to help soothe the sore muscles that resided there. If he had the time, or energy, he would have made a quick trip to the B&B for breakfast in hopes of catching Rhea before she started her day doing whatever it was she planned to do. However, he knew his mood needed improving first, otherwise he would not be good company. Just a few hours sleep. That's all he needed, and he would feel like an entirely new man. Toweling off, he headed towards his bedroom and flopped onto the oversized bed that had yet to be made, which is how he preferred it. Not even bothering with clothes, he slid under the covers and closed his eyes.

His eyes immediately flew open at the sound of Rugby whining in his face. The hopeful pale, brown eyes had him grinning and patting a hand on top of the covers. Eagerly, Rugby hopped onto the bed and settled at his feet. Claron rolled over to find a more comfortable position, and though he was exhausted, he could not fall asleep. He eyed the book on his bedside table: the Irish folklore purchase Rhea had asked to read with him. He reached for it and settled back against his pillows on a sigh. He could read for an hour or so and then fall asleep. That would work. Rugby eyed the book in disdain through narrowed eyes. "Just for a bit, bud." He opened the book and reached for his spare glasses on the nightstand, immediately bringing the words into focus. Brushing up on legends and lore was a good plan. It meant more conversation with Rhea. And if he was honest with himself, Claron realized that's exactly what he wanted.

∞

"I'll just park here and walk you inside." Riley nudged the gear shift into park and hopped out of the truck. Rhea slid out after him.

"Are you not eating with me?" she asked, as he draped his arm over her shoulders and began leading her up the sidewalk.

"Nope. I have to be at work."

"So, you brought me to Galway to drop me off at an eatery just so I can sit alone and then spend the day by myself?"

Riley laughed as he kissed the top of her hair. "I am not so cruel, Rhea."

"So, you *are* eating with me?"

He pointed ahead of her at a small table nestled by the front window of a cozy street café.

"Aunt Grace!" Rhea yelled and slipped from Riley's hold into the awaiting embrace of a familiar face. The perfectly cropped blonde hair, the ruby red lips, and the lightest blue eyes shined back at her. The women immediately began to blubber over one another, hands touching cheeks and hair. Hands gripped in pure happiness of reuniting. Rhea turned a watery smile to Riley. "Thank you!"

"See, not so cruel." He winked. "I shall leave you ladies to it then. If you need me, Rhea, you have my number. Grace." He tilted his head in a small nod. "You two have fun. I'll find you at the end of day to take you home."

"You're a dear, Riley O'Rifcan," Grace called after him as she cupped Rhea's face in her freshly manicured hands. "It is so good to see you, sweetie." She kissed Rhea's cheek and then motioned to the vacant chair across from her. "Sit. Let's catch up."

Rhea unfolded and folded the menu before her as she settled upon an omelet with bacon. She dropped two sugars into her cup of tea and stirred. "It is so good to see you, Aunt Grace. I can't even believe it really." Rhea giggled as she took a sip of her tea.

"You look beautiful, honey." Grace eyed Rhea closely, the inspection that comes from worry, but also as investigation for Rhea's mother. "Ireland seems to be treating you well."

"It is. I love it here."

"And it shows." Grace grinned. "Now you see why I never left."

"I certainly see the appeal."

"And I didn't have a handsome man escorting me around when I came," Grace prodded, wanting to know if Rhea and Riley had sparked each other's interest.

"Oh, Riley?" Rhea pointed over her shoulder as if he remained parked behind them. "He's just a good friend. He's sort of helped me out a bit since being here."

"And have you met his family?"

"All of them." Rhea's eyes widened in mock surprise.

Chuckling, Grace ran a finger over the rim of her tea cup. "They're a handsome bunch. And kind. No kinder family than the O'Rifcans."

"I agree on both accounts."

"So, your mom told me about Oliver." Grace reached across the table and lent a reassuring squeeze to Rhea's hand. "I won't pry, but it sounds like you are better off without him."

"More than better off. Relieved." Rhea eased back against her chair.

"Have you heard from him?"

Rhea rolled her eyes heavenward. "Yes. Every day. But that's okay, he'll eventually give up."

"Are you sure you want him to?" Grace asked and watched as Rhea's face blanched.

"Of course I do. Like you said, I'm way better off without Oliver. He obviously doesn't want me, so why should I want him?"

"But is that what you really want, Rhea?" Grace studied her further and Rhea shifted uncomfortably under her scrutiny.

"It's not like I have a choice in the matter," Rhea admitted. "He chose someone else. I can't trust him anymore. So even if I wanted to try it again, I could never trust him. Plus, the entire experience was humiliating."

"But now that the humiliation has faded some, you can gauge your feelings for him with a more open mind."

"And I'm still angry at him. I think it will take time for my feelings to fade completely," Rhea acknowledged. "But I'm willing to give it time."

"No hope for reconciliation?"

Rhea tilted her head and then crossed her arms. "Why are you asking?" Grace's face flushed. "Aunt Grace?" Rhea prodded.

"Oh alright." She waved her hands in defeat. "Oliver has been talking to your mom. Jeanie thinks he is heartbroken over the whole matter and asked me to see if there was still a chance."

"Mom?" Betrayal laced her tone. "She wants me to get back together with Oliver?"

"I did not say that," Grace pointed out with a firm shake of her head. "I think Jeanie just wants to make sure your decision wasn't made in the heat of the moment and that you aren't throwing away your future."

"What would you do, Aunt Grace?" Rhea asked. "You've never married, do you consider your life a waste?"

"Now sweetie, that's not what I or your mother mean. We just want to make sure you are happy with your decision and your move. If you say this has been the best thing for you, I will believe you."

"It is. It's going to be. I love it here. I'm already contemplating staying. That is, if I can find a job, and a more permanent place to live."

A slow smile spread over Grace's face. "I like the sound of that. Then I can see you whenever I want."

"Exactly." Rhea beamed as she accepted her plate from the waiter and immediately began cutting into her omelet. "Plus, Grandpa needs me. He may not admit it, but it's been nice spending time with him. I know he has the O'Rifcans, and Claron keeps tabs on him, but I would like to be able to take care of him."

"Roland can take care of himself." Grace pointed her fork at Rhea. "Don't take that responsibility upon yourself."

"It's not me feeling obligated, Aunt Grace, I actually want to. I want to be here for him. I know he has plenty of people looking out for him, but I just miss him and want to spend time with him."

Grace finished off her French toast and took a long sip of her tea. "So I should tell your mother you are completely over Oliver and are moving to Ireland?"

"Let's not jump too fast," Rhea warned. "One step at a time. You can tell her that yes, I am *getting* over Oliver, and I am *thinking* of moving to Ireland. That should ease her worry for a bit."

"Then that's what I'll say." Grace grinned. "Now, let me take you to a few of my favorite spots and then

I'll show you where I live. And you can fill me in on what all you've experienced so far." Grace stood and gathered her purse, leaving money on the table.

Rhea delicately wiped her mouth and grabbed her own bag. "Should I let Riley know where to find me later or did you two secretly already plan that out?"

Laughing, Grace took Rhea's hand and began walking up the sidewalk. "I do love that Riley. He's a sweet boy." Her tone was leading and had Rhea cringing.

"Don't even think about it, Aunt Grace. Riley and I are just friends."

"Oh, now Rhea, I wasn't implying—"

"Yes you were." Rhea laughed at the guilty gleam in her aunt's eyes.

"Okay, I was. You have to admit he's the handsome sort. And it is okay for a young, healthy woman to… enjoy the company of a young man."

"Okay, whoa." Rhea held up her hand. "Please stop." She couldn't help the smile at her aunt's meddling, but she also didn't want her aunt to get the wrong idea about Riley. "Let's not go there. Riley is handsome, and he is kind, but that does not mean I want more than the friendship he is offering. I need time before I consider another relationship."

"Well, there are more where he came from. I've seen the line up of O'Rifcan boys. When you're ready for the next step, I'm sure you can have your pick."

"Aunt Grace!" Rhea nudged her aunt. "They aren't fruit on a tree!"

Realizing now what Grandpa had meant about her being different from Aunt Grace, Rhea appreciated her aunt's candor, but knew deep down she did not want to end up like Aunt Grace after all. Men were more than items to be picked, and so was she. Her next relationship, whenever it may be, would be special and would mean something. She couldn't begin to understand frivolous relationships and how having those your entire life would be fulfilling. And as she listened to her aunt carry on about a few of her '*blitzes*,' as she liked to call them, the conversation filled Rhea with a sense of sadness for Grace. And though she sought a break from Oliver and the rest of the male species for a bit, Rhea knew she was designed for a relationship. For a family of her own. Her Grandpa was right in that assessment, and she inwardly thanked Riley for setting up the meeting with Aunt Grace so she could see that.

∞

"Ah, Clary, good to see you trudging in for the meal tonight. I wasn't sure you would be after such a long night last night." His mother clucked over to him and offered a quick peck on the cheek as she hurried back towards the counter and began beating bread dough with her fist. His sister, Lorena, stood at the stove stirring what Claron assumed was a giant pot of some sort of stew. He was early for the family meal by about an hour, but he had hoped to catch Rhea for a few minutes beforehand.

"I took a long nap this afternoon. Set myself a bit behind in planting for the week, but I will make up for it throughout the week."

Sidna surveyed his demeanor as he slid to a barstool and sat. "You look a bit pale. Are you feeling well?"

"Just tired, Mam. Feeling fine. Is Rhea about?"

"Oh, she's off to Galway with Riley for the day. They won't be in until late."

"Galway?"

"He's work there, as you know," she continued. "And he thought it a grand idea to take Rhea along for a visit to the city."

"I see." Disappointed, he rested his chin in his hand as he watched his mother work.

"Did you have a fun chat last night?" Mrs. O'Rifcan asked, trying to appear nonchalant.

"We did." Claron sat straighter as Lorena walked him over a cup of tea. "Thanks, Lo." She briefly patted his arm before going back to the stove. "I had hoped to talk with her a bit this evening as well. I've been reading the book we bought and thought to discuss it."

"What a grand idea." Sidna beamed. "I imagine she will be sorry she missed the opportunity." Heaving a heavy sigh, she flipped the massive ball of dough onto the counter and pressed her knuckles into it. Fold, flip, knead. Fold, flip, knead. Claron watched in a stupor until the back door opened and his father and Roland walked inside.

"Ah, Clary," his father greeted. "Come to feast with your sweetheart again, have you?"

Embarrassed, Claron shook his head. "Da, I do not have a sweetheart. I came for the meal."

"Course ya did." Senior clapped him on the back as he passed by to kiss Sidna on the cheek. Roland took the empty barstool next to Claron and patted him on the back.

"I see you survived Murphy this morning."

"Barely," Claron admitted with a smirk making his parents and Roland laugh. "He was kind enough to answer my call. Unlike Jaron."

"Always good in a pinch that Murphy," Sidna boasted proudly. "No kinder soul on the face of the planet."

"That might very well be true," Claron agreed, grateful that his older brother had shown up to help him for both milkings, having only been asked to help with the first round.

Voices flooded into the B&B and slowly progressed into the kitchen and dining room. Sidna herded everyone into the sitting room until she called for them, only Lorena and she remained in the kitchen. Until she turned to still find Claron sitting on the stool. "Best join the others, Clary. There's still half an hour left before serving."

"Aye. I think I'd prefer to sit in the quiet if that's okay, Mam."

Sidna handed the bread pans to Lorena, and her daughter diligently slid them into the hot oven. Sidna fisted her hands on her hips and eyed her son carefully. "Are you sure you aren't ill?" she asked, motioning for him to stand. He shook his head and remained seated.

"I feel fine. Just tired is all. Long day. Mind if I take a plate to go?"

"You don't want to visit, love?" Her concern deepened as he shook his head.

"Not tonight. Perhaps I will be fully rested tomorrow."

"Lorena dear, fix Clary a box to take home please." Without answering, his sister immediately did his mother's bidding.

"You will eat it all, Clary. I don't want you falling sick."

"I am not sick, Mam." He accepted the box from Lorena with a grateful nod and stood. The back door opened in a whirl, laughter flooding the room as Riley and Rhea stepped through. Rhea's smile only widened when she spotted Claron. Without stopping to hang her purse, she walked forward and enveloped him in a tight hug.

Surprised, he patted her on the back. When she pulled away, she walked around the counter and did the same to his mother.

"I see you had a marvelous day," Mrs. O'Rifcan chuckled as Rhea nodded.

"Galway was a blast." She beamed at Riley. "Thanks to Mr. O'Rifcan over there."

Riley bowed. "I only live to serve."

Rhea eyed the carton in Claron's hand. "Are you not staying for the meal?"

Kicking himself for jumping the gun to go home, he shrugged.

"Oh." He saw the light in her eyes dim a bit and felt a small sense of satisfaction that she wished for him to stay.

"Ah, Clary, there you are!" Layla waltzed into the kitchen looking as beautiful as ever in a fitted pair of jeans and navy sweater. "You're positively glowing, Rhea. How was Galway? Find you a handsome city fella?"

Rhea blushed. "Um, no. But I did have a great day with my Aunt Grace."

Claron turned towards Rhea to ask about her visit, but Layla tugged his arm. "I have a proposition for you, Clary. A business proposition."

"Would this have anything to do with renting out my cottage?"

Layla beamed. "Actually, it does. How did you know?"

"Because I've received phone calls all day from strangers wanting to stay in me bloody house, Layla. I had it in my mind to ask which of you listed the cottage on some website. I guess I now know who the culprit is."

"Don't look so dour, it's a good business venture. I've researched it. And for a small cut in the profits, I will even be your manager. Property manager," she amended.

"No."

"Clary, listen to me."

"I said no, Layla. I don't want strangers staying in my house. Besides, where would I stay?"

"Here." She pointed at the floor of the B&B. "Only on days you have people at the cottage."

"So, I will displace myself to make a few bucks? I'm doing fine. I don't need to rent out me house." Claron shook his head in disgust at the thought and Layla's back straightened. "Are you sure I can't interest you with eighty euros? Because that would be the fee for a night."

"Eighty euros?" Claron balked. "My house is worth more than a measly eighty."

"Your house, yes, but location, no," Layla added.

"The Gap is one of the most stunning views in County Clare, I'd say it's well worth more than eighty a night."

"It would be, yes, if it were located in a different place. Castlebrook is a bit off the beaten path, brother. There's nothing around for miles. So, we have to accommodate for that in the price."

"We accommodate nothing and no one. It is my house." Claron waved a hand of finality as he felt a light rub in the middle of his shoulder blades. Rhea offered reassurance as well as evening out the temper he assumed she saw rising in his red face. "The next time you wish to list my cottage on a property website, you'd best mention it to me first, Layla."

Layla shrugged unapologetically. "I guess Murphy and I will have to invest elsewhere."

"Murphy?" Claron asked.

"Aye. He thought it a good idea too. And he offered to spoil the dickens out of our guests at the local pub, of course."

"Of course he did." Claron shook his head. "You two are dangerous when your minds come together. You'd exploit my home to make some money for your pocket and him for his pub."

"It'd be linin' your pockets as well, brother," Layla pointed out.

"The answer is no. And that is final. The entire idea is absurd."

"Not so." Layla's hackles rose. "Just ask Rhea."

Claron turned angry eyes onto a surprised Rhea. She took a cautious step away from him.

"She's a Yank. I'm sure she could tell us if someone would want to stay in the place," Layla pointed out. "Wouldn't you, Rhea? Wouldn't you like to rent a quiet cottage set upon a majestic cliff in County Clare? The very place fairies were born, the land of legends and myths?" Layla spun her words eloquently, teasing her Irish lilt to exaggerate the advertisement.

"Well, I know people would love to stay in neat locations when they travel," she began.

"And?" Layla waved her onward to agreement.

"It is a lovely spot," she agreed.

"Ah, see. Rhea approves."

"I didn't say that," she added. "I just said it is beautiful. It *is* his home, Layla."

"As are all the houses listed on the site. They are peoples' homes. People willing to rent them out to travelers and line their pockets, as you say."

"Layla, drop this for now," Sidna interrupted. "The food is ready. Clary, best be on your way unless you intend to stay."

Rhea's hand rested on his arm as he continued holding his container of food. As he looked down at her light grasp, she slipped it away. "I would take the escape while you have it." She nodded towards Layla who leaned through the kitchen door and yelled to the rest of the family to gather in the dining room.

"Aye, I guess I should. I thought you would be having supper in Galway tonight."

She shook her head with a faint smile. "It would seem Aunt Grace had an important meal of her own tonight. Something about a man in a suit."

Claron offered a tired smile. "I see. Well, if I had known I would have held off on this." He held up his box.

"No worries. If you're like me, I'm sure you're exhausted. Actually, you're probably even more exhausted than I am since you had to work the farm today."

"But I did not have to deal with Riley," he pointed out.

Laughing, Rhea shook her head. "Only for the drive to and from Galway. Not so bad."

"Ah, that's good." Claron grinned. "But you are right, I am on the tired side. Some Yank kept me up until the wee hours of the mornin'. Absolutely no sympathy for me and my work."

She swatted him playfully. "I believe it was you who wanted the second piece of cake. I was just being polite in accepting."

"Oh really?" His brow rose as he watched her flush, both thinking back to how quickly she devoured the first and second piece of cake set before her the night before.

"Alright, truce. You get some much needed rest tonight, and I will do the same."

"And tomorrow we shall discuss our books," he finished.

Rhea fumbled a moment in surprise. "Our books?"

"The Irish folklore you wanted to read."

"You've been reading it?" she asked in astonishment.

"Well, you wished for me to, did you not?"

A beautiful smile spread over her face and he thanked every star in heaven he had fought off his nap for a bit of time to read earlier. "You are absolutely right. I just didn't know if you would."

Shrugging, he stepped out of the way as Declan walked towards the sink to wash his hands.

"I'd best go." Claron walked towards the back entrance off the kitchen and Rhea followed.

"What chapter are you on?" she asked.

"Four, I believe."

"Good. I'll be sure to be on the same come tomorrow. That way, whenever we do see one another, maybe we can talk about it. I do have a few questions."

"I'm sure you do." He grinned at her as he stood half way on the stoop and half way in the kitchen as his attention held on Rhea. Neither wishing for him to leave.

"Clary!" his mother called in feigned annoyance at the door standing open. He jolted and offered a self-conscious smile towards Rhea before saying farewell once more.

"I'll be seeing you, Rhea. Have a care." And with that, he walked out into the evening.

« CHAPTER NINE »

Rhea pulled the old rusted pickup into the small drive that led towards Claron's barn. All her strength was needed pulling the steering wheel to the left to make the turn due to no power steering. Though the truck had seen better days, the green heap Mr. O'Rifcan loaned her did achieve the task of moving her from point A to point B, and she couldn't complain. When she pulled into the drive, a small red car occupied the side yard, a shadowy figure seated inside. She reached for the picnic basket in the seat next to her and stepped out. She saw the cows lined up awaiting their turn to enter the milk barn, and she smiled. The sea of black and white dotted around the barn and she heard what she could assume were the sounds of milking taking place inside the barn mixed with the crooning of an eighties rocker on a stereo. When she stepped towards the door, a car door closed, and Rhea looked up to see Amelia heading towards the barn as well. Smiling, Rhea waved in greeting. "Hi, Amelia, right?"

Amelia did not accept the extended hand, but instead shouldered her purse.

Unaffected, Rhea slid her hand into her pocket and turned towards the barn entrance. "I'm enjoying the books I bought the other day." Rhea attempted conversation again, but Amelia remained focused on the doors ahead until she turned to face Rhea. "I prefer to speak with Claron alone for a minute. If you do not mind."

"Oh." Rhea trudged to a stop and forced a polite smile. "Of course. I'll just wait out here." She shifted the picnic basket into the crook of her elbow and stepped towards a small bench to the side of the door and sat. Amelia stepped through the doorway, shutting the barn door behind her. Rhea listened to the rocker and the shuffles of the cows' hooves. Though the air held a faint scent of dirt and manure, she found the light breeze and the every day work calming. She watched as cow after cow shifted for a closer position towards the barn, their udders full and ready for relief. A lone Jersey cow poked her head above the crowd and eyed Rhea closely. "I'm not here to bother you, sweet girl." Rhea spoke softly as she smiled and studied the Jersey in return. "You have better eyelashes than I do." She softly chuckled as the Jersey batted her long lashes as if understanding, and it was her womanly duty to show off her complimented features.

Rhea glanced at her watch. She'd wait a few more minutes before entering the barn. She wasn't sure why Amelia had come to speak to Claron. It was none of her business, or that's what she told herself, but she'd give them time alone. Her cell phone chirped, and she glanced at the screen. Oliver. Again. Sighing, she opened the text message.

O: "You haven't returned my calls. I'm worried."

R: "No need to worry, I am fine."

O: "We should talk."

R: "There is nothing more to talk about. Please stop calling, emailing, and texting me."

O: "Rhea, sweetie, this is ridiculous. I love you. So I screwed up. I'm human. But that doesn't mean I don't love you."

Rhea shoved the phone back into her purse. She was tired of the same old dribble. When would he get the hint that she was no longer interested? That she was no longer going to settle for a man who cheated on her. She stood, straightened her blouse and brushed away imaginary lint from her white capris. Her nude heels sunk into the grass as she walked towards the barn doors. Shaking away the moist earth, she studied the pretty Jersey cow a moment longer. She was the only brown speck in the vast crowd of black and white. She felt like that right now. She didn't quite fit in at home, and she didn't quite fit in here in Ireland. Not yet, anyway. Sighing, Rhea wondered if she'd ever find a place she fit, or if she was destined to stand out amongst the rest like her new-found friend, the Jersey cow.

∞

Claron glanced up and saw Amelia enter, and as he inwardly cringed at having to deal with her, he continued taking care of the cow before him. He never liked visitors to the barn during milking hours. Cows were fickle creatures, and the slightest change in routine or circumstance could cause a bovine uprising that typically led to an excrement purging chain reaction, flooding the floors of the milk parlor with manure and an even more oppressing stench than was typical.

Amelia had visited before, though it had been a year or so since her last visit, so Claron hoped she remembered the protocol. Do not speak to him until he comes to you. She cleared her throat and he held up a hand for her to give him a minute. He finished slipping the teat cups onto the cow before him and patted her side reassuringly and prayed for patience. He felt a tap on his shoulder and turned to find an impatient Amelia standing with arms crossed and a firm scowl etched on her face. He wasn't sure what he had done to warrant a personal visit with such disdain, but he was certain he was about to find out.

"Amelia," he greeted, his tone even so as not to upset the cows.

"I've called you three times in the last two days, Clary." Her voice rose, and he noticed a few of the cows nervously shift on their feet. "Why have you not answered or replied?"

"What can I do for you, Amelia? I'm a bit busy at the moment." Ignoring her question, he walked the circuit checking to make sure the feed troughs were full and that the cows were as comfortable as possible.

"Why have you been avoiding me?" she asked.

Sighing, he turned to face her. "I have not been avoiding you. I was in your store just this week."

"Yes, with that Yank of Roland's."

Avoiding the barb at Rhea, Claron shrugged. "Am I not allowed to converse with others? Last I checked, Amelia, we were not together anymore. Haven't been for quite some time. I do not see why it bothers you so that I enjoy the company of my friends."

"If you would return my calls, you would know that I ended things with Peter so that we could be together again."

"Oh, how fortunate for me." He cringed at the memory of catching Amelia in the other man's arms doing more than the *'talking'* they both claimed.

"I thought you would want to know. We had something, Clary. I do not want us to throw it away."

"*We* did not throw it away, Amelia. You did. *A year ago.* The moment you decided to leap into bed with Peter is when things between us changed. Nothing you say or do will steal that image from my mind. Nothing you say could ever convince me to trust you again. I'm sorry, but that's the way it is. I no longer have feelings for you in that way. I don't mind being friendly in public, but our relationship ends there."

"It's because of her, isn't it? That Yank."

"No. Though I enjoy Rhea's company, it is not because of her. I just prefer not to love someone who doesn't love me in return. Now if you will excuse me, I have work to do."

Amelia stomped her foot and her eyes grew glassy. "You can't just walk away."

"I'm sorry, Amelia, but I have. A long time ago. Best grow accustomed to the new way of things." He hated these conversations. It wasn't the first time he'd had to face Amelia and recite the same conversation. He knew this particular one stemmed from the fact that she had seen him with Rhea. Any time Amelia saw evidence of him moving on, she came around. Quite a nuisance really, but he kept the dialogue civil knowing they both would have to face one another in the village.

"You're making a mistake." Her voice became shrill, and he saw the stomp out of the corner of his eye as the leading cow twitched her ears and let her annoyance be known. He held up his hand for Amelia to calm down as the barn door swung open and Rhea stepped inside. "Claron! Hey!"

And with that, he heard the first plop of manure and felt the spatter hit his back and the side of Amelia. Rhea gasped as she stepped further inside. "I am so sorry," she called over the sound of the radio. Claron just dropped his head to his chest and closed his eyes awaiting the storm.

Amelia squealed as more manure splattered and each cow dropped their dung one after the other. Rhea jolted as the first splatter slammed into the side of her face. She closed her eyes as the small pit room erupted in flying excrement and cows stomped their displeasure sending even more of the liquid slosh flying every which way. The flood dams broke, and Amelia began to sob as her outfit and heart were battered. Rhea stood in shock as the other woman nudged past her and out the door, covering her tears.

Rhea looked to Claron apologetically as another plop sounded behind her and she felt the warm manure slide down the back of her arm. She sputtered before a laugh erupted. She tried to bite back the hysterical laughter but found herself unable to contain it as she looked down at herself and at Claron's stained appearance. Her white pants were covered in brown splotches and her arms and ankles sported a new squishy texture that was beyond disgusting. He just shook his head as he bit back his own smile and pointed for her to exit the barn. She tried to side step certain clumps of dung, but her heels betrayed her, and she slipped. Claron caught her from behind saving her rear end from hitting the concrete floor. He effortlessly hoisted her to her feet and escorted her outside.

Wiping a hand over his face, they both turned as they saw Amelia's car speed out of the drive, trailing a dirt funnel in her wake.

"I cannot believe that happened." Rhea looked down at herself and shook her head, but her grin remained. "This is so disgusting."

Claron ran a hand through his manure drenched hair and heaved a heavy sigh before letting his own laugh escape. Shaking his head, he motioned for Rhea to sit on the bench. "I'll be right back. Don't go anywhere, lass."

She saw the shifting of cows and a new line filtered into the barn. She looked down at her arms and hands and could not imagine the state of the rest of her. She lifted her arm up and sniffed, the putrid smell of cow manure had her recoiling and then laughing to herself. She had never seen anything like that before. She felt bad for Amelia and did not mean to cause such a ruckus that resulted in their outfits being ruined and for Amelia to run away in tears.

The barn door opened and Claron stepped out, rubbing a hand towel over his face, his glasses in his other hand. When he lowered the towel, he surveyed Rhea's appearance and then laughed again, tossing her the towel. She made quick work of rubbing it over her own face and neck.

"You're a sight now, lass. I apologize on behalf of my ladies." He motioned over his shoulder to the cows behind them.

Rhea's eyes widened in remembrance, and she stifled a giggle. "I am so sorry for causing such a... display. I had no idea that would happen!"

Claron chuckled as he reached for the picnic basket. "This for me?" he asked.

She nodded. "I know it's a bit past lunch time, but my intention was to let you know I'd be set up by the cliff after you were finished. It's a pretty day, so I thought it called for a snack out in the open. I'm sorry to have interrupted a conversation between you and Amelia. I honestly thought she'd have been wrapping it up."

"It was finished. You interrupted nothing." His tone lowered in distaste as he slipped out a bottle of water from the basket and uncapped it.

"And of course, this..." She motioned over the front of her outfit to the cow's handy work. "I'm sorry for this as well. Do they always do that?"

"Just when their norm is threatened. That'd be why I have the radio playing. It calms them and drowns out most new or loud noises for them."

"And then I come in guns blazing and yelling at the top of my lungs." Rhea shook her head on a laugh at her own fault. "Oh, man, I am sorry. And I did not mean to make Amelia cry."

"You didn't. She was crying before you walked into the barn."

His simple statement had her eyeing him and she saw the regret on his features. "I'm sorry to hear that. I hope I didn't make the situation worse, but I'm afraid I did."

"You made nothing worse." He flashed a reassuring smile. "If anything, you may have helped the situation. Your timing was impeccable. Despite the mishap." He flicked a piece of dried manure off his jeans.

"Yes, well I guess my plans for a delightful afternoon picnic discussing books may be postponed."

"Why is that?" he asked curiously.

She waved a hand down the front of her clothes. "Because I'm disgusting, and I smell."

"And so do I," he pointed out.

"Not exactly the most enjoyable of circumstances."

"The company would be."

She flushed at his comment. "Maybe a rain check." She stood and turned at the sound of an approaching vehicle.

"Seems everyone needs to visit with me today." Claron watched as Murphy slipped out of his truck and walked towards them, his smile spreading as he surveyed their clothes.

"A bit of a mishap?" He grabbed Rhea's hand and pretended to pick away poop before kissing her knuckles. "Lovely to see you, lass. I apologize for me dolt of a brother. He's never been one to understand the art of wooing a woman."

Claron shoved his shoulder and Murphy laughed.

"It was my fault, actually," Rhea admitted. "I was a bit disruptive and the girls let me know what they thought."

Murphy grinned. "They be nasty jealous of Clary's attention. I'd be upset too if a pretty lass waltzed in and swept him away."

Claron rolled his eyes. "What can I do for ya, Murphy?"

"Ah, well I came by to help you finish up the afternoon milking. Seems my arrival was perfectly timed."

"Why?"

"Why what?"

"Why are you wanting to help me this afternoon?" Claron asked suspiciously.

"Do I need a reason to be of help?"

"No, but you usually have one."

"Ah, well that's a wee bit hurtful, brother."

Rhea patted her thighs and stood, picking up her basket. "I will let you two get to work then. I am nothing but in the way right now, and I've already caused enough damage, so I will just head back to the B&B and clean up."

"Don't rush on my account lass," Murphy wriggled his eyebrows at Claron over Rhea's back as she bent to pluck a piece of grass from her ankle that had melded with dried manure. "I just wanted to help Clary a bit and discuss his cottage a moment."

"And there it is," Claron pointed out to Rhea. "The reason he's here."

Playing the innocent, Murphy appeared baffled.

"Don't play me for dumb, brother." Claron stifled a laugh at Murphy's amusing face.

"Oh alright," he admitted. "Layla and I have a plan for your cottage and we wish to pull you on board with it all."

"I should hope so, considering it's my house." Claron accepted the towel back from Rhea. "I told Layla last night that the answer is no."

"Ah, but that's before you had discussed the prospect with me." Murphy grinned and winked at Rhea. "I've a mind for this, Clary. Just you wait and see."

Rolling his eyes, Claron took another swig from his water bottle. "Rhea, I should very much like that rain check. Perhaps I'll swing by the B&B early— before the meal— and we can talk."

She nodded with a pleased smile. "Sounds like a plan. Murphy," she patted his arm. "Always good seeing you. You two boys take care. Don't upset the ladies." She tilted her head towards the cows and then made her way to Mr. O'Rifcan's truck. The two brothers stood outside the barn a moment longer to watch as she cranked the engine several times before it sputtered to life. On a wave, she backed away and turned towards the direction of the B&B.

∞

It was easy: the conversation, the laughter, the utter joy in which the O'Rifcan family lived their lives. Rhea found that her most favorite moments were while she sat amongst the family in the sitting room before dinner. She was never disappointed in the latest Layla and Riley argument or the teasing and pestering of Chloe. The way all the siblings held an esteemed love for one another despite conflict or jesting always managed to set Rhea at ease. The front door opened and Claron walked into the B&B to yells of welcome and the standard bone-crushing hug from his mother.

Trying not to seem too eager to see him, Rhea gave herself a moment to enjoy little Rose's delicate touch on her wrist as the small girl played with Rhea's bracelet. She'd had the bracelet since her sixteenth birthday. A charm bracelet. Each charm a chapter or special event from Rhea's life. The girl found the ballet slipper charm especially pretty. "Do you dance?" Rhea asked her.

Shyly the little girl nodded. "With the fairies."

Rhea tilted her head and tried to gauge whether or not the young girl was serious when Lorena leaned over. "That is the name of her dance class. They are the fairies."

Nodding in understanding, Rhea grinned. "I hear wonderful things about fairies. In fact, I've been reading all about them." Rose looked up at her in wonder.

"They live at Clary's house," the young girl said in excitement.

"Do they now?" Rhea tapped a finger to her chin. "I have yet to see one. Perhaps I should make your uncle show them to me."

Giggling, Rose squealed as strong hands scooped her up from behind and Claron nuzzled his nose in her neck. "Are we talking about fairies? Because I believe I've just caught one. What do you think, brother?" Claron tossed the young girl several feet through the air, a shrill squeal coming from her lips as Jaron nabbed her and soared her above his head. "Aye, I believe you did. Prettiest faery I've ever seen. Tom?" He then swooped the girl low over the ground before lifting her in the air and tossing her to another O'Rifcan brother. Tommy caught her and threw her over his shoulder. "Fairy? I don't see a fairy. Where did it go?" Rose giggled, her little feet kicking and squirming as he turned in circles looking for the elusive fairy. Finally, he flipped her over in his arms and gasped. "Why, there 'tis." Before he could kiss the young girl on her cheek, Murphy snatched the girl and plopped down into a free chair and snuggled her against his chest. "My fairy now. Don't you know to hold onto fairies, brother? For they're the best of luck." He kissed the girl's small cheek and winked. Rose sighed in pure pleasure from all the excitement as she settled comfortably against Murphy.

Rhea's cheeks ached from all the smiling, but the sweetness of the O'Rifcan family continually surprised her. Claron eased onto the couch next to her. "Evening, Rhea."

Her smile broadened as he leaned back against the cushions and rested his arm behind her. "I see you managed to clean up."

"And you," she pointed out.

"Aye, though I cannot claim to smell as lovely as you." He winked towards Roland who sat watching them, the older man chuckling and shaking his head at the flirtation, before Claron turned his attention back to Rhea. "You had a good day then?"

"I did. Despite the mishap at the dairy. Again, very sorry for causing an uproar."

He waved her concern away. "No need. It happens now and again. At least you taught Murphy a hard day's work."

Across the room, Murphy crossed his eyes and flattened his mouth into what Rhea could only call a frog face before his usual jolliness emerged again.

"I had hoped to be here earlier, but other matters seemed to come up at the farm," Claron continued. "I hope you will forgive me for yet again spoiling our plans."

A bit nervous, Rhea shrugged. "It's no problem. I know you're busy. In fact, I hate for you to make special time for something so... unimportant." She motioned towards the small side table that housed the book she'd currently been reading. "It was a silly idea to begin with really."

Claron scooted closer to her as Chloe weaseled her way onto the couch and forced the other occupants to move. "I don't find it unimportant." Claron's voice quieted as he studied her, the lamp casting a small gleam against his glasses and hiding his expression. "I'd still like to raincheck."

Again, she shrugged, and she noted his frustration with her response.

"Dinner is ready," Sidna announced and had everyone bustling to stand and walk towards the kitchen. Chloe hung back and linked her arm with Rhea's. "You give in too easily, Rhea," she whispered. Rhea's brows rose. "What?"

"Clary wishes to spend time with you. I can see it. Don't give up just yet. Give him time to work it into his schedule. Because he will. He's just not used to making room for a beautiful lass in his day."

"I don't want him to feel he has to. I just thought it would be fun, but I understand that he is busy. I don't want him to feel obligated."

"Trust me, he doesn't. Just... give him a couple days to figure out the balance of it."

"It's really okay." Rhea slipped into her chair and Chloe sat across from her next to Riley.

"Rhea love." Riley leaned onto his elbow as he spoke and flashed perfectly straight teeth as his eyes sparkled. "I'll be venturing to Galway tomorrow, if you wish to make another trip to see Grace."

Though Rhea did want to see her aunt, she'd hoped to kidnap her grandpa for a trip into Limerick. "I would, Riley, but I've booked myself already with a handsome gent."

"A handsome gent, you say?" Senior's voice boomed across the room as he eyed all of his sons. "And which is it, Rhea? Don't leave us in suspense."

Baffled that he assumed she meant one of his sons, Rhea sat frozen a moment before her eyes settled upon Claron down the table. He waited for her response just like everyone else. "Actually, Mr. O'Rifcan, I was just... um... I meant my grandpa."

She nodded towards Roland who wriggled his eyebrows. "Be jealous, boys," He taunted.

Senior's laugh thundered down the table and he slapped his knee. "And to think I thought we'd snagged a beautiful lass for one of our boys. Fate be a nasty devil at times." He winked at Rhea before digging into his meal.

"Where are you headed tomorrow, Rhea?" Layla asked.

"Limerick. I had hoped to look around and see if there were any apartments available, should I decide to stay in Ireland."

"We win you over that quickly?" Riley asked in glee.

"Not yet." Rhea held up her hands to ward off all the excitement from the group. "I'm just checking it out, just in case. I have yet to even venture to Limerick."

"Well, you know you always have a home here. As long as you need," Sidna admonished. "No quick decision in Limerick when you have a roof to hold you until you're sure."

"Thank you, Mrs. O'Rifcan."

"It's Sidna," she corrected in kindness as she handed a bowl of peas to Aine, Declan's wife. Rhea was glad to finally be able to meet and greet the kind woman. Aine was a nurse, and every aspect of her personality spoke of service as she spooned a serving on her own plate and then Declan's beside her before handing the bowl off to Riley.

"Declan could point you in the right direction, Rhea," Aine commented, narrowing her gaze at her husband to continue the offer.

"Ah, yes. I've worked in Limerick for years. There are some areas better than others."

"Whatever advice you have, I am all ears." Rhea smiled in thanks. "I'm hoping to spend the day there tomorrow, but we will be back for supper."

"I'll make a list and leave it with you before I leave." Declan accepted the tender pat to his thigh under the table as Aine acknowledged his kindness.

"Best not be gone too long," Layla said. "I had hoped to wrangle you into me plans to overhaul Clary's cottage."

Rhea looked down the table towards Claron for explanation. "No overhauling anything, Layla." He scowled. "Tis a test run, nothing more."

Beaming, Layla draped her arm over Murphy's shoulders. "Murph and I convinced him to rent out his cottage for tourists. We have our first run this weekend."

"Wow." Rhea looked to the siblings impressed.

"It was all me." Murphy proudly placed a hand on his chest and accepted the full support from Layla.

"I'll agree for now," she said. "But we shall see what the comment card reads after their lovely stay. For I plan to be an attentive host." She batted her eyelashes at Rhea and laughed as Claron groaned.

"And where will you stay this weekend, Claron?"

"Here. Or at least I plan to. I have yet to ask the owner of this fine establishment if I can room... for free." He smiled sweetly at his mother and she nodded.

"Always a home for my loves." Sidna went back to her conversation with Lorena as if never interrupted and Murphy clapped his hands. "See, all coming together, Clary."

"We shall see," Claron mumbled as he continued to eat his dinner.

"I think it a grand idea," Jaron confessed. "What's the point of living in the most beautiful spot if you do not intend to share it, Clary? And what better way of sharing than putting a bit of coin in your own pocket in the process?"

"My thoughts exactly." Murphy clinked glasses with his older brother. "Coins all around, I think. For the tourists are a couple of Yanks, like our Rhea." He nodded her direction. "Naturally, they'll wish to frequent the local pub and café whilst on holiday, which they will read all about in a wonderful type-up done by Layla... which will only add more bounty for us all."

"And then they'll realize there be nothing else in Castlebrook for them to do and then they will leave and wonder why they wasted a pretty penny on a cottage in the middle of nowhere," Claron muttered.

"Don't be such a spoil sport, brother," Murphy warned. "I feel your negative energy all the way down here. Layla and I plan for a success, and we shall have one."

"That's the best attitude to have," Roland agreed, though he sensed Claron's discomfort.

"You're welcome to my flat, Clary, should you not wish to stay at the B&B," Roland invited.

"Thanks, Roland. Call me spoilt, but I should think I'd prefer a bed to a couch." His eyes crinkled as he accepted the friendly pat to his back as Roland cracked up.

"And his mammy will enjoy having him in her nest once more." Mrs. O'Rifcan beamed over at him. "Clary needs a bit of fussing over for a change."

"Oy." He lowered his head and cringed as Layla and Murphy laughed.

"Your own fault, brother," Layla's voice chimed. "You escaped to the cottage too soon for Mam's taste. All of us had to succumb to her hoverin' over us. 'Tis your turn."

"I 'spose it is." Claron bit back a smile as he winked at his mother, the flush of pink to her cheeks telling him it pleased her he was agreeable.

"We will be neighbors," Rhea announced. "I'm in suite two. I'm assuming you will be in one of the other rooms upstairs." She looked to Sidna for confirmation and did not witness the excited gleam in the woman's eyes at Rhea's announcement.

"Aye, of course. He be in suite four, across the hall."

"I could easily sleep downstairs, Mam." Claron pointed to the small hallway off the back of the kitchen that led to a quaint bedroom spacious enough to accommodate him for a weekend.

"Nonsense, it be best that you are comfortable, especially after working so hard." Sidna waved away his suggestion and toned down her jittery nerves of excitement when her husband squeezed her hand. "It will be nice to have some company, I'm sure. Right, Rhea?" she asked.

Rhea agreed, still not catching the fact that Sidna's matchmaking wheels were not only turning but forging on through an entirely new countryside. "Maybe then we will finally have time for you to quiz me on what I've learned of Irish folklore."

Claron concurred with a slight nod and then began clearing his plate. "And on that note, I shall head home to *my* cottage. Best toenjoy it while I have it."

Layla looked up to the ceiling at his dramatics and then grinned as Murphy tugged her hair.

"Evening, all." He offered a wave as he handed his plate off to Emily, Lorena's oldest, and shifted his way behind chairs until reaching the entry to the dining hall.

"No dessert, Clary?" His mother had stood and followed him, already holding a wrapped piece of cake on a tea plate for him to take home. He accepted it while kissing her cheek. "Thanks, Mam."

"'Twill be nice to dote on you, lad, even if it be just a few days. You're too thin, Clary. Almost gaunt."

"I'm far from gaunt, Mam." Eyes twinkling, he lifted the small plate in thanks. "Sleep well."

Rhea watched Claron slip out and the worry etched on Sidna's face as she watched him leave. Though it added, what she assumed was an interruption to his routine, Rhea looked forward to Claron staying at the B&B. Perhaps then, as Chloe put it earlier, he'd make time in his schedule for her, though she kicked herself for wanting such a thing. She barely knew him, and she continued to remind herself of that as she followed the remaining O'Rifcan's into the sitting room for dessert and more laughter.

« CHAPTER TEN »

"*I find this to be* a complete nuisance, Layla." Claron handed her a bundle of sheets he'd stripped from his guest bed and she stuffed them into the wash.

"Oh, stop your bellyaching, Clary. It will feel nice to have a fresh home for their stay. I shall tackle your bedding on Thursday afternoon. You can enjoy your bed for a couple more nights."

"No, I might as well stay at the B&B that way you can do what needs done here. I'd just be getting in the way and messing it up again for you." He patted Rugby's head as he spoke, making a mental note to take his dog with him to the B&B. He would trust his house in another's care, but not Rugby. Or Holstein. He'd have to remember to track down his cat as well.

"Ah, and here you are being reasonable. I like it." Layla shut the lid to the washing machine and rested her elbow on his shoulder as they watched the timer set and the sound of water entering the machine promising that work was being accomplished. He slipped from her touch and began walking towards his back door that rested on the backside of the kitchen. He sat at the table and pulled on his work boots. "I'll be in the fields before second milking, if ya need me."

"I'll be fine." Layla's eyes surveyed his living room. "Are you attached to those curtains?"

He groaned, and she bit back a cheeky smile as he stood. "I thought you were enlisting Rhea to help you in the decorating realm."

"She's with Roland today, remember?"

"You still have two and a half days to recruit her."

"You want her to see your cottage in such a state?" Layla waved her hand around the house.

"It is nice."

"'Tis plain, Clary. Severely plain. Do you not wish for Rhea to think you have *some* personality?"

"Spoken like a true champion. And since when should I be concerned what Rhea or anyone thinks of me?"

"You're a fool pretending to be a man of scholarly pursuits if you think me blind to the fact that you fancy her."

Claron didn't respond and Layla knew he had not quite come to terms with his own feelings or thoughts on Rhea just yet.

"Despite your lack of vibrant personality inside your home, Clary, if it makes you feel any better, I think you've sparked an intrigue in Rhea as well. Though she'd never admit it."

"I have work to do. I've been foostering around here a bit too long." His mood darkening, he tucked his gloves into his rear pant pocket and Layla fought back the urge to taunt him even further.

"Look on the bright side, Clary, with Rhea around, you at least don't have to deal with Amelia anymore."

"You are aware that they were both in my milk parlor yesterday?" He pulled his cap onto his head.

"Aye, but from the sound of it, I doubt Amelia will be returning. Shut her down for good, I hear."

"Rhea told you?" he asked, surprised that Rhea would share such a story.

"No. Murphy."

"Should have known."

"Wait." She walked towards him as he reached for the door knob. She placed her hands on his shoulders. "Thank you for letting Murphy and I use the cottage. I know it displeases you not to be in your own space." She held up a hand to halt his interruption. "And I know you are still dealing with the great hurt and disappointment Amelia brought your way." Her eyes, normally gleaming with mischief, were sober as she studied him. "But I think, if you let them, the beautiful Rhea and time could perhaps ease those for you, brother."

He sighed as if tired of the topic.

"Don't disqualify her just yet, Clary, just because you're still healin'."

"Has it ever occurred to any of you that I am fine? That I enjoy my life the way it is? And heaven forbid I actually be over Amelia, because then what would any of you have to hold over me head? And if I act so heartbroken and depressed, please admit me somewhere, for it is not Amelia's doing. I'm long over her. I thought I was happy. But if me own family questions my happiness at every turn, *am* I truly happy? For you are all trying to convince me I'm not. Is what I thought was happiness just me being blind to the fact I'm still trapped and pathetically mourning an unhealthy relationship? Please, Layla, tell me your thoughts. Tell me that because I do not wish to pursue Rhea that I must still be holding onto hope for Amelia. Or better yet," he held up a finger as if he had a novel idea. "Please tell me that I must be blind not to pursue Rhea because what man in their right mind wouldn't want to?"

He paced. "Ah, but that must be it then, hm? None of you think me in my right mind. I'm lost, floundering, wasting away on my hilltop longing for love. That seems to be the consensus. What if I told you a secret, Layla?" He motioned for her to come closer and then yelled as she leaned towards him. "I'M COMPLETELY FINE!"

He stormed towards the door. "Now leave me alone about Amelia, and Rhea, and every other bloody woman in the world right now. When I want a woman, I shall find one. For now, I bloody like my life the way it is." And with that, he slammed the door behind him.

Layla heaved a heavy breath and looked down at the confused dog at her feet. "What are we to do with him, Rugby?"

The dog sighed as he shifted his head to his front paws and stretched out across the floor. "I guess you're right." Layla petted his head before moving on towards the hallway. "Best let him be."

∞

"Take the next left," Roland directed as Rhea turned the small two-door sedan Chloe had lent her down a side street leading towards downtown Limerick. "Looks like the building should be up on the corner." He pointed, and Rhea nodded, leaning forward to gaze up through the windshield at the buildings passing by. She pulled into a parking space and heaved a relieved sigh. "Not bad, dear." Roland patted her hand as Rhea unbuckled her seat belt.

"I'd say I'm improving. I mean, I only almost killed us twice, but hey, pretty soon I will be an expert at driving on the wrong side of the road."

"How very American of you, Rhea." He laughed. "It is not the *wrong* side of the road, just the opposite of what you're used to."

"That's what I meant."

"Ah, but not how some might interpret it. Be careful how you phrase things for some might have found that a rude statement."

"Good point, Grandpa. Thanks for the warning." She slipped out of the car and shouldered her purse taking a moment to wait for her Grandpa and to survey the building in front of her. "Odd that this is an apartment building. It looks like an office."

"The windows do make it seem a bit exposed, doesn't it? Perhaps the apartments are on the inside and face a wonderful courtyard."

"I guess we'll find out." Rhea linked her arm with Roland's and kept pace with his stride, his cane a silent companion. They entered the stark lobby, the solid glass walls and windows carrying not only around the exterior of the building but the interior as well. Rhea spied that there was indeed a courtyard in the center with small balconies overlooking a swimming pool and lush green grass.

"May I help you?" A woman, overly thin and dressed in the latest fashions, eyed Rhea curiously as she smiled in welcome.

"Hello, I'm Rhea Conners. I scheduled an appointment to tour some of your vacant apartments."

"Flats," Roland corrected with a smile and had the woman nodding in agreement.

"Let me look at the schedule and see which they've planned for you, miss. Then we can make the rounds. My name is Ceri, and I will be your guide today." She ran a cobalt blue nail down a list and then tapped the paper. "Ah, there you are. So you're looking at a two bedroom?"

"Yes."

Ceri reached under the desk for a metal ring that housed dozens of keys. "Shall we?" She motioned towards a hallway that lead to a pair of elevators and began rambling about the building's unique architecture. Rhea had been right. It was an office building turned apartment complex. Interesting concept, but an inimitable way of utilizing a structure that would otherwise be abandoned. After riding up two floors, Ceri led them down a hallway that overlooked the street and unlocked the door. She stepped aside as Rhea and Roland entered.

"Ah, now this is lovely." Roland stood to the side as the woman walked Rhea through room by room. The apartment was spacious, and the floor to ceiling windows facing the courtyard brightened the entire space, though she immediately began thinking of curtains for privacy. The rooms were large and the single bathroom shared between the two held enough space for both shower and tub. The kitchen was open concept and overlooked the living space and courtyard windows. Overall, Rhea liked what she saw, but again, questioned the privacy of such a place. She stared out the window and noticed most of the apartments across the courtyard had curtains or sheers pulled back to enjoy the pretty day, but she could easily see directly into their home. She smiled politely as Ceri led them back into the hallway and towards the elevator. When they reached the lobby, she handed Rhea a packet containing the price and floor plans of not only that apartment but others within the complex for her to take with her and review. Thanking her, Rhea and Roland made their way back to the car.

"Well," Rhea buckled her seat belt. "It was beautiful, but I'm not sure I feel comfortable with the building being made mostly of glass."

"Yes, you would need to be diligent about privacy."

"The price is reasonable though. Probably due to location, but I say we head to the next place and take a look." She eased into traffic and followed the sounds of her GPS.

"You know you could stay in Castlebrook," Roland began. "I happen to like my little flat, and there are others like it."

"I know. I just think that if I am to move here, I will more than likely find a job in Limerick and I'd rather be closer to work."

"And is this what you are planning to do? Move here? Work here? Permanently?"

She caught the slight hint of hope in his tone and her eyes sparkled when she turned to him a moment. "I think so." She pulled into street parking next to another building and turned towards Roland. "I love it here, Grandpa. Now," she held up her hand to stall any interruptions. "I know I haven't been here long, but I just feel so... at peace. And excited. For once, I would like to do something different. And why not move here? If I don't like it, I can always move back home."

"That is true."

"I know Mom and Dad will probably not like it, but I feel it's what's best for me."

"I'm sure they will fully support you, dear. But are you sure this is what you truly want? You're not just... escaping?"

Rhea's brow furrowed as she contemplated her answer. "To be honest, I think I am a bit. But it's not the only reason. I've loved meeting the O'Rifcans and the people of Castlebrook. I find it comfortable there. I love being near you." She reached across the console and grabbed his hand. "And the fact that it is far away from Oliver is an added perk." Her lips tilted a bit as she sighed. "It seems crazy, I know. But..."

"Right?"

She nodded. "Exactly, Grandpa. It feels *right*. For once, I feel like I'm in the right place at the right time. For what? I have no idea. But I'm liking the way it feels. And I think I need to give it a go."

"So then, now we must begin thinking of finding you a job."

"Actually, I've already been looking."

"You've only been here a week and a half, Rhea." With eyes of surprise, Roland gazed at his granddaughter and saw the sincerity in her face. Beaming, Roland gripped her hand. "Though I must say I am pleased with your decision. As I am sure the O'Rifcans will be as well."

"I hope so." She looked ahead and studied the Limerick street. "I see them being great friends."

"They will be." Roland watched as she continued staring straight ahead watching people walk by. "It is your choice, Rhea." His voice was soft as he saw the renewed anxiety creeping into her gaze. Turning, she offered a bittersweet smile. "It's right. I just... I've never been good with change. And in the last month my entire life has been one change after another. It's like I'm barely able to keep up, yet I feel relieved. And excited. And nervous. I'm afraid of failing or chickening out."

"Rhea honey, listen to me." Roland waited until her eyes fell on him and he knew he held her undivided attention. "You are a strong woman. Your life has been turned upside down and yet you survived and are taking control of your circumstances. You've made wise choices, you've made adventurous choices, and now you need to make the right choices. If this feels right to you, then make it right and go for it, sweetie." He squeezed her hand.

She swiped a tear before it could slide down her cheek and her bottom lip quivered as she forced a smile. "Thanks, Grandpa." She leaned over and hugged him tightly, breathing him in and accepting the unconditional love she always remembered as a girl. Leaning back, she cleared her throat and rubbed her hands through her dark hair. "Now, let's go do this." She unbuckled and slipped out of the car to head into the next complex.

∞

Claron dropped his bag in suite four as Rugby ran into the room and sniffed all the furnishings eager to settle in. "Don't shred anything, Rugby, or Mam will have both our hides." He waited until the dog settled in front of him, staring up at him. "Come. Let's see if she has us both a treat, hm?" Rugby's tongue lolled, and his tail wagged at the word *'treat'* as he bounded down the steps ahead of Claron.

A loud squeal echoed at the end of the stairwell as Claron rounded the final landing and watched as Rhea perched on her knees and accepted the excited licks and slobbers of Rugby. She rubbed the dog behind his ears and laughed as he tried to snuggle next to her and ended up knocking her over. The dog then took that as a positive sign and stood over her face licking away, Rhea's hands blocking his eager tongue.

"Rugby!" Claron barked, the dog snapped to happy attention and sat next to Rhea's head. He snuck a quick lick at her ear as she slowly eased to her elbows and looked up at his owner. Claron couldn't help but smile as she laughed, her hair tousled and eyes glowing. He extended a hand and she accepted the assistance getting to her feet. "Thanks." She dusted off her pants and beamed up at him. "He yours?"

"Aye. Though for that behavior I best pawn him off on Riley."

"He's gorgeous." She ruffled Rugby's ears and the dog looked up at her adoringly.

"Thanks. You look well. A good day in Limerick?"

"Fantastic. I think I wore Grandpa out though."

"Not so," Roland called from his usual chair. Claron spotted his father and Roland completing their crosswords.

"You're early, Clary," his father stated.

"Aye. I just dropped off a bag. Didn't want to worry about it later."

"You're staying the night?"

He nodded. "Layla has taken over the cottage and is cleaning away. I didn't want to be in the way."

"Probably wise." Rhea grinned. "It's good of you to give them a chance, she and Murphy."

"They'll make it grand, I have no doubt. I just don't like strangers in my space."

"I could see that. I wouldn't like it either." Rhea petted Rugby on the head as he pawed at her shoe.

"Sorry about him."

"He's cute." She cupped Rugby's jowls and planted a kiss on his nose before walking to sit on the couch amongst pamphlets and fliers from her day's quest in Limerick.

"I'll be back for supper." Claron looked towards his dad.

"The fields coming along?" Senior asked.

"A bit behind schedule, but nothing I can't catch up on this weekend."

"You need help, Clary," his father warned. "Buddy is grand, but you need more hands. You can't do everything, boyo."

Claron walked to the door and grabbed his cap, slipping it over his golden hair. Rhea looked up. "You milk twice a day, right?"

"Aye. In the wee hours and then again at three."

"Every day at three?" she asked curiously.

"Every day." He smiled and looked at the clock. "Which is in a few, so I best be headed back."

"Can I come?" She stood, gathering up her papers and pamphlets. "I'd like to help. Or watch. Whichever you're more comfortable with."

Stunned, Claron didn't know how to respond. "You best stay here, lass. It's not that exciting."

Rhea hoisted her papers in her hands. "Well, your dad pointed out you needed extra hands. I'm an extra pair of hands. I've already been splattered with manure, what else could possibly go wrong?"

Stuck between a rock and a hard place, Claron wasn't quite sure how to respond. Not that he wouldn't mind the extra help, but he still wasn't sure how he felt about Rhea in such close proximity.

"She's willing and able, Clary. Accept help when it comes your way."

Reluctantly, Claron nodded. "Alright. Come, Rhea, if you like."

"Yay!" Rhea pumped her fist into the air and patted him on the shoulder as she darted to the stairs. "Just let me put these in my room and change my shoes. I'll be right down," she called over her shoulder as she was already half way up the stairs.

Senior bit back a hearty laugh as his son looked to the door for his escape. "Will be good for her, Clary. She wishes to help. Help her feel useful."

"She is a fast learner," Roland chimed in. "Just be direct with her and she will be an asset."

"Aye, I'm sure she will be." A bit aggravated that he allowed himself to be talked into the extra help, he glanced at the clock again. Time was already ticking, and he knew his cows would already be making their way to the barn.

Rhea bounded down the stairs all smiles as Rugby jumped to his feet and did an excited spin.

"Stay here now." Claron patted his head and a disappointed Rugby hung his head as he made his way towards Mr. O'Rifcan. "Ready?" Claron asked Rhea.

Beaming, Rhea nodded. "Lead the way." She pointed towards the door and was pleased to see a rather new and spotless truck parked along the curb of the B&B. Claron opened her door and waited until she climbed in before shutting it.

He climbed inside and cranked the engine. "Are you sure you wish to help me?"

"I'm a woman of my word." Rhea rubbed her hands together in anticipation. "I promise to be quiet this time."

Claron's lips tilted as he recalled the mess that took he and Murphy too long to clean up. "That would be best, but perhaps I can teach you how to act inside the parlor. Like most ladies, manners are important to them."

Rhea snickered. "I will try not to disappoint."

« CHAPTER ELEVEN »

The lead cows entered the milk barn and Claron, after explaining what needed to be done, began work on sanitizing the cups and slipping them onto the cows. He noticed Rhea watching him on the first cow and then jumping in and executing the same task flawlessly.

He checked the feed troughs and circled back around to where Rhea stood watching the process.

"It's so amazing." She spoke in a hushed tone as he leaned close to hear.

"You can speak louder, lass." His green eyes sparkled as he tried to stifle a laugh. "Just no shouting is all."

"Oh," she rested her hands on her hips as she watched the cows eat while being relieved of their liquid burden. Speaking up, Rhea watched as he penciled something on a clipboard.

"So you do this twice a day, every day?" The same question from earlier had him smiling.

"Yep."

"Do you ever leave? I mean, Castlebrook?"

"Not often."

She nodded, eyeing every nook and cranny of the barn. "Hard work."

"Aye."

"What made you want to do this?" She waved her hand over the cow before her. "And that?" She pointed towards the exit indicating his farm lands.

Shrugging, Claron slipped the teat cups off the first cow and Rhea jumped into action as well as they worked the circuit once again.

"My granda and nanny ran this farm and dairy. They left it to me. The rest is history."

"Are those names what you call your grandparents?"

"Oh," Claron looked to Rhea and nodded. "Yes. They be the grands."

Nodding, she lifted the cups from the sanitizer bucket and slipped them onto the cow's udder. "I remember you saying it was their farm. But why you?"

He looked at her. "What do you mean?"

She grimaced as she didn't move her hand in time and the cow shifted and bumped her hand into the metal railing. She didn't complain in hopes that Claron would appreciate her help by the end of the day. "Why did they leave the farm to you? Why not one of the other brothers? Or your sisters?"

"No one else wanted it." He ducked beneath a railing and hopped onto the platform the cows stood upon and worked his way to a row of feed lines. He pounded his fist against one and seeming okay with the result, slipped back down into the pit where Rhea stood. "I loved helping my granda here. I loved the land and the feel of it beneath my fingers. I get to see the sun rise onto beautifully laid out and cultivated ground and see the miracle of plants growing. I get to see production, and new life both with the cows and in the fields." He paused as Rhea, again, followed his lead and the next rotation of cows circled into the barn. They worked in silence as they prepped for milking. When the pumps sounded, he turned back towards her.

"I always thought I'd be bored behind a desk. The same old job every day. Out there, in here, it doesn't matter what I may have planned for the day, it can all change in a heartbeat. I mean, I have my routine and schedule, but usually I'm working a different piece of land each day, sometimes different crops. Throw in some unexpected weather and it's a different challenge. I've got days full of activities that keep me on my toes. I never quite know what I'm to face that day until I get my hands dirty."

Rhea leaned against the pit wall and crossed her arms as she listened. "You're starting to make me regret being an accountant." She smirked as he pointed towards the cows and they quickly and efficiently rotated the next round.

"I'm sure you're grand at crunching numbers. It's just not for me. I hate handling the paperwork end of things. Just ask me Mam." He looked over his shoulder and grinned. "I often whine for her to take over the papers so I can be in the fields."

"Have you thought about hiring someone to keep your books?"

He shrugged. "A time or two. But it's just one of those things I keep putting off. Having to train someone in the way of things and such..." He cringed. "Takes time I don't have, and time I do not wish to give for that particular task."

"Hmm." Rhea stroked a hand over one of the cow's hides and watched as it chomped away at the sweet-smelling feed in its bin.

"I have to have room to breathe," he continued. "Working outside gives me that. I couldn't work in an office building for too long without going crazy or driving everyone else insane in the process."

"And that's why you love living out here too?"

"Aye. It's peaceful. I can't find that sort of serenity in the city. I love working as a beautifully painted sunrise emerges over the gap. I always take a moment to watch as it clears the ledge and highlights the fields. It's a wondrous sight."

Rhea jostled as a cow shifted behind her and bumped against her shoulder.

"They be done." He pointed for them to begin the rotation once more. "This be the last batch."

Rhea watched as the sweet Jersey cow worked her way inside. "Why, there you are." She patted the pretty brown cow's leg as she began sanitizing the cups.

"She be separate, Rhea," Claron stated. "We do not pump her milk at the same time."

"Oh." Rhea held up the teat cups, not knowing where to place them. He pointed to the rack lining the wall and she draped them over it. "Why is she last?"

"Her milk is different than the Holsteins. I only use her production for Mam. She will pump into a separate bin."

"What makes her milk different?" Rhea asked, as she saw him rig the Jersey to a different set of milkers.

"'Tis creamier... richer, I guess you could say. Mam likes to use it at the café. Makes her butter and things."

"Really?" Baffled, Rhea shook her head. "I feel as if I'm learning a whole new world here."

He chuckled. "Just a bit old fashioned, not new."

"I like it." She saw the genuine smile he cast her way as he finished without her help and she continually stroked a hand over the Jersey's leg as she milked. Realizing she was idle, Rhea cleared her throat. "Sorry, I was lost in the moment for a second. What do you need me to do? Clean the milkers?"

"They wash themselves. You're doing just fine, lass. Abigail seems to enjoy your company."

"Abigail, hm?" She turned back to the Jersey cow and softened. "Now that name definitely suits you."

"She's a beauty, that's for certain. Come." He motioned for Rhea to follow him into another room that housed the massive tanks the milk pumped into and several wash basins and control panels. He pointed to a row of oversized bottles as he grabbed a large pipe and disconnected it from one of the tanks and held it over a bucket. He filled two buckets full of milk before replacing the pipe. "Think you could fill those to the line here?" He handed her a bottle and pointed to the correct measurement.

"Sure."

He nodded and hurried back into the milk parlor.

Rhea did as she was instructed, mesmerized at the size of the bottles and wondered what he planned to do with them. She lined them up on a small concrete ledge that divided the draining floor from the entry way to the room. When he returned, she had filled the last bottle.

"Nicely done." He grabbed a wired basket from a shelf and lined the bottles up inside and handed it to her as he grabbed another basket and did the same for himself. "Come along."

He walked out the door towards the backside of the milk parlor and it was there Rhea noted a row of small pens that lined a covered platform full of manure.

"This be the lot. This is where the cows await us as we milk, and these," he motioned to the calves, "are our littles." He took one of the bottles and offered it to Rhea. She nervously took hold of it, and he guided her hands through an open slat in the pen. The small calf looked up at her with deep dark eyes and its mouth eagerly sought out its dinner. The calf pulled and tugged, and Rhea gripped the bottle tightly, so it would not be jerked away.

"He's hungry." She looked at Claron in wonder as the other little calves began stomping and wanting their own dinner. Claron winked at her as he settled the remaining bottles in metal holders fastened to the pens, so the calves could drink and he remained hands-free. He then slipped the bottle from Rhea and set hers in a holder as well. "You did good, lass."

"Thanks." Rhea placed her hands on her hips and looked around. "So is that it? Are we done?"

"I still have a bit of cleaning up to do, but you are welcome to head on back home if you like."

Rhea shook her head, thoroughly enjoying every moment working the dairy with Claron. She hoped she did indeed help him and he wasn't just tolerating her presence. But by the pleased look in his eye at her request for more work, she knew there was at least one more thing she could do. "I can help. What do you need me to do?"

∞

"'Tis not the most glamorous part of the job, lass," Claron warned.

"That's okay," Rhea assured. "Need I remind you I have been covered in cow manure from head to toe already. What could possibly be worse than that?"

He wagged a finger at her. "You've a point there." Hesitating a moment and gauging her sincerity, he finally reached towards a long water hose. "We clean the lot."

"This?" She waved her hand over the vast excrement covered cement.

"That's it."

"Okay. Where to?"

"Just towards the grate there in the middle. We will pump that later in the week and use it as fertilizer."

"Smart." Her quick acknowledgement made him smile as she angled the hose towards the concrete and nodded for him to turn the water on. He turned the nozzle and watched as she set about cleaning. Amazed that she handled the dirty task with enthusiasm, he walked to the opposite side and started his own hose.

It was quicker with two people. The milking, the calves, the cleaning. Though Murphy helped him now and again, his brother never stayed past the milking stage. Rhea's help with the calves and the lot afforded him extra daylight for the field he planned to finish planting. Of course, that was after he replaced the flat tire on the tractor. Which reminded him to discuss with Mam about his numbers to see if he was at a point to invest in another one. Would be helpful to have two, on the off chance one tractor failed him during planting he could immediately pick up the next day with the other and not lose time... as he had the last week due to tractor problems.

He realized he'd been ticking off his to-do list as he worked and noticed Rhea had disappeared. *Probably bored and headed home*, he realized, as he sprayed the last of the manure down the drain. He walked his hose back to the wall and turned off the water. As he wrapped it up, he spotted Rhea rounding the corner of the barn.

"Do you sanitize the bottles and buckets? I washed them out, but wasn't quite sure what to do with them next." She rubbed the back of her hand over her forehead, leaving a trail of grime in its wake. He'd never found a woman more attractive. "Claron?" she asked.

Frazzled with himself, he wiped his hands on his jeans. "They be fine for now, lass. Thanks for rinsing them."

"Sure." She shrugged. "What's next?"

Amazed, his face split into a dazzled smile. "I have not worn you of all this?"

"Not at all." She rested her elbow on his shoulder as they stood watching the calves banter back and forth in their pens. "They're pretty cute."

"Aye. They'll be headed out by week's end."

"Where are they going?" She studied the side of his face until he turned towards her. Her brown eyes full of concern for her newest little friends.

"Ah... well that is a whole other facet to the dairy business. But basically, I will be taking them to Clear to Granda, and will be bringing back some heifers in exchange."

"Your grandpa still farms?"

"'Tis in his blood." Claron began walking towards the front of the barn and his truck. "Keeps him busy and helps me out."

"I feel like all I've done today is ask you questions, but I find this all so fascinating. And I'm so impressed by you and what you do here."

He flushed at the extra attention. No one ever really noticed what he did. Not that he knew of any way, and why would they? He was just a farmer.

She noted his embarrassment and patted him on the back. "Seriously, Claron, it's amazing. And it fits you. Seeing you here, watching you work… I couldn't imagine you doing anything else." Her cell phone rang, and she withdrew it from her back pocket glancing at the caller ID. He noticed the name of Oliver, but she quickly declined the call and stuffed the phone back into her pocket. "Thanks for letting me join in today. So what do you do now?"

"I head to the fields. I've some planting to finish."

"And I'm guessing since I cannot drive a tractor, I am not much use now."

He squinted as he regretfully nodded in hopes she was not offended.

Snickering, she nudged a rock with her shoe. "Well, I guess I will head back to the B&B then."

"Here." He opened the driver side door to his truck. "Take this back."

"But what will you use when you're done?"

"I'll catch a ride with Layla." He pointed up towards his cottage where his sister continued to work, her small sports car parked out front.

"You sure?" Rhea asked. "It looks new. And though I am a confident woman… usually… I am a terrible driver here in Ireland. You know…" She motioned to the other side of the vehicle and he smiled.

"It's close by, and I trust you will be fine. You are right though, she is new, so know wanderin' from the main roads," he warned playfully as she hopped into his seat. Her feet barely reached the pedals and she pointed to the adjuster. He nodded. "I'll find my sweet spot once again, go on." He waited until she readjusted her seating and then shut the door.

She lowered the window and leaned over the sill. "It's beautiful here, Claron. Thanks for sharing it with me today."

He reached forward and lightly tucked a loose hair behind her ear. "Aye, have a care, lass."

He held her gaze a moment longer before stepping back and letting her crank the engine. With a small wave, she slowly backed out of the farm and headed towards town.

« CHAPTER TWELVE »

"She's completely unfathomable," Chloe complained as she rinsed the romaine lettuce in the sink and shook off the excess.

"Tis Layla, love, she will move on quickly and then you shall have your shot at Gage." Lorena patted her sister's shoulder in passing as she walked towards the oven to slide in two loaves of bread.

"Not the point," Chloe continued. "I don't want to have Layla's leftovers. I don't want to play second fiddle. A poor man's Layla."

"Ah, now..." Sidna walked over to her youngest and wrapped her arms around her shoulders. "You are not a poor man's Layla, Chloe. Now hear," she squeezed. "A wonderful man be waiting for you just around the corner, I imagine. No Gage needed."

The back door flew open and Rhea bounced into the kitchen bringing light, joy, and the heavy scent of cow manure. "I just had the most wonderful day!" She beamed as she hung Claron's keys on the hook by the door, the item not going unnoticed by his family, as Rhea walked immediately over to the sink to wash her hands. Chloe moved out of the way and shifted the lettuce from within reach. Her nose curled at the smell of Rhea. "Hey," Rhea greeted warmly, completely unaware of her pungent odor.

"Hey yourself," Chloe giggled. "You look a fright, Rhea."

Rhea's face fell. "What?"

Chloe guffawed as the other two women giggled in response as well. Mrs. O'Rifcan held up a sheet pan for Rhea to see her reflection and she gasped. "Oh my." Rhea flattened a hand over her wind-crazed hair and laughed. "I guess I do look a bit rough."

"What did Clary do to you out there?" Chloe asked.

Rhea lightly squeezed her arm before all but floating across the room to a stool. "It was amazing, Chloe. Did you know that he does all of that himself?" Amazed, Rhea just shook her head as she looked to the other women.

"We are familiar with his work, yes." Chloe bit back a grin as Rhea's bright gaze bounced from woman to woman.

She waved her hand. "Of course you are." She circled her finger next to her temple as if her brain was confused. "Any way, amazing. It's just amazing!"

"I'm glad you had a grand time, dear." Mrs. O'Rifcan shooed her off the stool on which she'd comfortably sat. "Now be on with you. Grab a shower and a change and then come tell us all about it."

"Mam's subtle way of saying you smell." Chloe winked as Rhea hopped to her feet.

"I'm too happy to take offense," Rhea beamed as her phone rang. She glanced at the caller ID and her lips slightly frowned before she stuffed it back into her pocket. "I'll be back in a few minutes." And she darted out of the room and up the stairs, barely clearing Rugby as he waited patiently at the top of the stairs outside Claron's door. His tail thumped as he looked pitifully up at Rhea.

"Awe, hi there, sweet boy." She bent down and ruffled his ears. "Have you missed him today?" She lightly ran a hand down his back and then stood.

"Want some company?" Rugby eased from his belly to his haunches. "Come on then." Rhea opened her door and Rugby barged his way into her room happily trudging towards the bathroom. "You already know where I'm headed, hm?" The dog sprawled out on the floor mat as Rhea quickly slipped into the shower.

She felt incredible. She had milked cows today! She could barely fathom it, but the brown slush dripping down the drain was proof that her day really had happened. She thought of Claron and what other work he had to accomplish. She was exhausted, and she only helped with one milk time. He had already completed one milking and worked in the fields by the time she'd arrived. And he would be working in the fields again the rest of the day. Farming was hard work, and she respected him all the more for not only doing it, but for *wanting* to do it as well.

He loved what he did, and it was evident in the patience he held for the cows, calves, and for Mother Nature. She liked that about him. Claron never seemed hurried. Never stressed. Just at ease. With himself and his surroundings. She found she slightly envied that about him. Perhaps the longer she stayed in Ireland she'd feel the same way. Once she'd found her footing.

The apartment hunt in Limerick had only whet her appetite further for making the move permanent. And with the full support of her grandpa, and she knew, her parents, she'd be making a decision quickly. At the moment, it looked to be the glass building that lacked privacy. She told herself she could double up the curtains and feel perfectly safe. And the fact that the price was almost half of the remaining apartments she'd toured made the decision easier.

Turning off the shower, she opened the door and Rugby raised his head. She toweled off and set about readying herself to help in the kitchen and for supper. She wondered if Claron was still in the fields and then kicked herself for thinking of him yet again. However, if she were completely honest with herself, she realized she liked thinking of him, his golden hair and bright green eyes. Him working alongside her. She'd thought her heart would leap out of her chest when his hand brushed hers in the milk room. But wasn't that foolish? She combed a brush through her dark hair and stifled a sigh. If she were acting the fool when it came to Claron, she liked the part. Fighting back the distrust and the disappointment of Oliver had her reminding herself of the last time she was fooled. Yet oddly, the sting of that rejection wasn't as sharp. And the fury that haunted her now seemed but a simmer. Perhaps her heart liked the idea of Ireland as well. Perhaps it was finally ready to move on. Her cell phone rang, and her audible groan at the thought of another call from Oliver had her forcibly grabbing it off the counter. Heidi. Her dread was immediately replaced with pleasure.

"Hello to you!" Rhea called into the phone.

"Hey you! So how's Ireland?"

"Amazing. I had the most fabulous day, Heidi. I milked cows!" Rhea laughed at her own amazement as Heidi's gasp resounded through the ear piece.

"Cows? As in moo cows?"

"Yep."

"What brought this about?"

"Claron."

"The sexy Irishman who rescued you from the flat tire?"

"No. That was Riley. Claron is his brother, but also sexy. He's a farmer."

"And I'm intrigued... go on," Heidi implored with a lilt to her voice.

"Long story short, Claron has a dairy and he let me help him."

"Wow. That was boring." Miffed, Heidi sighed. "And here I was hoping for a descriptive tale. One of sweaty muscles and handsome men."

"Well... there was that." Rhea giggled as Heidi baited her to go on. "It's just amazing, Heidi. I can't think of any other word for it. He's amazing. So patient and kind. He has the greenest eyes I've ever seen. Oh, and he also drives a tractor."

"As do most farmers," Heidi laughed. "But good to hear a handsome farmer has bewitched you for a spell. Now tell me about Limerick. I got your texts."

"I think I'm going to move here." Rhea blurted out the one thing she dreaded to tell her best friend. Silence rang over the phone before Heidi burst into cheers. "You aren't mad?"

"Mad? Why would I be mad?! I think it's fantastic!"

"Really?"

"Yes, really. Rhea, as your best friend I'm going to be brutally honest here, but Oliver cheating on you was the best thing to happen for you."

"What?" Rhea's brow furrowed as she sat at her vanity, an anxious Rugby sitting beside her on the floor. She stroked his head.

"You were bored here, Rhea. I mean, Baltimore has its perks, but take it from me, there are better places to live."

"You don't think I'm crazy to move here after such a short time?"

"Absolutely not. I'm a bit jealous, actually. And it only confirms that I will be visiting you sooner than later."

"Maybe I'll convince you to stay," Rhea teased.

"Perhaps. Though to be honest, I have been looking at heading back to Texas."

"When did this idea come about?" Rhea asked.

"When my best friend took off to go ogle over Irishmen and I was left in this boring place." Heidi chuckled at her own joke. "I came to Baltimore to follow Chase. We barely lasted six months and we ended things. I've been here for three years despite that. My heart isn't in Baltimore."

"That's the way I felt. Once I evaluated my feelings for Oliver, I realized that I needed a change."

"Likewise," Heidi agreed. "Speaking of Oliver, he's been a persistent pest lately. Hope you aren't mad, but I sort of let it slip that you were in Ireland. He just kept hounding me about you and needing to see you that I snapped. Told him it was impossible because you were in bloody Ireland. That he needed to give up. Unfortunately, I feel I may have made the situation worse. So, I apologize in advance if he's been hounding you. I think he was just completely shocked that you left."

"No worries. He was going to find out sooner or later." Rhea brushed her hair and sighed. "Maybe now he will see it is officially over." She smiled to herself as she thought about her day once more. "I love it here, Heidi."

"I hear it in your voice. And again, to say I'm a bit jealous would be an understatement. Plan for me to come visit soon. Once I'm done with taxes."

"Done. You just tell me when. Free place to stay. Whether I'm here in Castlebrook or Limerick."

"Woo!" Heidi chanted. "And ah, as your best friend, I look forward to an introduction to Riley."

"Why Riley?"

"He just sounds like my kind of man. I mean friend. Man. Friend. Man friend," Heidi bumbled, making Rhea laugh.

"Oh trust me, all the O'Rifcan men are eye candy. Prepare yourself... and pace yourself," Rhea teased.

"Now you have me already packing my bags."

Shaking her head, Rhea rubbed Rugby's ears. "I needed this conversation, Heidi. Thanks for calling."

"Of course. I miss you and your pretty face. Speaking of face... bruises gone?"

"Yep. And my ribs are back to normal. For the most part. I did cough the other day and felt a small twinge, but other than that, I feel great."

"See, Irish air already agrees with you."

"Exactly." Rhea grinned.

"Alright, well you enjoy your time with the fantastic farmer. Milking cows, plowing fields, whatever it is you are now doing." Her voice laced with humor as she smiled. "Love you, Rhea."

"Love you too. Bye." Hanging up, contentedly, she set the phone aside and stood. "Come Rugby. Now it's time to gush about my day to *more* women." The faithful hound excitedly ran to the door, as if he himself were thrilled to hear all about it once more.

∞

"Hello to the house!" Layla called as she stepped inside the back door and set a basket of cleaning supplies on the bar. Claron followed behind her and shut the door. He wiped his feet before removing his boots.

"You look spritely for one having a full day of cleaning," Chloe complimented as Layla eased onto a stool and rested her chin in her hands. "'Tis hard work cleaning a man's house."

"I would like to think it was not that filthy." Claron spotted his keys on the hook by the door and pointed to them. "Rhea home?"

"Aye. She beat you by an hour, brother. Looked completely caked in filth, she did." Chloe tisked her tongue. "What are we to do with you, Clary? You can't toss a woman around the barn and expect to win her over."

Claron ignored his sister and walked around the counter to give his mother a welcoming kiss on the cheek.

"Aye, but haven't you heard, sister?" Layla baited. "Our Clary doesn't want a woman. He so clearly told me just this mornin'."

"Wanting and needing are two different things," Lorena chimed from the stove with a tender smile towards her youngest brother. Claron acknowledged the comment with a light kiss to her cheek as well.

"Evening, Lorena." He walked to the sink and washed his hands as a pitiful meow flooded the room. Claron looked towards the door to the sitting room. "Holstein, there you are lad."

"Oh, my sweetheart." Mrs. O'Rifcan ignored her dicing and set her knife down and hurriedly wiped her hands on her apron before bending over and scooping up the black and white cat. She nuzzled its neck. "Tis a poor kitty, Clary. Coming for your sup, are you? No milk fresh from the pipe?" She brushed a hand over the cat's head as she reached into the refrigerator and pulled out a glass jar of milk and poured a generous helping into a small bowl Chloe provided. She then set it on the floor along with Holstein, brushing one last hand down his back and tail before heading to the sink to wash her hands.

"I wondered if he made the trip." Claron motioned towards the cat. "Placed him in me truck this morning with Rugby, but didn't see him when I pulled in. Guess he was too eager and made the jump early."

"He knows his way." Sidna gleamed at the cat who glanced up and offered a contented meow at her comment.

"Layla, perhaps you can help?" Sidna waved towards a stack of carrots, but Layla didn't move.

"I'm too tired, Mam. Clary's house wore me to the bone."

"Again, it was not that messy," Claron defended.

"Aye, it was not, to my surprise. But everything needs a fresh scrubbing for strangers. And though it be clean, there's a slight hint of a smell to it. Man and manure linger about. So, I had Chloe make fresh sachets for your linens and drawers. And spread about fresh lavender in vases and vanilla candles for scent and warmth. 'Tis looking more a home now than it did."

"You put flowers and candles in my house? And potpourri in my drawers?"

"Yes to all the above, brother." Layla straightened, ready for the argument that was sure to commence.

"I'm sure your work is lovely, Layla." Mrs. O'Rifcan's tone held warning towards Claron and he complied by making his way to the back stairwell.

"I aim to shower and look over my numbers for a bit before dinner. If I'm not down in time for the meal, just give me a ring." He darted up the stairs and grunted as he slammed directly into a descending Rhea. Their bodies crashed together in a tangle of limbs as both tried to maintain their balance on the steps and avoid crushing a passing Rugby. Neither was successful, the intertwining of their ankles had him miss his step and Rhea's arms tangling around his for balance sent them both tumbling and then crashing to the floor at the bottom stair. Claron took the brunt of the fall on his back as Rhea landed hard on top of him. Air whooshed from his lungs and he felt a sharp pain shoot up his elbow.

"My goodness!" Sidna stepped forward. "Clary you eejit," she swatted him with her dish towel causing his glasses to skew. "Runnin' as if you're blind. Rhea dear, you alright?"

Rhea raised her head off Claron's chest and grimaced. "Fine." She looked up at Claron and he forced a smirk. "So sorry. Did I hurt you?" she asked as she slipped off him and to her knees.

He eased onto his elbows and cringed slightly at the pressure to his left one. He lifted his arm and noted the scrape. "Nothing too bad. You?"

"I'm fine." Rhea stood and offered a helping hand as he stood.

"My fault for not considering you coming down." He ran a palm over his chest where her head had landed, his other hand still holding hers.

"I shouldn't have rushed down so fast," Rhea admitted. "I was just too excited to tell everyone about my day." Smiling, she squeezed his fingers and he realized he still held her hand.

"Ah, well, that's encouraging to hear. I haven't completely ruined you of Ireland, then?"

"Quite the opposite actually." Rhea beamed and Claron stood studying her in silence. Their gazes holding.

A throat cleared. "Best be on with your shower and work, Clary. Sup will be here before you know it." Sidna clucked.

Claron blinked and looked down at his and Rhea's hands. He brushed his thumb over her knuckles before releasing her. "Aye. I think I will." He nodded a quick farewell as he bounded up the steps once more towards his suite. After his tangle with Rhea and the tenderness in her eyes, work was certainly the last thing on his mind, but he also smelled, and that was enough to convince him to do his mother's bidding.

∞

"The invitation stands." Riley nudged Rhea with his shoulder as they sat on the couch and ate their dessert. The raspberry custard was rich and smooth, and Rhea savored each and every bite. "Whenever you wish to go, just let me know."

"Thanks. I do need to chat with Aunt Grace, especially after my trip to Limerick."

"Aye, I heard about that. I wasn't sure to believe it or not." He grinned. "So, you plan to stay in Ireland, lass?"

The room quieted, and all eyes fell on Rhea. She glanced towards her grandpa and he smiled.

"Well, it seems now is the time to share, I guess. The answer is yes. Yes, I plan to stay here."

Cheers erupted, and Riley threw an arm around her shoulders and pulled her into a tight hug. "Best news all day." He kissed her hair as Chloe and Layla weaseled into the seats next to her and both hugged her. "I'm so excited!" Chloe flashed a quick glance towards Claron, her brothers scowl surprising her. He quickly masked it when he noticed her appraisal.

Senior reached over and patted her knee. "Rhea, love," his voice boomed. "You are a welcome addition to Castlebrook."

"Actually," she held up a hand. "I plan to move to Limerick."

Quiet settled over the O'Rifcans. "Whatever for?" Layla pulled back.

"Well, I've lined up a job interview for next week, and Grandpa and I looked at apartments and I believe I've found one. It's not that far."

"'Tis good to stretch her wings." Riley winked at her as he took a sip of his coffee.

"I say we have just all been spoilt having her so close," Mrs. O'Rifcan doted, topping off Rhea's cup of tea and then several others' as well.

The sentiment warmed Rhea. The O'Rifcans cherished their time with her, and it had been too long since she'd last felt special. "I'm hoping you will visit me in the city." Rhea looked to the sisters and both nodded.

"For certain." Layla stood and walked to help herself to another glass of wine. "Imagine the fellas in Limerick, Chloe. So many to choose from." She wriggled her eyebrows and had all her brothers groaning.

"And what of Gage, sister?" Tommy asked. "You already move on from him?"

"Ah, that would be a no. I just like to plan for the future." She winked at Rhea and had Riley stiffening in his chair.

Rhea just shook her head and smiled.

"When do you move?" Claron asked, bringing her eyes across the room to settle upon him. She studied his stance, his posture relaxed, but his eyes sparking as if upset with the topic of conversation.

"Not sure yet. I don't want to move until I have a job in place. So I guess I will find out next week after my job interview."

"And it will go swimmingly." Roland beamed proudly as he stood to his feet. "Dinner was lovely,

Sidna." He patted Mrs. O'Rifcan's shoulder as he shuffled towards the front door. "This old man is heading home."

Rhea stood and walked to the door to give him a hug. "Thanks for supporting me, Grandpa." She whispered as she kissed his cheek.

He squeezed her hand. "Rhea dear, I couldn't be happier about your decision. I see great things happening here for you." He tapped her nose and then nodded his farewell to the rest of the room. She closed the door behind him and then squealed as strong hands lifted her off her feet and spun her on her heels into a dip. Murphy's cheeky grin had her laughing as he set her to rights and kissed her soundly on the lips. "'Tis exciting news, Rhea. Glad to have you stay. Come to the pub this Friday, we'll celebrate with a pint or two." He squeezed her waist and then walked towards the front door to leave as well. "Night to all." He waved and winked at Rhea once more before leaving.

O'Rifcan after O'Rifcan hugged Rhea as they left. When Riley finally stepped up and enveloped her in his arms, Rhea sighed comfortably. "You are a gem, Rhea love. And though I know Roland is pleased, I find myself pleased at having you around also." He pulled her tight against him and whispered in her ear. "And I don't think I'm the only one." He kissed her cheek before spinning her out and towards Claron. His younger brother suavely prevented Rhea from stumbling by spinning her into a friendly hug as well. "Night to the house," Riley called, offering his final farewell over his shoulder as the door closed.

The sisters sat on the couch and watched as Rhea slipped from Claron's grasp and lightly blushed. "We be waiting our turn, Rhea." Layla and Chloe stood. "It calls for wine and cake in your suite. Mam?"

"Oh yes. I will have it ready in just a few minutes." Sidna bustled out of the room to the kitchen.

"Clary, you up for joining?" Chloe asked.

He shook his head. "No, I'm afraid not. I have an early mornin' ahead of me."

He nodded towards his dad. "Night to you and Mam, Da."

"And to you, boyo." Senior watched as his tired son climbed the stairs, Rugby hot on his heels. Holstein darted out of the kitchen door and to the stairs.

"Well, who is this?" Rhea bent down and pet the cat as it passed by hurrying after Claron.

"That be Clary's cat, Holstein. He's a barn ruffian, but Clary has a soft spot for him. Didn't want to leave him while the Yanks stayed at the cottage," Layla explained. "Holstein knows his way of things. Mam spoils him when given the chance. I'm surprised he follows Clary and not you, Da." She looked to Senior and he shook his head.

"No cats in me bed. 'Tis a rule. Your Mammy knows."

"Aye," Layla walked over and kissed the top of her father's head. "But we all know you'd give Mam the world if she only asked."

"That be the truth of it, no denying it." His hearty laugh filled the room and had Rhea's heart warming at the sound and sentiment behind his statement.

"There's cake, berries, and wine." Mrs. O'Rifcan walked in carrying an overflowing tray of luscious food and drink. "This'll be for Clary." She pointed to a hot cup of tea. "Make sure he drinks it. He needs it." She eyed Chloe until the younger sister nodded. "Now, have a good long chat and celebrate." She hugged Rhea and kissed her cheek. "I believe you're growing used to me now. Not one flinch." She tweaked Rhea's nose.

"My ribs are finally feeling normal," Rhea admitted. "Ready and willing for more of your hugs, Sidna."

"Oh dear." Worry etched across Sidna's face. "All this time I've been hugging you something fierce and you had bruisin' to the ribs? I feel like a total ee—"

"Oh no," Rhea gripped her hands and shook her head not meaning to make the older woman feel bad. "Please don't feel bad. They were just what I needed." She kissed the woman's cheek in thanks. "All of you are just what I needed, and I thank you for showing me such hospitality over the last week and a half," Rhea assured her.

"Well, I hope so. I didn't know, dear, or I would have taken caution." Sidna nudged her towards the stairs. "Now celebrate."

Layla grabbed Rhea's hand as they all darted up the stairs to her room. Chloe handed her a cup of tea. "Take this to Clary and I will set out the rest in here." Rhea nodded as she turned and knocked on Claron's door.

He answered wearing a fitted white t-shirt and gray sweatpants. His hair was a bit disheveled and his cat circled around his ankles. Her heart skipped a beat. "I didn't wake you, did I?"

He shook his head and waved her inside. "No, not at all. Just going over my figures."

"Your favorite part," she said, remembering how much he dreaded the paperwork side of things. "Your mother insisted you drink this." She set the cup of tea on the small coffee table in his sitting area, her eyes roaming over his papers. "This for the calf exchange with your grandpa?" she asked, pointing to a slip of paper on top.

"Aye. I plan to make the trip Saturday. Come back on Sunday."

"Is it a long drive?" Rhea asked curiously.

"Not too bad. About 4 hours, give or take."

"Would you like some company?"

Surprised, Claron stuffed his hands into his pockets. "I'd be staying the night, lass."

"Oh, right. I understand if that would make you uncomfortable. I didn't think about that."

"No, that's not it." He flushed. "I mean, I'll be staying at my grands' house is all, and I tend to stay the night to give time for visiting."

Rhea made her way to the door unoffended, but slightly embarrassed.

"Wait," Claron walked around the table to try and catch her before she left. "I didn't mean for it to sound like I didn't want you to come. I just meant, it's a bit of a long trip. And I wasn't sure if you knew that."

A bit nervous, Rhea turned the knob. "No worries." Her polite smile told him she still wasn't convinced he didn't want her to go.

He ran a hand through his unruly hair. "Look, Rhea—"

"Claron, don't worry about it." She patted his arm. "It's okay. I understand if you would rather go alone."

"It's not that. I would love for you to come with me." His voice cracked a moment from nerves and he cleared his throat. "If you want to," he amended. "I just wanted to make sure you knew how long it would be for."

She tilted her head as if weighing if his words were true or not. Sighing, she leaned against the door. "You sure you would want some company?"

"Absolutely." He grinned. "It's a bit of a boring drive otherwise."

"Then I would love to go with you. I want to see more of the country."

"Perfect opportunity, then," he added. "Cape Clear is a different Ireland than even I'm used to."

"How's that?"

"'Tis a bit remote."

"I look forward to it."

A bang hit his door. "I think that's the girls telling me my time is up." Rhea shrugged in disappointment. "I've kept you from your work long enough, and you need rest." She opened the door and turned with a last thought and bumped into his chest. He muffled a groan and she threw up her hands to apologize. "So sorry. I didn't realize you were behind me." Her hands braced against his chest and she caught the slight tilt of his lips as she continued to babble. "I was just going to say..." Her words trailed off as her eyes met his. "Um..." She fumbled as her heart hammered in her chest. "I, uh..."

Claron gently brushed a strand of hair from her forehead and tucked it behind her ear causing her cheeks to heat and the flush carried clear to her toes.

"Rhea!" Layla called, another shoe flying across the hall and hitting the wall beside the door frame. She jolted and pure embarrassment swept over her features as she realized her hands were still on his chest. She quickly dropped them to her sides as Holstein wound around her feet with soft purrs. "I should— well, I'm to be— I'm going." She hurried across the hall, pausing at the door.

Claron waited until she turned to look at him once more. Her lips split into a shy, but dazzling smile. "Night, Claron."

"Night, lass."

« CHAPTER THIRTEEN »

Rhea eased the suite door closed and inhaled a deep breath to relax. *What had just happened?*

"You alright there, Rhea?" Chloe's concern had her turning to find the youngest sister watching her carefully.

Relaxing, Rhea bobbed her head. "Fine. Where's Layla?"

"Inviting herself over for the night." Chloe pointed to the washroom. "She's in the bath. No doubt using all your luxurious salts and scrubs while sipping her wine." She placed a reassuring hand on Rhea's shoulder. "You sure you're okay?"

Touched at Chloe's sincerity, Rhea knew of all the O'Rifcans that she'd be an easy and trustworthy ear. "Just... can I tell you something in confidence?"

"Of course." Chloe waved her to the small sofa and poured Rhea a generous glass of wine and handed it to her as she sat with her legs folded under her.

"I'm a bit out of sorts," Rhea admitted, taking a sip of the dry red. "Claron... well..." She shook her head as if to clear her thoughts.

"He hurt your feelings, love?" Chloe's eyes sparked at the thought.

"Oh, no. Nothing like that." Rhea shifted uncomfortably at the weight of Chloe's scrutiny. "I just— it's just— aghhhh." Rhea placed her face in her hands and growled.

"Ah, I see." Chloe giggled. "He's put you in a tizzy, has he?"

Without removing her hands, Rhea nodded. She slowly peeked through her fingers until Chloe playfully pulled her hands down. "Tell me."

Rhea stood and with her glass of wine began to pace. "I can't explain it, Chloe. One minute I was chatting with him about traveling to your grandparent's place this weekend to swap the calves for heifers, the next thing I know I'm in his arms and feeling *way* to comfortable there." Rhea paused and widened her eyes for effect. "I mean, *way* too comfy," she said again. "And it was weird because for a moment I thought…"

"Thought what?" Chloe asked.

"I thought he was going to kiss me." Rhea leaned her face into her palm as she eyed Chloe in dismay. "Is that crazy?"

"Crazy? No." Chloe leaned back against the cushions. "Did Clary do anything? Did he make a move?"

"That's just it. No. I think it was all me in the physical department. On accident," she quickly pointed out and had Chloe snickering. "But his eyes… Chloe I could have sworn he was thinking the same thing I was."

"Perhaps he was. No way of knowing unless you ask."

Rhea gasped. "I'm not going to ask him. '*Oh, hey Claron, remember last night when I groped your chest? Did you want to kiss me then?*'" She gawked at her own questions.

"You groped his chest?" Chloe giggled at Rhea's embarrassment. "Again, it was not on purpose. I just sort of ended up there," she placed her hands to the air as if they rested against him. "And stayed there... lingering."

"Lingering, were they?"

"Okay, okay." Rhea tossed a berry at Chloe as the sister laughed. "It just felt different somehow. Not our normal interaction."

"And is there something wrong with that?"

"Well, no, I guess not. I'm just not looking for a relationship right now."

"Who said anything about a relationship?" Chloe asked. "Perhaps it's nice to have a flirt every once in a while and it not go anywhere."

"I guess." Rhea took a long sip of her wine in confusion.

"Always nice to have a good flirt!" Layla called from the bath. "Can you two bring the conversation in here? I'm tired of straining me ears!"

Chloe rolled her eyes playfully. "Seems we are both in your confidence, Rhea, due to Layla's expert earwigging."

"I heard that!" Layla called out and had them both laughing.

"Coming!" Rhea called, gathering the bottle of wine. "Might as well, right?"

"Indeed." Chloe grinned as they walked into the bathroom and Layla's head rested above a cloud of bubbles. A hand emerged from beneath the froth to grasp her glass and she took a sip of wine. "Seems you've made yourself at home, sister," Chloe commented.

"Always." Layla pointed to the chaise and a vanity stool and the other women sat. "So you're turning a glad eye on our brother, now are you, Rhea?"

"What? Oh... no. I just... well, I think he's great. Maybe. I don't know." Chloe patted her knee.

"Either you are or you aren't," Layla stated. "If you fancy him, do something about it. After all, you two will be living in such close quarters the next few days and all. Might be the perfect opportunity."

Rhea's eyes widened. "I couldn't possibly. I'm not even sure I am ready for a flirtation, much less a relationship. And I don't think it fair to force my intentions on Claron if he is not interested."

"Ah, true. Best start with Riley then if you're looking for a bit of fun. Clary's the more serious one."

Rhea held up her hand. "Whoa. I did not say anything about *fun*." Aggravated with herself and the line of thought Layla had followed, Rhea looked to Chloe for help. The younger sister did not disappoint.

"Not everyone is about gaming the men, Layla. Rhea's got much to sort out with her heart towards Oliver and the prospects of something new with someone else."

Layla waved her hand as if bored. "She's already finished with the Oliver fellow. He no longer be a concern."

"Perhaps, but the remnants of his betrayal impact future decisions," Chloe explained.

"I'm right here," Rhea reminded the two sisters as they spoke around her.

"Right you are, Rhea. Forgive us." Chloe sipped her wine. "'Tis alright if you had a moment with Clary. We are allowed moments every now and then. Perhaps it is meant as an encouragement for your heart. The fact you could feel a bit of a flutter with Clary means your heart is healin' from Oliver."

"Maybe you're right."

"Unfortunately she usually is." Layla admitted begrudgingly.

Chloe flipped her red hair over her shoulder. "Tis true." She winked at Rhea. "Either way, Clary or no Clary, can we please just celebrate that we've Rhea living amongst us now?"

"I will toast to that." Layla raised her glass as Chloe and Rhea did the same.

"To our new friend and sister," Chloe toasted, and they all sipped.

A knock on the suite door had Rhea jumping back to her feet. "Someone's at the door? What time is it?"

"That'd be half past eleven." Chloe walked to the doorway of the bathroom as Rhea continued on to the main door. She opened it a peek and then further as Claron stood on the other side looking exhausted.

"Claron." Rhea lightly rubbed a hand over her messy ponytail, the gesture making Chloe bite back a grin.

"Rhea," he greeted.

"Are we being too loud? Can you not sleep? I'm so sorry." Her hand reached out and hesitated before dropping back to her side.

"Um no." He eyed Chloe and nodded. "I thought I would come by to see if you wished to help me in the morning, but I can see you ladies are having a fun night of it, so I won't bother."

"What?" Rhea looked to Chloe and back to Claron. "For the morning milking?"

"Aye, but 'tis no worry, Rhea. Another time." He turned to leave, and she gripped his arm.

"Wait."

He slowly turned back around.

"I would love to help you. What time do I need to be ready?"

"'Tis eleven, lass. Late. I didn't realize the time when the idea came to me."

Chloe crossed her arms and rested her chin in her hands, her fingers covering up her smile as she watched her brother and Rhea tip toe around one another.

"I want to help you. What time should I be ready to leave?"

"I plan to head that way at two."

"I'll be ready."

"Listen, Rhea, it's alright if you'd rather have fun tonight. I can—"

"I said I would help, Claron. And I want to."

He placed a hand over hers as it still rested on his arm. "That'll be the way of it then." He flashed a tired smile. "I'll meet you in the kitchen later."

"You'd best sleep at some point, Claron."

"Aye, I should. Unfortunately I've let me papers pile up. I've a bit of time yet." He squeezed her hand. "Night, Rhea." He took a small step towards her, hesitating a brief second before leaning forward and placing a tender kiss to her cheek. He then quietly slipped back across the hall.

Rhea turned and found a smug Chloe watching her. "Glad eye, indeed," she muttered.

"What happened?!" Layla called. "What'd I miss?!"

A laugh bubbled forth as Rhea walked back towards a smiling Chloe and a nosy Layla. Chloe offered a brief pat on the back as she draped her arm over Rhea's shoulders and they continued bantering towards an awaiting Layla.

∞

He checked the clock above the stove and noted it was just three minutes shy of two in the morning. He couldn't blame her if Rhea had fallen asleep, especially after celebrating with his sisters. He stirred his coffee and pressed the lid onto the travel mug. He eyed the tea he'd made her and lifted it to pour it in the sink when he heard footsteps down the back stairwell. Rhea emerged with a tired smile. She pointed to the hovering mug. "Were you about to give up on me?"

"Aye, almost." He set it down and pressed a lid onto the mug and handed it to her.

"Thank you." Her voice held a slight hoarseness either from lack of sleep or too much wine the night before, but she took a grateful sip before stifling a yawn.

"Listen, lass, I appreciate you being willing to help, but I completely understand if you're needin' a bit more sleep."

"I'm awake now, so I might as well work. I don't think I could fall back asleep." She walked towards the back door and cringed as the hinges creaked.

"They sleep like stones, love, don't even worry about it." He followed after her and watched as Rhea slipped into the driver's side of his truck. He grinned as he reopened her door. "You'll be drivin' then?" He motioned to the steering wheel in front of her and she gasped around another yawn.

She slipped out of the truck and bumped into him as she found her footing. "Sorry. Guess I'm a bit out of it still." She rounded the truck and made herself comfortable in the passenger seat. He knew she fell asleep as soon as he pulled onto the road, but he let her take the few minutes needed as he drove the few short kilometers to his barn.

As he pulled in, he spotted his cottage. The tourists arrived today and would be setting up shop all weekend. He was thankful he'd be leaving town while they occupied his home. He wasn't quite sure he could handle watching someone use his space while he worked. The cows were already lining up as he quietly exited the truck. He left Rhea to sleep a bit longer as he turned on the barn lights and set the radio to humming.

He might as well get started, and Rhea could join him when she was ready. He opened the milk parlor and the lead cows began entering. He made quick work of sanitizing milkers as he slipped them onto each cow. When he'd just placed the last of the bunch, Rhea walked inside, feet shuffling.

"You didn't wake me." She rested her hands on her hips as she surveyed his work and then faced him.

"This be the first batch, still time enough for you to help. Thought you could use the few extra minutes of sleep."

"You mean few minutes of sleep. There's nothing extra about it."

"You girls didn't sleep?" Claron asked.

"No. Every time Chloe or I would start fading, Layla would nudge us or start hounding us about some other topic of conversation." She smirked. "She could talk forever."

"Aye, 'tis true. I'm sorry, lass."

"Don't be. I loved every minute of it." She grinned. "What about you? Did you sleep?"

"Unfortunately, no."

"Claron." Her voice held annoyance. "Why not?"

He bit back a grin at her sassy tone. "Much to handle on the paperwork end of things. I feel fine though. I'm a bit used to the crazy schedule."

"So operating on no sleep is a norm for you?"

"Not a norm, no. Just not a foreign concept." He winked as he began rotating another group of cows, Rhea hopping to attention and helping. They worked in tandem with one another. Though she'd only helped once before, she moved almost as expertly as he did. And not once did she complain if one of the girls decided to flick their tails or slosh their dung about. He could almost get used to having her help him, but he quickly shut that idea down. She was moving to Limerick. She was finding her own job, her own way. Castlebrook, their time together, was just a stepping stone in her new life she was anxious to begin paving. And he couldn't blame her. Her excitement for being near the family meant she'd come around often, but to think she'd want to help with milking when she came back, or help ever again, would be setting his hopes too high. He dared not. And he forced himself to begin erecting a wall around his emotions. Because though he would not admit it, and though he was not looking for it, Rhea had somehow made an impression on him.

There was no denying it. He knew Chloe was on to him, and perhaps Riley. But he had yet to venture to the point of no return. Tomorrow would be two weeks. Two weeks was all he'd known her and yet he felt as if she'd always been a part of their lives. Limerick. It wasn't *that* far, he admitted to himself. He darted to Limerick often, for parts or seed, what harm would a small side trip to visit Rhea really do?

He shook his head as he realized he was finishing the last group of cows himself and Rhea had disappeared. Unoffended that she'd given in to her sleep deprivation, he finished the last girls and sent them on their way. He then headed to the milk room to gather milk for the calves. It was there he found Rhea rinsing out bottles.

"What are you doing, lass?"

"Finishing up." She smiled over her shoulder as she set the last bottle upside down to drain on the sink rack.

"You fed the calves?"

"Yep. We are finished." She clapped her hands together as she linked her arm with his and rested her head briefly on his shoulder. "Do we scrape the lot in the morning?"

"No, just at end of day."

"Good, because I'm beginning to drag." She sighed as they reached the truck. "Was there anything else you normally do in the morning?"

Baffled that she'd operated the calves without him, he just shook his head in silence.

"Is something wrong?" She waited as he opened her door.

"Thank you," he said. "For helping."

A soft smile spread over her gorgeous face and she rested her palm against his cheek. "Don't mention it. Now take me back to the B&B so I can scarf down everything and anything your mom has cooked. I'm starving."

Chuckling, he nodded. "Aye. I'll do that. I feel I could eat a cow meself." He playfully cringed as he looked over his shoulder to see if any of his beloved ladies overheard him.

Rhea's laugh sung through the air. "Cute. Now get in, because I'm serious," she teased further as he obeyed and swiftly hopped into the truck and cranked the engine.

They rolled up next to the B&B at half past six and both sluggishly made their way to the back entrance off the kitchen. His mother, bless her, had two steaming platefuls of fresh eggs and bacon and two mugs of hot coffee awaiting them at the small dinette table in the kitchen. He greeted her with his usual kiss to the cheek.

"You two best fuel yourselves." Sidna walked over and brushed a hand over Claron's hair as she watched them both dig into their breakfast with vigor. "You've a nice party last night, Rhea?"

Yes, thank you again for the treats."

"Aye, you're most welcome, dear."

Rhea's gaze lingered upon Mrs. O'Rifcan a moment as she sensed a hint of worry in her tone. "Is something wrong, Sidna?" she asked, her question causing Claron to glance up at his mother.

"Oh dear," Mrs. O'Rifcan flopped into the spare chair between them and fretted over the towel in her hands. "I hate to be the one to darken your day, lass."

Claron set his fork down and reached for his mother's hand. "What is it, Mam?"

Rhea nudged her plate aside and accepted Claron's other hand in support. "Grandpa?" Rhea asked nervously.

"Oh no," Sidna shook her head. "Nothing like that. Roland is fine as feathers. Praise be. Unfortunately, 'tis to do with your Oliver, I'm afraid."

"Oliver?" Surprise lit Rhea's face as she looked to Claron and then back to his mother. "What about him?"

"He phoned the B&B not but ten minutes before you arrived."

"He found me." Defeat rang in Rhea's voice and she squeezed Claron's hand before releasing it. "When does he arrive?"

"Not sure, love." Sidna regretfully stood. "I am sorry, Rhea dear. I did not know 'twas him calling. The way he asked if Rhea was about I thought it a friend. 'Twas towards the end of the conversation he told me his name. If I had known, I would have denied your presence."

Rhea rubbed her arm in consolation. "No. You were honest, and that is always best. It was bound to happen sooner or later. My friend, Heidi, told me she let it slip I was in Ireland. I'm sure it didn't take him long to remember my grandpa lived here."

"He did not say if he was in the village, just wanted to speak with you."

"I guess it is a good thing I will be leaving town tomorrow." She offered a relieved smile towards Claron.

"Oh?" Sidna asked.

Rhea nodded. "I'm traveling with Claron to Cape Clear."

"Is that so now?" Sidna's joy barely tampered as she beamed at her son. "I think it a grand idea to be sure. Fresh air will do you both nicely."

"I guarantee Oliver will show up here, Sidna. And if he does, well... please let him speak to Grandpa if I'm away. I'm hoping he won't, but with Oliver... well, you never really know what he will do."

"Aye, I'll be prepared for 'im and will let Roland know as well."

"Thank you." Rhea took another bite of her breakfast and then set her fork aside once more. "And I'm sorry for putting you in such a position."

"'Tis not your fault he be a fool." Sidna swished her hand towel as if the matter meant nothing. "Dodgy lads deserve what fate hands them. You will not stress on it, dear. You enjoy your time with Clary at Clear and don't think on it." She offered one more reassuring squeeze to Rhea's hand before rising to her feet. "I best tend to the bread. The café will be bustlin' before we know it." She rose and walked back towards the counter and shuffled mixing bowls and canisters until her work space was set just how she liked. She made sure, however, that her ears were primed for eavesdropping as Claron and Rhea continued eating their breakfast.

He could see the worry etched on Rhea's face, the avoidance of eye contact, and the hurried way she ate spoke volumes compared to their easy banter before. She was worried Oliver would walk through the door at any moment. And if he admitted it, he was too. He finished his breakfast as Rhea nudged her plate forward as well and stood. She reached for his plate and carried it to the sink as he topped off her mug of tea and handed it to her when she came back towards the table. "Thanks." She offered a small toast as she took a sip. "I think I will go shower and rest, if my bed is empty. Though I imagine Chloe or Layla took it over this morning."

"If you need a place to sleep, you can use my suite," he offered. "I need to make some rounds in town before second milking."

"No, you need sleep." Rhea's gaze narrowed until he flushed under the scrutiny.

"'Tis true. But it will have to come later for me, I'm afraid."

"Clary, town can wait. Leave a list and I'll have your Da see to it," Sidna called to him in her no-nonsense manner.

"Mam, I don't wish to trouble Da with errands."

"No bother, he'd be glad to, I'm sure of it." She nodded to a pad and pen on the edge of the counter. "You're ghosts walking, the two of you. Both of you need rest. I suggest you take it while you can. I'll make sure you're up for second milking."

Feeling a bit chuffed from her mothering, Claron held his mother's gaze so she sensed his disapproval. "Don't be eyein' me, boyo," she scolded. "A mother knows when to interfere. Rest it will be for you. Now go." She nodded towards the stairs.

"And Rhea dear, kick those daughters of mine out of your room so you have the comfort of your own bed."

Claron steered Rhea towards the stairs so as to avoid further orders from his bossy mother. As they trudged up the steps, he apologized. "She doesn't realize we are adults sometimes."

Rhea grinned. "She's a mom. And you're her baby. She only wants to take care of you."

"A baby once, yes. I'm far from a wee baby now," he grumbled, and she snickered as she laced her arm through his.

"Yes, far from it now." They reached the hall and stood outside their doors. "Rest for both of us."

He nodded. "It would seem."

"Promise me you will sleep and not work on your papers?" she asked.

He tilted his head. "Now why would you think I'd avoid a direct order from me Mam?"

"Because I see the wheels in your head turning and going over the list of things you want to get done." She tapped his temple and then gently rested her hand on his shoulder. "*Rest*, Claron."

"Aye, I will. If only to give you two ladies peace of mind." He winked and appreciated the quick smirk Rhea flashed his way as she walked to her door. "If you need me, just knock."

Rhea paused with her hand on the knob. "Oliver is my problem, Claron. Though I appreciate the offer." She rubbed her fingers over her forehead to erase some of the strain. "I'm sorry, that was rude. I meant—"

"I know what you meant," Claron added, unoffended. "And I understand completely. Been there, done that." He shrugged with a playful grimace and her frown eased into a tired smile.

"Yeah, so I've heard. Remind me once I'm fully functional again to ask how you did it."

"'Tis a long, drawn out saga, I'm afraid."

"Good thing we have a long drive tomorrow then, huh?" She cracked her bedroom door. "Sweet dreams, Claron."

"And you, lass." He waited as she walked into her room and quietly closed the door out of respect for the two sisters that had decided to crash inside. Sighing, he meandered into his own room and mentally struggled with whether he should give into his exhaustion or work on his papers. As he made his way into the shower and felt the hot spray on his aching muscles, he knew the answer was definitely sleep.

« CHAPTER FOURTEEN »

"*You've all you need?*" Mrs. O'Rifcan asked as she handed Rhea a basket full of culinary gifts to carry on the trip.

"I believe so." Rhea accepted a hug from Chloe who handed her a bouquet of flowers, the vase just large enough to nestle amongst the bags without spilling. "These are beautiful, Chloe."

"Thanks. Just make sure Nanny knows they are from me and not Clary." She winked at her brother as he tossed a duffle bag into the backseat of his truck.

"I'll make sure he doesn't steal your thunder." The women hugged.

"And you have a brilliant time, Rhea. Enjoy the peace and beauty of Cape Clear and enjoy your time with Clary," Chloe whispered in her ear before pulling back. Rhea slightly flushed at the comment and Chloe patted her arm before stepping back to stand next to her mother.

"And best take the turns slowly, Clary," Sidna warned, her motherly clucking seemingly ignored as he adjusted a few items in the back of his truck. "The bar may be long, Rhea dear, but keep Clary talking and the trip shall pass quickly"

"The bar?" Rhea looked to Chloe for interpretation.

"The road," Chloe explained with a grin.

"Ah." Rhea giggled as Sidna grabbed her for another hug.

"Take deep breaths of the fresh air, dear, and encourage Clary to do the same. He needs it."

"Mam," Claron walked up and kissed his mother's cheek and enveloped her in a tight hug. "We'll be fine. Everything will be grand." He tapped a finger to Chloe's nose before climbing into the truck. Rhea eased into her seat and buckled up as he offered one last wave to his family before pulling away from the footpath out front of the B&B. Their trailer occupants also echoed sentiments of farewell as they made their way out of Castlebrook.

"You'd think I never leave town." Claron eyed his rearview mirror as his family watched until they rounded the corner.

"It's sweet." Rhea shifted in her seat to comfortably tuck one leg under the other. "I think your mom just likes having all her eggs in one basket. When one of you wanders off, it unsettles her."

"Right you are there," he grinned. "Mam loves having us all close. If she had her way, we'd all still be living in the B&B fighting over washrooms and food.

"You all lived in the B&B?"

"For a bit. Though Lorena married quite young, so she and Paul moved across the river. Your suite be my old room."

"Really?" Intrigued, she rested her elbow on the center console and looked at him. "Has it always looked the same?"

"Oh no, Mam and Da had quite a bit of remodeling work done when they decided to make the change from house to bed and breakfast."

"When did you move out?"

He glanced at her for a second before turning his eyes back to the road. "I believe I was seventeen at the time."

"SEVENTEEN?!" Shocked, Rhea studied him harder. "Why so young?"

Claron chuckled. "I had a lovely cottage awaiting me, and my work was ready for me. No need to stick around." He reached for her hand and squeezed before placing it back on the wheel. "Do me a favor, will you?"

"Sure." Rhea straightened in her chair and waited.

"Reach in me bag back there, front pocket, and retrieve what's in there."

Rhea turned in her seat to do his bidding. "Ahh… were you planning on getting some reading done, Mr. O'Rifcan?" She held up his copy of their shared book and smiled.

"We have yet to discuss it, so I brought it along just in case you wished to."

"And is this you avoiding the subject of yourself?" Rhea's right brow rose as she narrowed a knowing gaze at him.

He laughed. "Very much so."

She tilted a smirk at him. "I'll let you off the hook this one time." She ran her fingers through the pages to find his last location. "Where did you leave off?"

"I'm finished with it."

"Finished?" Rhea looked up in surprise. "And when have you had time to read?"

"I make time here and there."

Impressed, she reached into her own bag and pulled out her own copy. "In my defense, I've had several books to read, not just the one." She showed him that she had a few remaining chapters and he shook his head in mock disappointment as he kept right to follow R525. She playfully swatted his shoulder. "Alright then, what is your favorite part?"

"Favorite part? I guess you mean story?"

"Sure."

He grinned as he watched her flip through several pages. "I've always been a fan of The Voyage of Bran. I like the idea of a quest across the sea."

"And The Island of Women has nothing to do with it, I'm sure," Rhea replied dryly and had him laughing.

"Aye, I guess you could say it was a factor." He winked at her as she shook her head and laughed.

"Men." She rolled her eyes as she flipped another page. "I liked the story of Midir and Etain."

"Aye, that be a good one too. Though it does not end well for Eochaid Airem."

"But he's not the point." Rhea pointed to her book. "He was just in the way."

Claron bit back a smile as Rhea continued retelling him the story he'd heard since he was a child. Passion leapt from her voice as she talked of their transcending love.

"It brings a whole new light to 'love conquers all.'" She looked to him and he nodded quietly. "And obviously I'm getting way too into this, because you think I'm crazy." She blushed as he shook his head.

"Not a'tall. I think it grand. 'Tis a brilliant story. And one of the few that ends happily for those involved. It was one of my favorites when I was a wee lad. Etain the beautiful. Midir continually searching and fighting for her love."

"If by fighting, you mean playing chess, then yes, I suppose he did."

Claron laughed. "Ah, I forgot about the chess match."

"If you were Midir, you wouldn't have stood a chance against Eochaid Airem in chess. Better stick with the sword."

Claron turned in genuine surprise at her cheeky comment and she wriggled her eyebrows. He reached across the console and gripped above her knee, the tickling causing her to squeal and shift further against her door on a laugh. "I would like to point out I beat Roland in me last chess match, thank you."

"For the first time, if I recall."

"A win is a win." He laughed as he turned to head further south. "Eochaid Airem would not have stood a chance against me on the board, not when it came to my Etain." He grinned as he snuck a quick peek at Rhea smiling while she continued to flip through the book.

"So here's a question: What's up with all the untimely downfalls?"

"What do you mean?"

"Why are so many Irish legends and myths full of tragic endings? Don't you guys believe in happily ever after?"

He chuckled. "As you so cleverly pointed out, lass, Midir and Etain had a happy ending."

"Right, for them. But like *you* pointed out, Eochaid did not. He spent the remainder of his life searching for her. And he wasn't the only one. Most of the stories involved two lovers finding one another and then one, if not both, die." She snapped her fingers. "Just like that. No happy ending. No time to actually spend time with the love of their life, just—" she snapped again. "It's a bit depressing if you think about it."

"Aye, but the point is the love. Most have immortal love that transcends beyond this world. So do they ever *really* die?" He countered.

"True." She bit the inside of her lip as she pondered his statement. "That at least makes me feel better."

"'Twas the point." He smiled as she reached into the basket his mother had provided them and fetched a bag of crisps. Opening them, she offered them his way before digging in herself. They munched a moment.

"So your mother mentioned we would be taking a ferry ride to reach Cape Clear."

"Aye."

"That's kind of exciting." Rhea's eyes sparkled, and he pointed to a sticker on his windscreen.

"This be our pass."

"I've only been on a ferry boat once when I was younger," Rhea admitted. "I remember every minute of it though. It was beautiful. I can't even imagine a ferry ride off the coast of Ireland."

"It is very pretty," Claron agreed. "Cape Clear is an interesting place. You will see your fair share of ruins. Nothing extravagant, but some interesting spots we can amble to."

"I would love that. I would love to see a castle." Rhea's eyes lit up at the prospect.

"There's no castle on Clear, but we will pass one on the way. We may not be able to stop on the way there, lass, but on the way back, I promise to take you to one. With the calves, we are a bit on a schedule."

"Oh." Though disappointed, she completely understood. "On the way back is fine."

"There be a lighthouse and an old church ruin that is close to where we land off the ferry. We can do a quick pass today, or we can visit most of the sights tomorrow. 'Tis up to you, lass."

"I don't want to cut into your time with your grandparents, so we can do any touristy adventures on the way back. I'm fine with waiting."

"I imagine my grands will wish to beguile you with stories of the island. They love a new audience."

"I can't wait to hear them."

Claron semi-grimaced.

"What?" Rhea asked.

"Well," he took a moment before continuing, his eyes darting to his rearview mirror as he slowly changed lanes. "One thing you need to know about me grands is that, well, they're a bit eccentric."

Her eyes widened. "Really?" Intrigued, Rhea rested her chin in her palm on the console.

"They speak mostly Irish, as do most people on Cape Clear. My nanny speaks English a bit more than Granda, but should you find it hard to interpret what they're saying, just ask me. T'will not offend them in the slightest if you do not understand them. They do it mostly for fun around new people... especially a Yank."

"Wow. So, do you speak Irish?"

"Of course I do. How else would I be able to talk t—" he turned and saw the wonder on her face. "Aye, I do," he amended with an embarrassed smile.

"I can't wait to hear it. I love listening to you already, I can't imagine hearing you speak another language."

He blushed at that comment and she leaned back against her seat to stare out the window. "Say something to me in Irish."

"Now?"

"Yes." She turned and flashed a dazzling smile his way.

"What do you want me to say?"

She shrugged. "Anything. Something sweet."

"Alright." He scratched his stubbled chin and eloquently spoke. "Lean an bóthar sin agus ceann ó dheas."

"Oh my," she gushed. "What did you just say?"

He laughed at her excitement. "Follow that road and head South."

She shoved his shoulder and laughed. "I guess you can literally say anything and it sounds beautiful."

"I imagine Granda will offer you lovely conversation. He has a soft spot for pretty faces. And should he find you taken with the language, I am sure he will talk the night away."

Rhea grinned. "I can't wait."

∞

The drive was too short in his mind. The easy conversation, the laughs, and the awe Rhea provided had the journey seeming like minutes instead of hours. He pulled to a stop on the ferry and stepped out of the vehicle and waited for Rhea to join him on his side before making the trek to the top of the boat. If he could not show her the sights today, he would at least give her the best seat to watch the island come into view.

The wind teased his hair as he emerged on the second level, and as soon as Rhea stood by him, her gasp had him smiling. "Well, lass, what do you think?"

She spun in a slow circle to observe her surroundings and just shook her head in bafflement. "I cannot believe I'm on a ferry in the south of Ireland. It's breathtaking." She tucked her hair behind her ear as the wind sent it splaying from the pins that had previously held it in place.

He watched as she leaned against the railing, her eyes soaking in every detail as they sailed across the water towards Clear. Wonder and appreciation sparkled in her creamy brown eyes until joy flashed across her face. She hopped towards him and wrapped her arms around his neck in a fierce hug, her eyes never leaving the view in front of them. Laughing, he held her as she rested her head against his chest and continued to soak in the experience. When they began to reach the dock, Claron slipped from her grasp and nodded towards the stairs. She followed, her hand in his as he descended the steps and opened her passenger door.

"If we see nothing else while here, this was enough."

He turned to see her appreciative gaze.

"Thank you, Claron, for letting me tag along."

"You're most welcome, love." He held her eyes a moment longer before they heard the horn sound and the few cars on board before them began rolling forward. "Let's just hope you feel this way after a night with the grands."

Rhea's smile only broadened as she leaned against the seat with a heavy sigh of pure satisfaction.

"As we head towards their house, we will pass— what the devil?" He slammed on the brakes and had Rhea gripping the arm rests as she waited to see what had caused him to stop so abruptly. He unclipped his seat belt and hopped out of the truck.

"Claron? What is it?" Rhea leaned over the console to see where he'd stepped.

"Sióga ar an mbealach." He laughed as he said it and though Rhea had no idea what he'd just said to her, she grinned. As if realizing his blunder, he added, "just some faeries in the road." A boisterous laugh resounded as Claron disappeared from the doorway again.

"A lass, have ye? Here for a craic no doubt." The bellowing voice drew closer as an old man peeked through Claron's door. Rhea offered a small wave and the man slid into the driver's seat. "Fáilte!" He reached for Rhea's hand and kissed it. Claron peeped into the truck and caught Rhea's amused expression.

"This be Granda," Claron introduced. "Or also known as Aodhán. Granda, this is Rhea Connors."

"Connors?" The man asked, eyeing his grandson curiously. "Roland?"

"Aye. Gariníon," Claron explained, then looked to Rhea to translate. "I was letting him know you are Roland's granddaughter. He enjoys Roland's company. Your grandfather has traveled with me several times."

"I see." Rhea smiled and squeezed the man's hand in greeting as he still held onto it.

"Bean álainn." Granda's eyes glistened as he eyed Rhea once more and then slipped out of the vehicle and patted Claron on the back in congratulations.

"Aye. Rhea is a good friend," Claron tried to clarify, but his grandfather just shook his head and laughed as he headed towards his own vehicle. Claron slipped into his seat and turned to Rhea. "Apologies for the abrupt stop, Rhea."

"No problem. He's cute."

Amused, Claron snickered as he slipped the truck back into drive. "Cute, hm?"

"Yes. He seems kind. Though I can't understand him, his eyes give him away. They're kind."

Observant, he thought. But then, why should he be surprised? Rhea had been soaking in every detail of the trip thus far, and she seemed keen in her observations. "Aye, he is."

"What was that he said at the end? Something 'Bean?'

Claron flashed her a grin. "He said you were a beautiful woman."

Rhea placed a hand on her heart. "Awe, that is so sweet. What a nice thing to say."

"He only speaks the truth," Claron commented as he turned into the drive leading to his grandparent's house.

"Your eyes are almost the same color," she added. "A vivid green."

"Aye." Charmed, he reached over and squeezed her hand. *Observant, indeed.* "We relate in looks, but I'm afraid his personality was inherited by Riley. Two peas in a pod, those two."

"You know," Rhea tapped her chin in thought. "I can easily see that."

He laughed as he parked the truck and trailer, his nanny waving a kitchen towel from the doorway beckoning them to enter. "Come." He walked over to her door and opened it, the surprise on his grandmother's face not going unnoticed as he escorted Rhea towards the house. "There's more for you to see." He placed his hand at the small of her back as they walked towards the excited arms of Nanny.

∞

The smells, similar to the B&B, permeated of fresh bread and a stew of some sort simmering on the stove top. However, a light hint of sea air tinged the overall aroma of the comfortable home. Rhea watched as Claron's grandmother wrapped him into a tight hug, her sharp eyes never leaving Rhea's face. Small-boned and wiry, Rhea could not envision this woman giving birth to either Sidna or Senior, but the man's voice, eyes, and jolly disposition told Rhea these were Senior's parents. O'Rifcan through and through. She felt a small hand on her shoulder as Aodhán proudly introduced her to his wife. She heard her grandpa's name and assumed he was telling of her relation to Roland.

Claron had left, more than likely to do what needed to be done with the calves, and Rhea hesitantly stepped forward as the woman kindly took her hand. "'Tis a pleasure to meet you, Rhea. So glad Clary brought you along. He enjoys surprising us with guests."

"I apologize for making an abrupt arrival. I thought Claron had told you I was coming as well."

"Oh no bother, dear. We love company, especially a lovely lass like yourself. Clary has never brought one of those before."

Aodhán nodded in agreement and grinned.

Feeling a bit awkward, as if they thought she were special, she tried defending Claron's reasoning for allowing her to come. "Claron's kind enough to let me tag along. I've only been in Ireland a couple weeks and wanted to see more of the country."

"Of course, dear." The old woman patted her hand and led her to a chair in front of the fireplace. The weather in Castlebrook held a light warmth to the emergence of Spring, but in Clear, the air still held a nice bite to it on a good wind, and Rhea appreciated the added warmth from the low flames. A mug of what she assumed was tea was nudged into her hands. "Clary be along shortly. Anchoring the calves, I'm sure."

Rhea took a sip of her drink and restrained a cough as the thick brew's stoutness made her eyes start to water. She covered it by lightly clearing her throat. Aodhán winked at her as if he knew her secret and had her blushing.

"So, me name is Aibreann."

"Av-Rawn," Rhea repeated. "It's lovely."

The woman smiled. "Thank you. 'Twas me mam's name."

Claron walked inside and walked to the sink to wash his hands. When he entered, he rested a hand on Rhea's shoulder in a reassuring squeeze. She tentatively reached up and rested her hand on his to let him know she was fine. "I see you've gotten a cup of Nanny's famous tea."

His grandfather laughed as Rhea appreciatively held up her mug. "I did. Would you like some?"

"Ah, that'd be a no for me, thanks. I know better." He winked at his grandmother as she sat unoffended, reaching for her knitting needles.

"'Tis a strong brew that wards off the chill and ailments. Only the strong can handle it." She nodded in approval at Rhea as her eyes briefly took in their joined hands on Rhea's shoulder. Rhea withdrew her hand quickly as if caught with it in the cookie jar. The woman's lips twitched, but she said nothing.

"You be around long, Agra?" Aodhán asked.

Rhea, unsure of what he just called her, nodded. "I am to move to Ireland permanently."

"Rhea will be looking for work in Limerick next week," Claron added.

"Lovely," Aibreann commented. "Not too far from the farm, Limerick. Easy to travel back and forth for certain." She knitted without looking up.

"Yes," Rhea added. "I've seen the farm. It's beautiful. I understand that was your home before Claron's?"

Aibreann looked up and nodded. "Angel's Gap was a beautiful home. We cherished our time there. Clary takes tender care of it."

"He does," Rhea agreed and felt a slight wave of relief as Claron sat in the empty chair beside her.

"Rhea has learned the way of the dairy," Claron continued. "She's a steady hand in the milk room."

"Dat so?" Aodhán gleamed. "Aye, be a steady lass you have there, Clary, if she be willing to take on the cows."

"Better than Murphy, that is for certain," Claron added, making both his grandparents laugh.

"He be seein' to it while you're here?" His grandmother asked.

"Aye. Thankfully. I'm glad to be here, as Layla and Murphy had it in their minds to rent out my cottage to a couple Yanks for the weekend."

"Dat so?" Aibreann asked. "Anything to make a bob, that Layla. She settle yet?"

Claron laughed. "That would be a no. She has a glad eye for one of Riley's friends at the moment, until Rhea can whisk her away to Limerick for a day."

"Níor chóir go mbeadh roinnt áilleacht in ann tóir a dhéanamh," Aodhán replied.

"True, but Layla has her choices. She only wishes to irritate us all by choosing those close to us."

"'Tis her way, as a younger sister, to irritate her brothers." Aibreann chuckled. "What of you, Rhea?"

Confused, Rhea fumbled over how to respond and then looked to Claron.

"Ah," he realized she did not know what his grandfather had said that had sparked the conversation. "Granda said some beauty cannot be tamed... in regard to Layla."

"Oh, I see."

"And what of you, Rhea?" His grandmother asked again. "Can you?"

"Be tamed?" Rhea didn't like the word, but she knew it meant was she hoping to settle down one day and have a family of her own. "Eventually. I want a family. If my time here has taught me anything, it is definitely that."

Pleased with her answer, Aibreann nodded kindly and went back to her knitting. "Sidna be just like Layla when she was a lass. Only took our Claron to tack her boot to the floor. One look at the other and they were meant. Now look at them. Ten beautiful children and a lovely home between them. 'Tis all it took was the look."

"They have both been so welcoming and kind. I've been staying at the B&B," Rhea commented.

"Are you now?" Aibreann looked pleased. "Sidna feeding you well enough?"

"More than enough," Rhea laughed as the older woman nodded proudly.

"And Chloe, how be our little one?" She looked to Claron.

Rhea placed a palm to her forehead. "Oh, Claron, we forgot the flowers."

He stood. "Aye, good thought, Rhea. I'll go fetch'em." He was back within seconds with the crystal vase full of blooms.

Aibreann's eyes sparked. "G'way!" She accepted the vase and smelled. "Chloe and the fairies seem to be getting along." She stood and nestled the vase atop the mantle, nudging small fairy figurines out of the way. "Clary, you should take Rhea for a spin before tea."

Rhea looked at her almost full mug in front of her and Claron chuckled, taking her cup and setting it on the table. "She means supper, lass." He stood and offered his hand to Rhea. "We'll see a few sights and be back in time." He led Rhea to the door and helped her into the light jacket he insisted she bring.

"Head on now," Aibreann called. "Before the chill."

Stepping outside, Rhea inhaled a deep breath of fresh air, and the salty mist in the air had her turning to walk to the side of the house. It was then she saw how close to the island's edge the O'Rifcans lived. "Wow."

"Yep. They traded one cliff for the other." Claron grinned.

"I'd say." Rhea smiled up at him. "They're wonderful, Claron."

"Aye."

She walked forward and slipped her arms around his waist and gave a small squeeze before stepping away.

"And what was that for?" he asked.

"For being you." She snickered at his confusion. "For bringing me here. For being a good man. For caring for your grandparents. For continuing their legacy at the farm." She shrugged. "I could go on."

"Please don't." His face flushed as he nodded towards a barn down the small slope of green grass.

"I didn't mean to embarrass you, I just... am impressed."

"Don't be. I owe them everything I have, so loving them comes easy."

"And that right there." She pointed at him as they walked. "You're gracious."

"And so are you," he pointed out. "No need to make a big deal out of me."

"And humble," Rhea continued. "Except when you win at chess," she modified and had him laughing.

"Aye, I am not ashamed of that one," he joked, sliding his hands into his pockets as they watched the new calves find their way around the grassy land around them.

"Thanks for bringing me here, Claron." Rhea linked her arm with his and rested her head against his shoulder as they enjoyed the view before them. "It's just what I needed before my life gets a bit hectic."

"Ah, Limerick," he commented.

"Yes." Rhea rested her chin on his shoulder and stared at his profile until he turned. He lightly tweaked her nose and she smiled. "Is it crazy of me?"

"Not at all. Sounds as if there is opportunity for you there. A place to plant your feet."

"I'm hoping so. I need a change from Maryland, and I already love it here. Grandpa is supportive. I talked with my parents yesterday and they are sad, but supportive. Heidi is thrilled." She chuckled at the thought of her best friend. "So why am I still so nervous about it all?"

"'Tis a big change, lass. You have the right to be nervous. Any sane person would be."

Her sigh held a resigned "yeah" as it floated on the wind. He withdrew her arm from his and draped his over her shoulders in a friendly hug. "It will be grand, Rhea. You'll see." He squeezed as he turned her back towards the cozy house. "But first, I'm afraid you will have to suffer more of Nanny's terrible tea." With a small giggle, they ducked back inside the cozy home on the cliff.

« CHAPTER FIFTEEN »

"'Tis never long enough, your visits."
Nanny hugged Claron tightly as he attempted to pack away his and Rhea's bags back into the truck.

"Will not be long before I'm back. Perhaps I can convince Rhea to come again." He nodded towards Rhea as his granda led her to the cliff's edge by gently holding her hand. He could see him telling her grand tales and Rhea's answering smile warmed Claron through and through.

"She be lovely, Clary. A keeper for sure," Nanny chimed in as they both watched.

Claron startled a moment, not realizing he'd been staring. "She's an asset to be certain. A good friend in the making."

"Just a friend?" Nanny asked, looking up at him.

"Aye."

"Clary." Her tone was soft with understanding. "You need to move on, lad."

He squeezed an arm around his grandmother's shoulders. "I have, Nanny. Don't you worry about me."

"But she's so lovely." Nanny nodded in Rhea's direction.

"She is," he agreed. "But she needs time."

"Ah." Nanny nodded. "I see. Well, show her the sights on the way home. The air is full of promises today. It helps with healing, a good day of fresh air."

"Aye. I plan to take her by Kanturk."

"Good choice." She squeezed his waist and stepped towards her husband when he and Rhea walked up. Her flash of perfectly straight teeth told Claron that Rhea had enjoyed her conversation with his granda.

"Ready, Rhea?"

On a reluctant sigh, she slipped her hand from Granda's and stepped towards him. "I guess so. I wish we could stay longer, but I know we need to take the heifers to your place now."

"We will be back before you know it." Clary gave a reassuring nod as she slid into Nanny's embrace.

"Thank you for having me."

"Oh, it be our pleasure, love. And you be welcome any time, whether Clary is with you or not."

Smiling, Rhea backed away. "Thank you."

"I hate to let a fairy slip through me fingers, but the fates seem to have other plans for you today, Rhea." Aodhán hugged her tightly one last time, casting a glance over her shoulder at his grandson. "Clary, you best be careful with this one. No crazy driving on the way home. For Rhea is to come visit us again."

"Yes sir, Granda." Claron shook Granda's hand and pulled him into a hug.

Claron opened Rhea's door and she slid inside the truck and buckled her seatbelt. She offered a final wave to his grandparents as they slowly pulled away from the cliff and headed back towards the ferry.

"You think they know?" Aibreann turned to her husband and his eyes gleamed.

"Not a clue, those two."

Aibreann snickered. "Same look of Sidna and our Claron, they do."

"To be sure." Aodhán agreed. "Clary's always been a patient one. He will wait for the proper time."

"Proper time," Aibreann scoffed. "There be no time like the present."

"Not always, love." He began leading her back to the house. "Not always." He offered a final wave to Claron as they stepped inside.

Claron sighed. Leaving his grandparents was always hard. He loved his time with them, and he knew, as with all things, time was unpredictable and never promised. He hated living so far from them, but he knew they loved Cape Clear and the peace of the cliffs.

"They're wonderful, Claron." Rhea reached over and squeezed his hand as if she knew he were struggling leaving them behind.

He turned his hand over so their hands rested palm to palm and lifted her hand to his lips. "Aye. 'Tis always a bit hard to leave them."

"I imagine so. I feel that way about Grandpa. Now that I'm here, I cannot imagine going back to the states and leaving him here. I think my parents understand that a bit. Though they're a little sad."

"They will need to visit to experience Ireland themselves, then."

"That's what I told them. It's been years since they've come here. Maybe now they'll have a good reason to." She pointed to herself.

"The best reason, I'd think."

Rhea shifted her feet underneath her as she continued holding his hand on the console. He didn't release his hold, and he wondered if she even realized she held his hand. It wasn't a huge gesture, but something had shifted between them. A comfortable agreement of the heart. He felt it in himself, and though he knew she still needed to fully release the pain from Oliver's betrayal, he could feel the shift in her as well. They'd have to broach the subject eventually, but he'd give her time. Let things progress organically. He was used to doing that any way. It seemed natural for him.

They fell into a comfortable silence, the scenery passing by as they made their way back towards Castlebrook. He exited, taking the turn slowly so Rhea could appreciate the scenery about to come into view. When he heard her gasp, he knew he'd made the right decision in bringing her to Kanturk.

"It's a castle!" She squealed in excitement as she leaned forward to peer out of the windscreen to catch a better view. "It's gorgeous!"

He pulled to a stop and turned off the engine. "Would you like to go inside?"

"We can walk in there?" Bewildered at the prospect, she nodded eagerly. "I can't believe this." She hopped out of the truck faster than he could move to open her door and she awaited him with an excited grin. She slipped her arm through his as they made their way towards the looming structure.

"Now see, this is what I envision when I think of Ireland."

He laughed. "There's plenty of them."

"They're so magical and... gorgeous. It's easy to imagine all the myths and legends taking place in structures like this."

"I'm afraid Kanturk Castle doesn't have that whimsical of a tale, but it be a beauty."

They walked into the castle and Rhea's eyes shot up the stone walls to the open air above them. "It's amazing to me that structures like this were built by hand."

"Aye. Talk about a hard day's work."

She eyed him with a small smirk. "Coming from the man who works just as hard if not more so."

He shrugged. "Different type of labor."

They weren't the only couple walking around the interior of the structure, but Claron didn't mind. Rhea's enraptured state had her blocking out everyone but him and the castle. She tugged him towards a window that looked out over the property. "It's a perfect spot," she whispered. "The trees are beautiful. You can feel the breeze filtering inside."

He lightly tucked a strand of her hair behind her ear as she spoke, her eyes focused on a couple of birds hopping from tree to tree. When she faced him, her caramel eyes glistened with unshed tears. "It's like a dream, Claron. Thank you for bringing me here."

Without thinking, he slid his hand to her cheek and she briefly closed her eyes at his gentle touch. The calluses on his work-tainted hands didn't seem to bother her. When her eyes opened and focused on his, he pulled her towards him, his lips lightly pressing against hers. He paused a moment, unsure if she was ready for what he was offering, and to see if he himself were ready, but Rhea answered. Her lips accepting and surrendering to his. It was slow, testing, and way too brief for his liking, but again, he was patient. When he broke contact, Rhea leaned her forehead to his and inhaled a small shaky breath.

"We should head on." He whispered, his hands gently rubbing up and down her arms to grip her hands. She nodded, and they exited quietly so as not to disturb the other amblers.

∞

They rode in silence. Neither one bringing up what had happened at Kanturk. Should she say something? Should she ask why he'd kissed her? Why would she, the answer was obvious. Or was it? Did he care for her? She sensed he did, but Claron was quiet as well. Was his head spinning with questions as well? She bit back a sigh as she worried her bottom lip.

She'd enjoyed the kiss. Oh, who was she kidding? She'd *loved* his kiss. The way it sank deep into her bones and turned her stomach into a bundle of jittery nerves of anticipation. The way it made her heart pound in her ears all while silencing out the remainder of the world. She'd never felt a kiss like that. She'd never realized a kiss was *meant* to feel like that. It was what she saw in movies or read about in books or even in the Irish folklore she'd been absorbing since her arrival. A kiss that steals your breath and heart in one jump simply did not exist outside of those parameters. But now, she knew it did. Her pulse was still unsteady at just the thought. And her mind was whirling replaying it over and over and over. She cast a cautious glance Claron's direction and caught him staring at her. A nervous smile twitched his lips as he turned his eyes back to the road.

So should she bring it up? He obviously knew she was thinking about it as well.

"So…" Rhea began, her voice unsteady. "I, um… we ah…"

Claron sat quietly, flicking his blinker to take the exit that would then take them on towards Castlebrook. They were almost home.

"You…" She had no idea what to say, and the fact that he continued to sit in silence had her fumbling with nervous energy. "Can you just say something?" she asked finally and had him laughing. She stifled her own grin as he reached for her hand. She gave it to him willingly and he kissed the back of it, the thrill of the small contact making her heart leap.

"I've no words at the moment, Rhea. I am sorry, but I'm still a bit out of sorts."

His honesty had her relaxing. "Me too."

"So we let it be for now?" He offered a quick glance her direction.

"For now." She nodded in agreement with a shy smile as she turned to continue staring out the window and watched as Castlebrook's streets came into view. He navigated towards the B&B first, probably to drop her off, she realized, before setting out to the farm to handle the new heifers. When they pulled to a stop outside Sidna's B&B, Rhea reluctantly slipped out of the truck. She wasn't quite ready for their trip to end, but she could see Claron's work-filled mind already circling around the trailer full of heifers. His eyes surveyed them as he waited for her to meet him on the sidewalk.

She slipped her arm through his and they walked to the front entrance of the familiar home. When they stepped inside, Rhea called out the O'Rifcan greeting, "Hello to the house!"

Several faces littered the sitting room, but her eyes zeroed in on one and the color and joy drained from her face. Oliver.

∞

Claron felt Rhea tense beside him and it did not take much to realize the strange man sitting amongst his family was Oliver. The slicked back hair, the tailored suit, the polished shoes. The man reeked of business success and Claron suddenly felt like punching him in the face. Surprised at his harsh thought, he shut the door behind him and began leading Rhea further into the room. His mother hopped to her feet.

"There you are!" She hugged them each in turn and cupped Rhea's face. "And how was the trip, dear?" Her eyes held apology as she waited for Rhea's response and then did the same to Claron's face.

"It was wonderful." Rhea forced a smile as she walked towards her Grandpa's chair and bent down to kiss his cheek. She hugged Chloe and Layla as well.

"Clear seems to have freshened you up a bit." Layla tugged Rhea's ponytail with a knowing grin as she darted her eyes towards her brother. Rhea's blush confirmed her suspicions.

"And how be my cottage, sister?" Claron asked.

"Still in one piece, thanks be to me and Murphy."

"Good to hear."

Rhea avoided Oliver until she'd made her rounds to Mr. O'Rifcan and Jaron, the only other O'Rifcan sitting in the small room.

Oliver cleared his throat and Rhea's eyes fell upon him. Claron could feel the heat behind her stare from across the room. "Oliver," She greeted. "This is a surprise."

She didn't walk towards him, but instead, walked towards Claron and slid her arm around his waist. "Do you need help with the heifers?" Looking down at her pleading gaze, he felt torn.

She needed to face Oliver, but he also wished to whisk her away from the man that'd caused her so much pain.

"I think Murphy and I can manage for now. Walk with me?" He motioned out the door and she nodded.

"Be a minute," Claron commented to the room as they stepped back outside. As soon as he closed the door, Rhea's bravado vanished and she shook her head in dismay, covering her face. He wrapped his arms around her and she rested her forehead against his chest. "I don't know what to do, Claron. Why is he here? What do I say?"

He smoothed a hand over her hair. He felt her shudder and pulled back to lift her face. He could see the tears threatening to fall. "Don't do it, Rhea. Not yet, love. You be strong."

"But I don't even want to see him." Her eyes darted nervously to the door.

"And he knows that," Claron added. "That's why he is here."

"I just..." She paused a moment and he watched as the tears faded and anger replaced them. Fire sparked in her brown eyes and he grinned. "And there she is." He winked. "You handle him now, lass, or he will never give up."

"I'm just so angry at him. Not at what he did. I'm over that for the most part. I'm mad he's here. How dare he come here? After I specifically told him not to." She stomped her foot and she shook her head, holding a palm over her cheek to calm down. "I'm sorry, Claron. I just... I had such an amazing time with you and for it to end on this note just... and well—" She looked at him as if all her self-control went into her next words. "Well, it just makes me want to burst I'm so mad." He gently rubbed her arms and then linked his fingers with hers, gently placing a kiss on the back of each of her hands.

"Don't let it sour our time together, love."

She shook her head and looked up at the sky as she blinked back tears. "A man like Oliver will not give up until you show him you're serious. He needed to see you in person. He believes he can convince you to be with him."

"There is no way he c—"

Claron held a finger over her lips silencing her comment. "Then show him, Rhea. He's a man that has to be shown. Show him you've moved on. Show him you're serious." He pulled her into a reassuring hug. "Do you wish for me to stay?"

He could see she was torn. "No. Go." She waved her hand towards his trailer. "You need to tend to them. I can do this."

"That'a lass." He released her.

"But will you be back for the meal later?"

"Of course. I wouldn't miss it."

She stepped towards him and gave him one last hug. "Think you could just—"

He kissed her soundly on the mouth, his lips firm, his contact brief as he knew she needed a quick burst of strength and reassurance.

"And all of a sudden I feel like I can take on the world." Rhea nuzzled her nose in his neck as she hugged him once more.

"Be on with ya now, Rhea, or I shall never leave." He brushed a hand over her ponytail and lightly tugged it. He felt her smile into the curve of his neck before she pulled away. "I'm only a call away."

"I know." She waved as he hopped into his truck and drove away.

« CHAPTER SIXTEEN »

Her hand rested on the knob a brief moment to collect herself before stepping back into the B&B.

When she crossed the threshold, Oliver was there waiting for her. "How about we take a walk, Rhea?" He nudged her back out the door before anyone else interfered. His hand on her elbow did not go unnoticed by her or the remaining people in the house as he shuffled her down the front stoop and guided her through the busy café tables towards the back of the building. The familiar trails and benches along the river centered her. She tugged her arm from his grasp and motioned towards a bench. "How about we sit?"

He waited until she did so and then sat beside her, turning to face her.

"What are you doing here, Oliver?" she asked.

"I should think it quite obvious, Rhea. I've come to take you back. Obviously we belong together. The foolishness that happened is in the past. We will move on and be stronger than ever. Just like we've done before. We will only be a better couple. Overcoming mistakes does that to people. It only makes us stronger."

Baffled that he assumed she'd even consider flying over the ocean with him, much less leave the bench they sat on, she turned to him stunned. "You honestly think it is that easy for you? That you can just waltz into my home and drag me out."

"Home?" He motioned to the B&B. "This is not your home. Your home is with me in Maryland."

"No, it is not. It never has been. My home is here now. These people are my family."

"Family?" He chuckled and shook his head. "Your grandfather needs to be in a home. He hasn't moved from his chair since my arrival. We can even take him back with us, if that would make you feel more comfortable."

"I'm not just talking about Grandpa. And no, he does not need to be in a home. The O'Rifcans are my family too." She felt her temper rising and her pulse race.

"These people?" He motioned towards the café. "Rhea, you barely know them. How could you possibly think that after just a few short weeks that they will just adopt you into their oversized family? Sweetie, I'm sorry, but that's just ridiculous. It's our turn to start a family together. You and me. Like we used to talk about."

"No."

His eyes narrowed briefly. "Rhea, honey, I messed up. But I'm owning up to it. It won't happen again. We can and will move past this."

"I said no, Oliver. I don't want to move past this with you. I just want to move on. I *have* moved on."

He studied her a moment and then an eerie smile spread over his lips. "Oh, you cannot be serious?" He covered his mouth as he laughed. "The farmer?" He shook his head as he tried to regain his composure. "Oh, Rhea. No. That man cannot provide for you."

"Claron is none of your concern, Oliver."

"He is, if you think you have feelings for him."

"I don't think anything. I know. And it doesn't matter how I feel towards him or anyone else for that matter. What matters is how I feel towards you. And all I feel is anger and disgust. You disgust me, Oliver."

He retreated back against the bench as if she'd slapped him. "Excuse me?"

"That's right. I'm just going to say it. I've never been more disappointed or disgusted in one human being than I have been by you. The fact that you can cheat on me and then tell me you love me? Did you tell the other woman the same thing? Does she hang on your every word? Does she believe you?"

Rhea stood and looked down at him. "We are through, Oliver. I never want to see your face again. I want you to move on. I want you to be happy. But I do not want it to be with me. Please do not contact my family or me again. Do not show up here again. And for goodness sake," she motioned towards his suit. "Buy a new tie already!"

He blanched at her insult and then stood as well, straightening his jacket. "I'm appalled, Rhea."

"Me too."

"At you."

"And I at you," she countered, not backing down. She heard a familiar whistle coming up the path and knew it would be just a moment before Riley stumbled upon them. She wondered if he knew Oliver was in town or if he was just making his routine walk down the path.

"You will regret this."

"I highly doubt it. I have not regretted it one moment since being here, Oliver. Not one moment. And the longer I stand before you now the more I cannot stand to even look at you. Good bye." She turned to leave, and he snagged her arm, his eyes flaming with untamed fury. "You dare not walk away from me, Rhea."

"I believe she has there, lad." Riley's arrival could not have been more perfectly timed. Relief washed over Rhea as Oliver's fingers dug into her arm. "It'd be best if you let her go now." Riley flicked an uninterested glance towards the river as he waited patiently for Oliver to remove his hand from Rhea.

"You're needed at the house now, Rhea." Riley nodded for her to go and with a final tug, she removed her arm from Oliver's reluctant grasp.

"Rhea…" Oliver's tone held a warning as she began walking away.

She turned.

"Done here, Rhea?" Riley asked.

She nodded and turned back towards the B&B and began walking. Oliver stepped her direction and met a solid wall of muscle. "It'd be best if you let the lady be and be on your way now, Oliver."

Surprise that the man knew his name wore off as it did not take long for Oliver to realize it was another O'Rifcan standing before him. "I will not be bossed. I have unfinished business with Rhea."

"No. You do not. She has made her wishes clear. I suggest you go on now. And best if you don't return."

"Or what?" Oliver pulled at the cuff of his suit jacket as Riley stepped closer, his blue eyes sharpening. "Or it will be more than me you'll be dealing with." He nodded up towards the house and several O'Rifcan brothers now covered the back steps.

"Threats?" Oliver asked. "I do not take kindly to threats, Mr. O'Rifcan. And I am not scared of a bunch of small-town Irishmen."

"'Tis not a threat. It be a promise. You come to hurt our Rhea again, and we will do the same to you." Riley's gaze narrowed as Oliver studied him a moment longer and then looked to the other looming brothers who'd made their way down towards them.

Aggravated, insulted, and a bit tired of it all, Oliver huffed. "Fine." He rolled his shoulders back. "She's not worth the time anyway," he mumbled. He turned to leave as a fist flew from one of the brothers and landed against his nose. Blood spattered, and a gasp of horror slipped from Oliver's lips. He cast a nervous and surprised glance at Riley and then hastened his steps as if he finally realized his welcome had worn out.

Riley turned surprised eyes to his older brother. "That be a shot, Declan."

The other brothers looked to their more passive brother in glee as Declan shrugged. "Rhea is one of ours, no man disrespects her in such a way as that and gets away with it."

Riley grinned wickedly. "Though Rhea will hate to think us fighting her battles. I'd say this be the way of it. Best let Clary know of your quick jab. He'd be needing to treat you to a pint." He slapped Declan on the back as they all made their way up to the B&B with wide grins of pleased victory and brotherly pride.

∞

Claron parked the trailer near the barn and set about opening gates to the pens as Murphy stepped out of the dairy barn sweaty and shirtless.

"Clary!" He spread his arms in welcome as he walked up and patted the side of one of the heifers. "Mighty fine ladies you have here, brother." He helped Claron open the trailer doors and let them filter out into the pen. "You have a nice trip with Rhea, brother?"

"Aye, it was." Claron grimaced as he used a burst of his strength to nudge a stubborn cow out of the trailer.

"And where she be?" Murphy peeked into the truck.

"At the B&B. Oliver showed up."

Murphy froze a moment. "Olly what?"

"Showed up. As in he was sitting having tea when we arrived."

"And?" Murphy asked, concern furrowing his handsome face.

"And what?"

"And what has become of him, then?"

"I don't know. I had heifers to tend to."

"You left her to fend for herself?" Murphy, appalled, fisted his hands on his hips.

"'Tis her life, Murphy. She needed to handle it on her own."

"And you are not bothered that she might run into the man's arms and be swept away."

"No."

A slow grin spread over Murphy's face. "Ahh... and why are you not worried, brother? Something happen between you and our Rhea?" He wriggled his brows.

Claron, ignoring him, walked into the dairy parlor to check the status of Murphy's afternoon clean up. "You going to leave me wonderin', Clary?" Murphy called, walking into the room. "I just finished hosing the lot, if you must know," Murphy continued. "Was about to wrap it up for the day." He followed his younger brother back outside and offered a wave towards Claron's cottage. Claron glanced up and saw two feminine figures return the wave in enthusiasm. His brother's smile turned goofy.

"Please tell me you have not messed with the Yanks while I've been away." Claron cringed at the thought.

Murphy laughed and slapped Claron's back. "Not a'tall. I just be the local talent." He winked. "Smiles, flirtations, and a bit of fun to be had at the pub. Best to keep the customers happy."

"Is that why you be working without your clothes?" Claron's brow lifted at his brother's laugh.

"Possibly." Murphy shrugged unapologetically. "Turns out I'm a hit with the Yanks. Might put a few extra bob in our pockets, hm?"

"Exploiting yourself, now are you, Murphy?" Claron shook his head but laughed.

"Not exploiting, per se. Just a bit of marketing."

"Marketing, hmmm..." Claron shut his truck door.

"They leave today," Murphy added. "Shame really, for I've come to like having a fan club the last several days."

"I imagine so." Claron rolled his eyes.

"Good to see you in high spirits, Clary. Glad your trip with Rhea was swell. Did you romance her a bit?"

"A bit," Claron added as he clasped the gate lock closed and trudged back towards the trailer.

"Atta lad." Murphy hopped into the passenger side of Claron's truck as Claron pulled the trailer towards the other pieces of equipment parked in a longer barn closer to the fields. They made quick work of unhitching the trailer.

"You be headed back to the B&B?" Murphy asked.

"Aye. My cottage is still occupied, is it not?" Claron asked.

"That it is."

"Then yes."

"Drop me off at the pub on the way?"

"Aye, I can do that." Claron shifted the truck into gear and set out towards Murphy's Pub listening to his brother tell of his adventures with the visiting women from America. But his mind was on Rhea. And though he felt something had changed and stirred between them on their trip, he dreaded Oliver and what the man may say. He prayed Rhea remained at his mother's when he arrived. He prayed she stayed in Ireland.

∞

A knock sounded on Rhea's door, but she didn't answer. It wasn't until she heard her grandpa's voice that she stood and turned the knob. His gaze washed over her tear-stained face. "Oh, my dear." He walked into the room and shut the door behind him. He sat on the edge of her bed as she did the same, and he immediately wrapped his arms around her in a tight hug. When it seemed her sobs had subsided, he pulled back to hold her face in his hands. "It is done now, dear. All is done. Oliver has gone."

"I know."

"And you are sad because he is gone?"

"No. I'm so upset with him and myself that I just can't seem to get ahold of my emotions at the moment. I'm so embarrassed the O'Rifcans had to witness him. That Claron—" she trailed off.

"What of Clary? He didn't seem bothered by Oliver's presence in the slightest. Did he tell you otherwise?"

She shook her head. "It's just... we had such an amazing time in Cape Clear, Grandpa. Things were... good. And then Oliver was here when we arrived, and... Claron was understanding, but I just know he is going to take a step back because, well why would he want to deal with a woman whose ex randomly shows up and confesses his love to her? I've completely ruined things."

Roland bit back a smile as she wiped her eyes on the edges of her shirt.

"I think you give Oliver too much credit, Rhea dear. Claron is a strong lad, he would not have left if he did not feel you could handle the situation."

"But I didn't handle it. I watched from up here." She pointed towards the hallway. I saw Declan punch him."

Roland rubbed her back. "That he did. And not one brother down there seems disappointed in you. They love you, Rhea honey, that is why they helped with Oliver."

"I'm just embarrassed."

"You cannot be embarrassed for Oliver's actions. He is his own man. And the way he acts has no bearing on you."

She shook her head and sighed. "I'm glad I will be gone tomorrow. I just don't want to face anyone right now."

"And where will you be going?"

"Limerick. My job interview."

"Ah, of course." Roland patted her knee. "And what of supper? Will you be coming down to join us for supper?"

She shook her head. "No. I need... I just need a break for a night."

"And what of Clary? He's more than likely going to check on you. And he's still staying across the hall."

"I don't know, Grandpa. I just need time to myself right now."

Nodding, Roland stood. "Well, then I will leave you to it then. I'll have Sidna keep you a plate warm in the oven for later. You can retrieve it once everyone has gone."

"Thanks, Grandpa."

"You're welcome, sweetie. Though I will say again. You have nothing to be ashamed of. Oliver is gone. You should be celebrating with those who care about you."

Acknowledging his comment, Rhea walked him to the door as Claron was coming up the stairs. Their eyes briefly met, and he took a step in her direction at seeing her tear-ridden face. She held up her hand for him to stop and he obeyed as Roland turned one last time towards Rhea. "Good night, sweetie."

"Night, Grandpa."

Roland patted Claron on the shoulder as he passed to walk down the stairs.

"How are you, lass?" Claron asked, keeping his distance.

"I just need a minute, Claron. If you don't mind."

He nodded. "Of course. You are well though?"

A soft smile tilted the corner of her mouth. "Yes." If he only knew all she wanted was to be wrapped into his arms and held by him. "I just need..."

"Space?" he asked.

She nodded.

"Very well. If you need me, all you have to do is ask."

"I know." Rhea watched as he walked to his bedroom door. "Thanks for understanding, Claron."

He turned with a half a smile. "I've been there, remember?"

Nodding, she leaned against the door jam. "It sucks."

He snickered. "That it does. But it will be better from here on out."

"I know. It's just so..."

"Weird. And hard," he finished.

"Yes." Relieved someone understood her exact feelings, she flashed a sad grin.

He stepped towards her and gently brushed his fingertips over her cheek. Her eyes closed at his touch. "Rest, love. The mornin' will be better."

She exhaled a deep breath and then opened her eyes to find him gone. Wishing she had a moment longer with him, but relieved to escape back into her room, she slipped back through the door with a slight edge of disappointment. A hot bath was needed. A hot bath with a long night of sleep. The morning, she decided, would definitely be better.

« CHAPTER SEVENTEEN »

It had been two weeks. Two weeks of Rhea accepting the job in Limerick. Two weeks of her moving into her apartment and getting settled. Two weeks of the space she requested. And two, long weeks of finding his patience slipping. He'd given her ample time after the Oliver situation. He'd attempted to stay out of her way, as did most of the brothers, as she focused on moving and ignoring the male species. But how long was he to wait? They had yet to even discuss what happened at Kanturk Castle. Did it mean nothing now? Was she too busy? Too distracted? Too... uninterested now? He felt the slap on his back before he heard the cheerful greeting of his brothers.

"'Tis high time you leave this barn, Clary." Riley grinned as he and Murphy eased onto the vacant seats of various pieces of farming equipment and watched as Claron continued tightening the fitting on one of the tractor's hoses. "You've been squirreled away for weeks."

"Once you reclaimed your cottage, you've disappeared, Clary," Murphy chimed in. "Are you feelin' low?"

Claron glanced at his brothers. "Just busy."

"More like makin' yourself busy," Riley corrected. "Ignoring your phone, your friends, and your family."

"Not ignoring." Claron stood and tossed his wrench into his tool box, carrying the load to his work table. "Just busy."

"Layla and Chloe plan to visit Rhea in Limerick for the weekend," Riley baited. "Something about a house party to meet her neighbors tonight."

Claron's back stiffened as he listened. He had not received an invite. Not that it should surprise him. Rhea probably assumed he couldn't come due to milking. "And you two?"

"What?" Both brothers asked in tandem.

"Are you two going to the big party?"

"No," Riley stated with a confused brow. "I was not invited."

"Nor I." Murphy feigned being wounded.

"We would only damper the mood, being big brothers and all. Our sisters can't feel the freedom to flirt with brothers lurking about."

"So it be a party to meet the local talent then?" Claron could not help the sting in his voice.

Riley and Murphy exchanged a quick glance. "For Layla's sake," Murphy amended. "I believe Rhea wishes to meet a few neighbors in the building, but Layla has her own agenda, as she always does."

"Have you heard from Rhea recently?" Riley asked knowing full well what the answer would be.

"No, I have not. I'm sure she is busy." Claron walked over to the water hose as a tired Rugby shuffled forward, his tongue lolling out of his mouth. Switching the water on, Claron filled a giant water bucket while giving Rugby a thorough rub down.

"And I'm sure she would love to see you. Told me so herself just yesterday," Murphy added. "Bumped into her at McCarthy's restaurant."

"She was in Castlebrook?" Claron asked, finally offering them a glance.

"Aye." Murphy replied. "She and Chloe were enjoying a break in their shopping. Furnishing a new apartment had them traveling all the way to Galway and back. I believe Rhea's Aunt Grace has provided extra reinforcements on the furnishing part."

"I see."

"She asked after you," Murphy continued. "Told her you had turned back to your hermit ways. At least until Layla and I rent out your house again."

"Which better not be soon," Claron grumbled as he gave Rugby one last pat and made his way towards the dairy barn. The brothers followed. Holstein meowed as they approached and Claron watched as Rugby darted after the cat and had him climbing the nearest tree. "Leave him be, Rugby," he warned.

"Anyways," Murphy continued. "The party starts at seven from what I hear, right brother?"

Riley nodded. "Seven, aye. At Rhea's new apartment."

Claron ignored them as he darted into the milk room and grabbed an extra water hose and began traipsing up towards the cottage. His brothers could keep talking, but he'd keep walking and working.

"She be living in the high-rise she and Roland looked at." Riley watched as Claron screwed the hose to the spout and then began watering the flower garden around the cottage's front yard. His brother diligently tended to his home and his land. Always had. But for once, Riley wished to rip the hose from Claron's grip and beat him over the head with it.

"Anyways," Murphy clapped his hands together and eyed Riley. "We best head on. Pints at the pub don't serve themselves. Especially on a Friday. Have a care, Clary."

"And you." Claron nodded his farewell as he continued his work and ignored their departure.

"Think he will go?" Murphy whispered as they walked towards Riley's truck.

"Not sure. Let us hope so."

∞

"I tell you now, Rhea, these drapes need to be open for the party." Layla swung back the curtains and exposed Rhea's living space to the bright sunshine. "Oh, would you look at that." She giggled as she offered a wave to the handsome man that lived across the courtyard from Rhea. "Did we invite him?" she asked.

"Aye," Chloe chimed from the kitchen counter. "Everyone received an invite. Your mystery man included."

Chloe turned to Rhea beside her and rolled her eyes at her sister's flirting. Rhea stifled a laugh as she continued slicing cubes of cheese for the tray she was preparing.

"Well, I certainly hope he comes." Layla tossed her hair over her shoulder as she walked towards them and slid onto one of Rhea's brand new bar stools. "You've made a lovely home here, Rhea. All fresh and crisp."

Rhea grinned, her eyes traveling over the soft grey tones of her fluffy new couch and the white throw pillows scattered about the cushions.

"So clean feeling," Layla added. "Though I wish I could just add a red rug or throw somewhere about. Add some color."

Chloe snickered. "Layla only lives for the bold."

"And what is wrong with that?" Layla asked as she popped a grape into her mouth, Chloe showing her disappointment in Layla's lack of help as she narrowed her gaze.

"Neutral tones are calming for the mind," Chloe continued. "Nothing wrong with wanting a peaceful home."

Scoffing, Layla grabbed the bruschetta loaf and began slicing. "Clary took all my cottage additions and shoved them in a closet. A closet!" She shook her head in disgust. "They sit to collect dust until I rent his house out again. Which I could have already done three times, but he's refused. So all the beautiful color I brought into his home is wasting away. I could bring some items with me next time I come, Rhea. Spice it up a bit in here."

"'Tis her home, Layla. Not yours."

"Aye. I know that. Just offering."

"Why don't you put them in your own house?" Rhea asked.

"Too cluttered already." Layla explained. "Besides, I'm not the one needing color."

"Chloe brought me color." Rhea motioned towards the several flower arrangements scattered about the room.

"And good thing she did," Layla continued.

A chime filtered through the air and Chloe quickly wiped her hands on a towel before answering her phone. "Conor McCarthy," she greeted warmly. "I'm in Limerick for the day, best tell me your mam is not needing new flowers for her tables today." She paused, and her eyes widened before she slapped a hand to her forehead. "Oh no! I completely forgot." She shook her head and walked towards her purse and fetched her pocket planner. She flipped through it. "Yes, yes, I know. For Friday. I see it marked... Oh, now Conor, I hate for you to do that." She sat on the edge of the white armchair and fingered the edge of the armrest. "You'd be a doll for doing so. You might as well stay once you arrive. We're having a party at Rhea's new apartment to welcome her to Limerick... Aye... See you then." She hung up. "I ordered the cheesecakes from Conor's mam and completely forgot to cart them here. He's bringing them. Hope it's okay to invite him."

"Of course," Rhea smiled. "It will be nice having a friend from Castlebrook. I still can't believe none of the brothers could come."

Layla and Chloe cast each other a glance.

"What?" Rhea asked. "What was that look?"

"What look?" Layla played innocent.

With narrowed eyes and fist on hip, Rhea eyed them both. Chloe melted under the scrutiny. "Layla did not wish to invite them because she felt they'd get in the way of you relaxing around other... men." She grimaced as she waited for Rhea's disapproval.

"So I'm having a party and I'm not inviting some of my closest friends?" Rhea reached for her phone. "They probably think me a snob now. And Claron? Is that why I haven't heard from him? His feelings are probably hurt knowing I'm throwing a party and didn't invite him."

Layla grabbed Rhea's phone before she could dial anyone. "Rhea love, just let it be. They don't take offense. This party is for you to meet your neighbors." She motioned over her shoulder to the apartment across the courtyard. "If Riley or Murphy show up you will spend the majority of your time with them because they're a comfort. And if Clary showed up, well, then you would completely disappear, I'm sure of it."

Rhea blushed at that comment, but still wished to invite them. "I feel bad."

"Don't. Chloe and I are the ones throwing this party in your honor. Let it be our fault if they wish to blame someone. Besides, Clary is too busy to come. Riley probably already has plans. And it be Friday at the pub, which means Murphy couldn't slip away either."

Disappointment settled over Rhea. "You're probably right. I just... I just haven't heard from Claron in a while and was hoping he'd come."

Layla waved her concern away. "If you wish to see Clary you know you can always find him covered in manure, spending time with his ladies in the milk parlor."

"Layla!" Chloe's tone was full of disapproval.

"What?" Layla shrugged. "'Tis true, is it not? Meanwhile, there's plenty of people for you to meet here." She spun on the stool and faced the windows that overlooked the courtyard, her gaze flashing to the apartment that housed her latest interest.

Chloe stood and walked back to her post behind the counter and squeezed Rhea's arm. "If you wish to invite them, Rhea, go ahead."

"Well, it's a bit late now, I think. I mean, the party starts in half an hour. It would be a little last minute. I hate them to feel obligated or for them to feel hurried." Rhea set her phone down and went back to dicing cheese cubes.

"We promise it will be a fun evening no matter who comes." Layla clapped her hands as she walked towards the refrigerator and withdrew a bottle of champagne, making quick work of popping cork and pouring into glasses. "Time for us to start the party now." She grinned as the other two women held their glasses up. "To Rhea's new life in Limerick." Glasses clinked and Rhea, though she sipped, longed not only for a nice life in Limerick, but found herself also longing for a manure-smelling milk parlor.

∞

Claron straightened his crisp buttoned shirt as he shifted to close his truck door. Taking a deep breath, he eyed the building before him. He was here. *Uninvited*, he reminded himself. But here. Why did he feel like turning right back around and heading home? He was never the nervous sort, but he found his feet stuck to the parking lot.

"Clary, a hand?" A familiar voice called out to him and had him turning. Conor McCarthy reached into his backseat and withdrew two large boxes. "Conor? What the devil are you doing here?"

"'Tis a party, is it not?" He winked, his usually scraggily beard neatly trimmed.

Surprised that Conor received an invite and he didn't, Claron tried not to let the disappointment and shock show on his face. He grabbed one of the boxes from Conor.

"Chloe had the mammy make some cheesecakes for tonight. Chloe forgot them. I received an invite out of necessity, methinks." He laughed heartily as if it didn't bother him. "'Twas the only way her cheesecakes would make it to Limerick. But a chance to hang with lovely ladies is worth whatever invite a man can get, right?" He nudged

Claron's shoulder and Claron couldn't help but grin at his friend.

"Smart thinking, Conor."

"Anyways, I hear it's to be a big night." He made his way through the lobby of the apartment complex towards the elevators and Claron followed.

"You know which one it is?"

"539, Chloe says." Conor pushed the button for the fifth floor. "Cheerful place, isn't it?" He looked out of the glass elevator as it rose over the courtyard. "The only green in Limerick, I wager." He chuckled as he shook his head. "Don't know how people live in cities." The doors slid open and Conor turned left and quickly turned the other direction. "Looks to be this way. Come along, Clary."

Claron followed at a steady pace, his gaze surveying the layout of the building. Though it wasn't his taste, he could see the appeal. The building rested downtown, close to Rhea's work, from what he gathered from Chloe. Close to other businesses, restaurants, and shopping. Location was key in a city, and it seemed Rhea chose well. Conor's mammoth fist pounded a knock on the door of apartment 539. Hesitantly it opened a crack and then flew back in welcome. "Conor!" Rhea's voice made Claron's pulse jump. He stood to the side of the door, his presence not yet known. "Come in." Rhea stepped back.

"Thank you, Rhea." Conor leaned forward and barely kissed her cheek as he hurried inside. Rhea started to shut the door when Claron stepped into view. She gasped and hopped back a step before realizing it was him. Her hand over her heart, a slow smile spread over her face. "Claron." She jumped towards him and wrapped her arms around his neck in a tight embrace. Taken aback, he stumbled back a step as he tried to balance the box of cheesecake and an excited Rhea. Conor, laughing, set his cheesecake on the counter and then quickly took the one from Claron.

Rhea leaned back and stared up at him. "I can't believe you're here." Her eyes glistened as they roamed over his face. She then hugged him once more. Claron wrapped his arms around her and held her close, a contented sigh slipping from her lips as he did. He kissed the top of her head. "And how's Limerick, Rhea?" He asked quietly, his sisters and friend diverting their attention to various tasks so as not to appear to be eavesdropping.

"It is so much better now that you are here." She pulled away and tugged him further into her apartment. "What made you decide to come? Did you ride with Conor? How are the cows? How is Rugby?" Her questions fired off one after another as she continued leading him towards her living room and to her plump sofa. Sitting, she gripped his hand in her lap. "I've missed you," she finished, a light flush working its way to her cheeks.

Claron studied her a moment and she shifted uneasily under his inspection. "Limerick seems to suit you. You look well."

"It's only been a couple of weeks, but it's been good. I like my job." She shrugged her shoulders as if that were one of the few things she enjoyed.

"That's good, lass." He brushed his thumb over her knuckles. "I've missed you too, by the way." His voice lowered, and he watched as relief flashed into her eyes. A beautiful smile bloomed across her face as she quickly leaned forward and claimed his lips with a quick, hard kiss. When she pulled away, she placed her hands on her red cheeks. "I cannot believe I just did that!" She giggled nervously. "I'm sorry, Claron, I just... wow, I, um..."

He laughed as he scooted closer towards her and gently turned her face towards his. "You were only reading my own mind, Rhea." He gently kissed her lips and heard the room fall silent behind them. He rested his forehead against hers. "And here I thought I would have to steal you away at some point tonight to have a chance to speak to you."

"I'm sorry I haven't called you," she said. "I was so wrapped up in the whole Oliver visit, new job, and moving that I sort of... put you off." She lowered her head. "I'm sorry for that."

He lifted her chin with his finger. "No need to be. I was trying to give you your space. Though I admit I was starting to grow weary." He tilted a smirk as she squeezed his hand in hers. "Not knowing where we stood after Cape Clear. I hoped we'd... well, I planned, that is, that I could... maybe we could try for a little something more than just friends. What say you of that, Rhea?" He inhaled a deep breath as he watched his words sink in.

"I think," she began, "I would absolutely love that, Claron." She kissed his cheek before enveloping him in another hug. When she pulled away, a tear slid down her cheek.

"What is this?" He gently brushed it away and she shook her head to clear the rest away.

"I'm sorry, I'm just... I'm so happy right now." She sniffled a laugh as he pulled her to him and draped his arm around her shoulders and kissed her temple.

"Aye, me too, love. Me too."

They sat silent a moment, enjoying the comfort and thrill of one another's presence. Claron felt his heart swell at the thought of Rhea in his life as more than just a family friend, as more than just the loud Yank who'd stormed into his dairy parlor weeks before. And as she rested her chin on his shoulder, he leaned in to kiss her once more, but not before Layla began assaulting them with grapes.

"Enough of that for now." She smiled and wriggled her eyebrows at them. "We have a party starting. Conor," Layla called towards their friend standing by the door. "Let them in."

Continue the story with...

Book Two of
The Siblings O'Rifcan Series

**All titles by Katharine E. Hamilton
Available on Amazon and Amazon Kindle**

Adult Fiction:

The Unfading Lands Series
The Unfading Lands, Part One
Darkness Divided, Part Two
Redemption Rising, Part Three

The Lighthearted Collection
Chicago's Best
Montgomery House
Beautiful Fury

Children's Literature:
The Adventurous Life of Laura Bell
Susie At Your Service
Sissy and Kat

Short Stories:
If the Shoe Fits

Find out more about Katharine and her works at:
www.katharinehamilton.com

Social Media is a great way to connect with Katharine. Check her out on the following:

Facebook: Katharine E. Hamilton
https://www.facebook.com/Katharine-E-Hamilton-282475125097433/

Twitter: @AuthorKatharine
Instagram: @AuthorKatharine

Contact Katharine:
khamiltonauthor@gmail.com

ABOUT THE AUTHOR

Katharine E. Hamilton began writing a decade ago by introducing children to three fun stories based on family and friends in her own life. Though she enjoyed writing for children, Katharine moved into adult fiction in 2015 with the release of her first novel, The Unfading Lands, a clean, epic fantasy that landed in Amazon's Hot 100 New Releases on its fourth day of publication and reached #72 in the Top 100 Bestsellers on all of Amazon in its first week. The series did not stop there and the following two books in The Unfading Lands series released in late 2015 and early 2016.

Though comfortable in the fantasy genre, Katharine decided to venture into romance in 2017 and released the first novel in a collection of sweet, clean romances: The Lighthearted Collection. The collection's works would go on to reach bestseller statuses and win Reader's Choice Awards and various Indie Book Awards in 2017 and early 2018.

Katharine has contributed to charitable Indie anthologies and helped other aspiring writers journey their way through the publication process. She loves everything to do with writing and loves that she can continue to share heartwarming stories to a wide array of readers.

She was born and raised in the state of Texas, where she currently resides on a ranch in the heart of brush country with her husband, Brad, and their son, Everett, and their two furry friends, Tulip and Cash. She is a graduate of Texas A&M University, where she received a Bachelor's degree in History.

She is thankful to her readers for allowing her the privilege to turn her dreams into a new adventure for us all.

Made in the USA
Monee, IL
12 July 2022